HEART OF A WARRIOR SERIES / BOOK 3

SURRENDERED

Kariss Lynch

FaithHappenings Publishers

FaithHappenings Publishers
7061 S. University Blvd., Suite 307
Centennial, CO 80122

Cover Design ©2015 Chasya Lynch
Book Layout ©2013 BookDesignTemplates.com

Surrendered/ Kariss Lynch. -- 1st ed.
ISBN (Softcover) 978-1-941555-04-0
This book was printed in the United States of America.

To order additional copies of this book, contact:
info@faithhappenings.com

FaithHappenings Publishers,
a division of FaithHappenings.com

ENDORSEMENTS

"There is something so authentic and relatable in Kariss Lynch's writing. From the opening pages of *Surrendered,* I felt like I was hanging out with friends -- ones whose journey of romance, healing, and hope settled in my heart. An absolute delight to read and a wonderful conclusion to the *Heart of a Warrior* series!"
Melissa Tagg, author of *From the Start* and *Like Never Before*

"As Lynch rounds out the captivating story of Nick and Kaylan, she gives us what we want in the form of suspense, drama, and romance. She also gives us what we need . . . an image of surrender. It's a beautiful story of letting go of the things we cannot control, in order to whittle down to what matters most. A hearty well done to end this captivating trilogy."
Heather James, author of *Unholy Hunger* and *Hands of Darkness*

"*Surrendered* is the fulfillment of anticipation, excitement, and mystery that stirred our hearts in the *Heart of a Warrior* series. Kariss has once again given the reader a glimpse into the clash of family, love, and military sacrifice in a thrilling love story that highlights faith within the fight."
Navy SEAL

"Where is love when the battlefield of love demands courage, sacrifice, and forgiveness? *Surrendered* . . . will love survive the ultimate test of facing the truth about the past?"
DiAnn Mills, author of *Deadlock* – Tyndale Publishers

To the men and women who fight for our country and to your families … thank you for showing me what it looks like to have the heart of a warrior.

NOTE FROM THE AUTHOR

The *Heart of a Warrior* series has come to a close and even now my heart is a little sad. I have loved sharing the story of the Richards family, Nick, and the SEALs. Over the course of these books, I have been able to meet and talk with several men and women who fight for our country, and every time I am inspired to fight harder, love stronger, and never, ever give up. Nick and Kaylan's story may be over but my journey to developing a courageous heart is only just beginning. And I hope yours is, as well.

It amazes me that the Lord often brings our most rewarding journeys from our deepest struggles. In 2009, I graduated from college a week after I turned 21, wide-eyed and panicked about what to do next. Life had dealt tough blows my last semester of college, and my future seemed to drop off into a black hole with no end in sight. I was terrified.

But God knew.

A few weeks after I graduated, I packed the car and headed to the Colorado mountains where I lived for two months with forty-eight strangers while attending Focus on the Family Leadership Institute. I entered the summer incredibly broken and bitter with God. I finished the summer with lifelong friends, a humbled heart, and a start toward healing.

As I prepared to walk across the stage with my new friends to graduate and re-enter real life, my advisor pulled me into a hug. "Be bold, Kariss. Be bold," she whispered in my ear. My feet hit the stage with my head in a fog as I contemplated her words. I felt broken, unable to be bold. Incapable of courage and a strong heart. Less than a year later, *Shaken* and the *Heart of Warrior* series were born out of this painful season.

Some days I still don't understand what it means to be bold, but I do understand that it is closely tied with surrender—surrender to a loving Father who desires to give us good things. Even His "no's" are out of His desire to give us better things than we know to ask Him for. I do know boldness is a choice every day. It isn't something I can fail at. It is something I can continually grow in. And it is an opportunity to daily trust Him more than the day before. It is the decision to let my faith be bigger than my fear.

I can't wait to share more stories with you. To stay up to date with all the latest book news, contests, giveaways, and my random thoughts, visit ***karisslynch.com*** or connect with me on Facebook, Instagram, and Twitter. As always, I love to hear from you!

Until next time, my friends, I'm praying you continue to develop the heart of a warrior.

Be bold,
Kariss Lynch

It's like in the great stories, Mr. Frodo. The ones that really mattered. Full of darkness and danger they were. And sometimes you didn't want to know the end. Because how could the end be happy? How could the world go back to the way it was when so much bad had happened? But in the end, it's only a passing thing, this shadow. Even darkness must pass. A new day will come. And when the sun shines, it will shine out the clearer. Those were the stories that stayed with you. That meant something, even if you were too small to understand why. But I think, Mr. Frodo, I do understand. I know now. Folk in those stories had lots of chances of turning back, only they didn't. Because they were holding on to something ... There's some good in this world, Mr. Frodo. And it's worth fighting for.

— Sam, *Lord of the Rings* by J. R. R. Tolkien

PROLOGUE

Anya Petrov pulled her legs to her chest and took deep breaths. The walls closed in more every second. If God existed, he hadn't built her for prison. She shivered in the cold that seeped through the dull concrete walls. She was somewhere in the United States and somewhere with brisk air and a chill that burrowed deep into her soul. Or maybe that was more the result of captivity.

The orange jumpsuit irritated her skin, but she'd worn worse. As a child. As a young adult under Soviet rule. She was safer here than she had been behind the Iron Curtain. But she longed for her yacht, an expensive meal, and the rich taste of a bottle of wine.

A scratching sound caught her attention, and she jerked in the direction of the door. Funny how the smallest noises magnified in silence. Her thoughts seemed louder, too. Almost deafening. She crawled from her thin mattress and reached for the corner of a dirty off-white envelope slipped halfway beneath the metal door.

She stood on her toes and scanned the hallway just outside her one-room cell. She was tired of confinement. Tired of fear that ate away her sanity, tired of her jail mates. She dug deep, reaching for a calm she didn't feel, but the longer her sentence stretched, the louder the roaring in her heart.

What happened to the cool spy who'd once stupefied the West? She ran her finger beneath the envelope lip and pulled out a single sheet of paper. The hand that had once fired a gun without hesitation began to tremble.

The familiar scrawl nearly stopped her heart. No.

Her legs hit the bed frame as she backed up. She tumbled back onto the mattress, the springs squealing in protest. She curled up against the wall, hugging it as she would her brother Andrei ages ago.

He'd found her.

The paper rattled in her hands despite attempts to hold the single sheet steady. It wrinkled beneath her tight grip and crackled where a single sentence sprawled.

I am coming.

But the signature, the single letter ending the note, made her blood freeze.

S

She was as good as dead.

CHAPTER ONE

The battlefield, pockmarked with old cars and metal remains, yawned before Nick Carmichael and his fellow SEALs. He'd never fought a battle quite like this before, nor faced a more formidable opponent.

He crouched behind a beat-up red pickup truck. The insides had disappeared at some point, leaving the shell to the mercy of enemy fire. Nick dug his boots deeper into the mud, evidence of rain the night before, although the deceptively blue sky showed no trace of it now. Despite the cool temperature, moisture seeped from beneath his armor. He hated feeling stuck and sweaty.

He folded his body behind the tire to avoid the peppered shots coming from the other side and glanced down the line to Micah Richards, his best friend and the brother of his fiancée, Kaylan. The enemy had them pinned for now, but Nick grew tired of waiting.

"I thought you said she knew how to shoot," Nick shouted over the cacophony of paintballs striking the truck bumper.

Micah lifted his face mask and rolled his eyes. Yellow paint splattered above his head and dusted his nearly black hair. He ducked.

"Masks on!" shouted the referee from across the field. Micah slapped his mask down again just as a pink paintball splattered near his feet.

"I said we taught her. Not that she was good." He shrugged, his voice muffled beneath the plastic. "At least they are hitting somewhat close to us."

The San Diego paintball course affectionately named "The Fuel Depot" stretched the length of half a football field. It reminded Nick of a deserted old gas depot in some podunk Southern town. Nick peeked from behind the tire to get a better lay of the land. Old cars, painted to look rusted and long since retired, lounged scattered in something resembling a horizontal line formation from one end of the field to the other. Barrel obstacles sat stacked two tall and two wide throughout the course, providing the perfect cover for their wives and girlfriends currently regaling them with colored paint. The girls had insisted on playing with one fewer teammate, convinced they could still dominate.

Across the field members of their Navy SEAL Support Activity 1 team, Titus, Jay, and Colt, crept from obstacle to obstacle, avoiding fire until they finally huddled with Nick and Micah. David and Seth Richards—Micah's brothers visiting for the week—joined from the other end of the painted metal line.

They could shoot. They just couldn't aim.

"Come on out, fellas!" Titus's wife, Liza, yelled as another barrage of fire peppered the air. Her frizzy black hair stuck out at odd angles beneath the elastic strap holding her mask in place.

"Yeah, don't be chicken," Megan, Kaylan's roommate, hollered from behind a barrel. Nick had the sudden urge to add some color to her normally dark clothes.

"Says the girl at the back of the course," Jay shouted back. He spat in the mud and crouched behind the truck with Nick. Self-titled team prankster, he clearly didn't see the current predicament as challenge enough for his skills.

Nick pulled a piece of Juicy Fruit from his pocket and popped it in his mouth. "Colt, you got eyes on all the girls?"

Colt's grin sparked beneath his mask. As team daredevil, taking on the ladies doubled as the perfect job for him. He'd even brought a date, Jia, a leggy redhead more skater girl than hipster. Where most of the guys dreaded the repercussions of shooting the girls and hearing about it later, Colt didn't carry that emotional stake just yet. "Jia is to our right about fifteen yards behind the brown Chevy. Liza is the closest behind that jacked-up blue bug."

"My sister is hiding out behind a couple of barrels off to our right and back about twenty yards," Seth huffed beneath his mask. The single barrel he crouched behind barely concealed his tall, full University of Alabama linebacker frame.

"Anyone else?"

At their silence, Nick rolled over again, trying to gauge the direction of the paintballs with the locations he now knew. His sniper skills served him well in moments like these. Melody, David's girlfriend, popped from behind a single barrel at the back right of the field to fire a shot. He grinned at her shoot-and-hide approach. That left one more.

"Jay, where's your date, man?"

"My what?"

Micah bent next to him and slapped him across the chest. "Gorgeous blonde, successful lawyer, way out of your league, responds to Bree. Ringing any bells?"

"Oh, right." His bored expression caused Nick to chuckle. "She's got guts. She's behind the car right next to Liza and sneaking pretty close to our line."

A movement caught Nick's eye, and he fired. A frustrated cry met his ears. Bree stood tall with her hands over her head, rounding one of the barrels. "I'm out. You happy?"

"Well, one down." Nick rolled and sat up, wiping the drying mud from his cargo shorts. "Jay, if you don't like her, why'd you bring her?"

"Because Megan won't go out with me. Now, for the love of everything sacred, can we please put them out of their misery?" Jay begged as he readied his gun. "Whose idea was it to play paintball with a bunch of women anyway?"

"I can't take much more of this. They think they're winning," Colt huffed.

"They have to be about out of ammo," Titus said as he swiped a bead of sweat rolling down his neck. "Those guns only hold so much paint."

The January sun hovered in the California sky, heating the metal around them. Nick sighed. "Kaylan bruises like a peach. I'm going to hear about it for the next two weeks."

Jay flipped his mask up, his blue eyes incredulous. "That's what's holding us back? Man, forget this!" With a whistle, the men took off in twos and threes, taking cover behind the rusty-looking metal. Gunfire erupted in earnest. The SEALs were out to win.

Micah slapped Nick's back. "She's your problem now, my friend. No refunds or exchanges." He chuckled as he scurried off.

"I haven't married her yet," Nick muttered. Feminine cries filled the air around him. He might as well help end this quickly. He rolled onto his belly beneath the truck and readied his weapon. He watched Kaylan creep closer and take cover behind two metal barrels fifteen yards away. She took aim facing away from him, her green eyes intent beneath her mask. Nick grinned. Why not up the stakes a bit?

"Yo, Seth! Feel like picking on your big sister?"

Seth shuffled closer and leaned down to hear as the carnage continued, the SEALs now fully engaged and decimating the enemy. "What do you have in mind?"

Nick's smile spread wider in anticipation, his breath heating the air in his face mask. "How 'bout a game of catch? Keep her distracted while I sneak up behind her. I'll take her hostage, and we'll force the girls to surrender."

Seth smirked. "You do remember this is paintball and not BUD/S, right?"

Nick remembered well his days training to be a SEAL, but it's what made this faux war even more fun. "You're playing with SEALs, son." He slapped Seth on the back and crouched low to take his position before Seth could toss another jab his way. He needn't have worried. Seth trained his sights on his sister instead.

"Hey, Kayles, we taught you to shoot better than that."

His taunt worked like a charm. Kaylan fired. The shot went wide, causing Seth to momentarily duck and snicker. His head popped up as he continued his teasing, fulfilling his role of little brother. Nick ran to the next barrel. A shot zinged from his right. He swiveled, aimed, and fired in a fluid movement. With a grunt, Megan lost her balance and fell rear first into the mud. There. Now he'd added a bit of color.

"Seriously?" Megan shrieked. She swiped at paint on her protective vest as she stood to her feet and stalked off the field. "I hate pink."

Nick smirked, imagining her in the pink bridesmaids dresses Kaylan had picked in honor of Sarah Beth, her best friend who had died in the Haiti earthquake almost a year before. He shook his head. Only two barrels remained between Kaylan and him, but Kaylan only had eyes for Seth.

His shoes squished in the soft earth as he ran to the next barrel, assessing the scene. Bree, Megan, and Jia slumped off to the side, watching the guys clean shop. Jay stood fuming next to them, paint on the center of his mask and covering his thigh. “Let’s end this, boys,” he shouted. Only Kaylan, Liza, and Melody remained in the game. Nick knew just how to force their hand. With a final sprint, he pounced on Kaylan.

“Nuh-uh, gorgeous. Just drop the gun nice and easy.”

She squealed and tried to swivel around in his arms. “Nick Carmichael, this is paintball, not war games, and I am trying to shoot my smart-mouth little brother.”

“I’m afraid I can’t let you do that. He may be a smart-mouth, but he’s on my team.”

“I heard that, traitor!” Seth shouted.

Nick pulled Kaylan to her feet in front of him with his arm wrapped around her and his gun held at the ready in his other hand.

“All right, all right. Game’s over, ladies. Time to give it up,” Nick called across the field to Liza and Melody.

“Don’t think because you’ve got Kaylan, we won’t still shoot,” Liza hollered. Titus had married a spitfire. A spitfire he was about to extinguish from the looks of it.

“Liza, look out,” Melody and Kaylan yelled from different sides of the field.

Liza spun and fired at Titus just as Colt let loose a round that splattered against her back. A howl ripped from her mouth. The look she shot at her husband probably stung more than paintballs. Nick smothered a grin as Titus tried to appease her. David put a quick end to Melody with a shot to her toes peeking out from beneath an old, dented Cadillac, and the game came to a close.

Kaylan swung around in Nick's arms, her green eyes sparkling. "That, my dear fiancé, was world-class cheating."

Nick bit back a chuckle. He pulled her face mask off, placed a finger under her chin, and lifted her green eyes to meet his. "When you learn how to actually shoot, we might call it a game."

"You jerk," she squealed. "I grew up in the South. I can outride and outshoot most other people."

Nick crossed his arms over his chest as Kaylan's brothers and Melody joined them at the barrels in the center of the field. "First of all, not everyone in the South rides a horse, so don't perpetuate the stereotype. Second, remember who you are playing with. You will never outshoot us. And third, your brothers epically failed to teach you how to shoot at anything."

"Hey there, don't blame us. We tried." Micah popped Nick on the back of the head.

"She finally shot a coke bottle a couple of years ago," David said as he threw his arm around Melody. The petite blonde folded her arms and leaned into him, her smile evidence of her familiarity with Richards' family banter.

"Actually," Seth interrupted, "I kind of shot that bottle and let her take the credit." He ran a hand through his sweaty russet hair. His sheepish expression almost made Nick feel sorry for Kaylan. Almost.

"Seth Richards, I really am going to kill you." Kaylan's face went red as she took off after her brother. She was no match for the sophomore collegiate football star. He let her chase him before turning around and flipping her over his shoulder. He trundled back to his family as she screamed.

"Shall we?" he motioned to the parking lot where the rest of the guys and their wives and girlfriends waited.

"I'll take her," Nick responded, bracing himself as Seth dumped Kaylan into his arms. Nick swung her into a cradle position and followed David, Micah, Seth, and Melody to the gravel parking lot. Laughter drifted on the breeze, and Nick thanked God for the family he would join in just a short time.

He gently placed Kaylan on the ground and they hung back for some alone time, Kaylan's eyes following her brothers. "You know, sometimes I hate that my brothers are all much stronger and taller than I am. I think God made a mistake by not giving me a sister." A sadness stole across her eyes, tugging at Nick's heart.

He pulled her into a hug. "You had one, babe," he murmured, thinking of Sarah Beth. Joy. That word always came to mind when he remembered the bubbly blonde Kaylan had grown up with.

"I know."

They walked in companionable silence and climbed into his Jeep. Nick allowed the quiet to linger as he pulled onto the road behind his friends and headed back toward Imperial Beach and the tiny house he lived in with Micah. Gravel crunched beneath the tires and a thin layer of trees lined the back road as they pulled away from the pop of other paintball games behind them.

"Speaking of sisters ..."

"No, Kaylan."

He felt her eyes on his profile but kept his gaze glued to the road. He added pressure to the gas pedal.

"Nick, we've got to talk about it. You've got to talk about it. It's already been a couple of months since you learned of her existence. I know you've been busy with work and then Christmas and now my brothers visiting, but you need to meet her."

He met her eyes. "I thought we were talking about Sarah Beth. When are we going to talk about her?"

"That's not fair, Nick."

He gripped the steering wheel, regretting the low blow. "I know. I'm sorry."

"January twelfth is in four days. I can't believe it's been a year since the Haiti earthquake. A year since she . . . you know. I'll figure something out. It's just hard. No one here knew her."

"Your brothers are here and they did. And I met her too when we first started dating. Let's do something to remember her while they are in town."

The wind grew louder in her silence, and he glanced over. She sat rigid, her jaw tight, her eyes moist. She swung her gaze to meet his, and the fierce look surprised him.

"I promise I will figure out a way to grieve and celebrate Sarah Beth if you promise to plan a time to go meet your sister."

"Kaylan . . ."

"Promise."

He gripped the steering wheel harder, the hot rubber uncomfortable beneath his sweaty palm. "I promise."

"I want her at our wedding, Nick."

His heart leapt at her quiet statement, but he said nothing. Instead, he ground his teeth and punched the button to turn on the radio.

A cloud drifted over the sun and a cool breeze chilled his skin. He didn't want to deal with this. He didn't want to deal with any of it.

But he no longer had a choice.

CHAPTER TWO

The sweet smell of icing drifted from Carla's Bakery as Nick held the door open for Kaylan. Cake tasting. One more thing to check off her wedding list, and she didn't even have to bribe Nick to come. And she was lucky that Carla, the owner, had agreed to come in on a Sunday. She tucked a loose strand of hair behind her ear, noticing a streak of paint from their morning game that hadn't washed off in the shower.

"This is going to spoil my dinner," Kaylan muttered as Carla led them to a counter where several samples waited for them.

"Ruin dinner? Babe, I'm making this my dinner." Nick licked his lips and rubbed his stomach.

Kaylan rolled her eyes. "Sure. You get to eat anything you want and somehow maintain those abs. I eat one bite and gain one pound on my hips."

His hands came to rest on her waist, causing her to jump at the unexpected touch. His breath warmed the side of her face, his nearness and touch sending a chill down her spine. "Lies. You are gorgeous just the way you are," Nick whispered. He placed a quick kiss on her shoulder and then pulled her chair out for her, flashing a mischievous grin at the woman helping them.

Kaylan's cheeks flushed, but she couldn't let it rest. "Are you going to be one of those guys that tells me I look amazing every time I ask if I look fat?"

Nick tapped his chin and studied her. "Well, that depends. Are you going to be one of those women who is constantly asking that?"

"Probably not."

"Well then, don't worry about it. Besides, my honest streak would kick in soon enough. But for the record, I always think you look gorgeous."

Carla, a woman with deep brown skin and hazel eyes, cleared her throat and with a knowing smile began to explain the selections. Vanilla with buttercream. Chocolate with raspberry topping. Red velvet with cream cheese.

"Mm, this one," Nick mumbled, his mouth still relishing the red velvet option.

"For a wedding cake?"

"For whatever. You can't go wrong with red velvet."

"I think you are supposed to go with chocolate or vanilla options at a wedding."

"Says who?"

Kaylan blinked. "Says . . . everyone?"

"That doesn't work for me." Nick crossed his arms over his chest.

"Nick Carmichael, there are unwritten rules about weddings that you just wouldn't understand."

"Babe, no one can tell me what cake I need to prefer at my wedding." He pointed to the red velvet cake. "Carla, we're going with this."

"Whoa." Kaylan threw up her hand. "Carla, can you give us a minute?"

She chuckled. "I'll do you one better. I'll give you a few."

Kaylan turned to her fiancé. "I think we should go with the vanilla for the wedding cake and chocolate for the groom's cake."

"Vanilla for the main cake. Red velvet for the groom's cake." He shot a thumb in the direction of his rock-hard chest. "I'm the groom, remember?"

Kaylan poked his ribs. "Not if you don't cooperate." Kaylan knew she'd made a mistake a split second too late. "Nick, don't." She jerked and started laughing as his fingers struck all the sensitive places in her rib cage. "We are in public," she rasped, trying not to squeal.

He wrapped his arm around the back of the chair and leaned in close to her face. "Who cares?" His lips found hers, warm, smooth, with just a hint of red velvet. It really did taste good.

"You win." She pulled back, her eyes still closed. "A red velvet groom's cake."

Nick pumped a fist in the air, his muscle highlighted beneath his thin sweatshirt. "Success. See? Compromise already."

Carla joined them again. "Did you work it out?"

"I think so. We are going to go with the vanilla for the main cake in the design I gave you." She stole a quick glance at Nick. "And red velvet cupcakes for the groom's side."

"Wait, whoa. Cupcakes?" Nick shook his head and removed his arm from the back of her chair. "No way. We are not doing cute cupcakes with all my buddies coming."

"Compromise, remember?" She knew she was poking a tiger, but she couldn't help her sly grin.

Nick's face told her she was in for trouble later. "Right. Carla, we will take vanilla cupcakes for the main cake, arranged like Kaylan asked for in . . . what's that word again?"

"Tiers?" Carla prompted. Kaylan smirked. Great. Nick had yet another admirer. Thank goodness he still hadn't won Megan over yet or Kaylan would never have people on her side.

"Exactly. Tiers. And we will take a red velvet groom's *cake*," he emphasized, his blue eyes coming to land on Kaylan, sparking with playfulness.

Kaylan thought about it for a moment, envisioning a tiered cupcake arrangement in beautiful ivory, with maybe a few coral-colored roses mixed in for a pop of color.

She nodded slowly. "I think that will work."

Carla finished writing on her notepad. "Got it. Great! We will make sure that is ready for you." She leaned forward as if to share a secret. "And can I just say, you two make a gorgeous couple."

Now Kaylan really knew Carla had taken a liking to her fiancé. Seriously, he could charm a barracuda and leave it swooning.

"She just radiates enough beauty for both of us. Ready, Kayles?" Nick wrapped his arm around her waist and kissed her cheek.

With a nod to Carla, they stood and exited the sweet-smelling shop.

Cool air twirled around Kaylan, but not quite as brisk as an Alabama winter. Kaylan shed her heavy jacket. "Oh man, I miss seasons at home. Why is California so warm in January?"

"It's sixty-three, Kayles. That's cold." His jeans and light sweatshirt told another story. And he once again had persistently worn flip-flops.

"But back home it gets even cooler than that. Most of the time, anyway. You know, sweater weather, fun coats, cute boots, and scarves." She laughed at the face he made. "Fine. You could care less about winter fashion."

Nick held open the door to his Jeep and waited as she climbed in. "Well, who knows. Maybe we will be stationed in Virginia Beach one day, and then I'll be the one complaining about the weather." He closed her door and walked around to the driver's side, climbed in, and eased the car out of the shopping center. Saturday night traffic taunted them with the glittering array of red bumper lights. "Maybe text your brothers and let them know we might be a few minutes late for dinner."

They sat in silence as traffic crept in front of them. "Kayles, do you really miss home that much?" Nick's voice broke through the monotony.

She turned to look at him, sensing hidden emotion in his tone. At times she found it hard to cut through the neutral veneer he erected. It kept him calm as a SEAL but shielded her from his thoughts. "I think it's harder after being at home and then coming back." Her thoughts drifted to the holidays—Thanksgiving with Megan back in Alabama, holiday parties with the Teams in California before going back to Alabama for a home-style Christmas. She'd gone for a ride on Black-eyed Pea; made apple cider with Mom; talked to Pap and Gran for hours; beat her brothers in Monopoly; gone for runs with Seth; spent time with David, Melody, and Melody's little girl; built a model ship with her dad. Then they'd flown back to California, and time with her brothers here kept home close by. But they were leaving in two days, right after they celebrated Sarah Beth.

A well of nostalgia and longing bubbled up, threatening to engulf her. She wanted to give in, but one look at Nick's blue eyes and the tide passed. She reached for his hand and threaded her fingers through his, once again noticing how well they fit together. She'd found the home she'd always longed for with a man who belonged at sea.

She squeezed his hand and looked to the road ahead of them. "I'm right where I should be."

"Yes, you are." He brought her hand to his lips and placed a gentle kiss on her fingers. "Right next to me."

The pang that too often flitted across her heart bore down with gentle pressure. She took a deep breath to maintain control of the fear she constantly held at bay. The one she had chosen to bury the last few months. "Should we talk about what that looks like when you aren't right next to me?"

He stole a quick glance at her. "You lived through a couple of short deployments with Support Activity 1. Didn't those help? My Team will only deploy for about six months."

"I don't know that those are quite the same. You'll be deploying for real in the next year. What does that look like?"

He squeezed her hand as he pulled the Jeep into the parking lot of their favorite seafood place. The engine ground to a halt. Nick turned to face her. His hesitancy surprised her. Why wouldn't he talk about this? He usually initiated the conversations, quick to reassure her, determined to walk her through every step, a champion for fighting her every insecurity. But his silence? That was unusual. It sent every nerve in her body running scared.

"Nick?"

"Kayles, can we—" His phone rang. In the gathering shadows, she watched his face morph from hesitant to hardened. His Navy SEAL mode kicked in full force. "I need to take this. I'll meet you inside?" His fingers tightened on hers and then let go as he answered the phone.

She crawled from the car and headed inside. It was difficult knowing he probably wouldn't be able to share the details of the conversation with her later. The closer the wedding date, the more removed Nick became about anything deep or personal. She could handle deployments. She could handle being away from home. But there was one lesson couldn't handle again, one she couldn't tolerate for long –

the idea of being cut off from Nick, her best friend, and being isolated and alone.

And right now, his presence of body and absence of emotion scared her more than any deployment could.

"Jake, what's up?" Nick didn't feel like small talk with his old friend in the CIA. Jake wouldn't call unless he had a reason, and Nick dreaded finding out the "why."

"Hey, man. How's life in sunny Cali?"

Nick ran a hand over his face. I guess they were going to ease in. "Oh, you know. Probably about the same as it is in Virginia."

"Nah, much colder. And we get that cold, white, powdery stuff instead of the warm, brown, grainy stuff that gets stuck everywhere."

"Yeah. I'm perfectly content with my sand." Nick gripped the steering wheel and stared at the restaurant. "Jake, seriously, what's up?"

"Just wanted to let you know your mom is talking and partnering with us."

Nick gritted his teeth, knowing his friend couldn't give him full details over the phone. The identification of their relationship was meant to determine his emotional state. He decided to play neutral.

"Well, isn't that sweet of her." Nick paused, trying to figure out the best way to determine if she was still locked away or if she had been moved to Virginia. "Is she enjoying all that snow?"

"You know she prefers the cold. But I think she misses her yacht."

Nick released a breath. At least she wasn't headed back to California, free to roam as she pleased.

"Well, I hope she gives you what you need."

Silence lengthened on the other line.

"Jake?"

"That's the thing. I think she could help more if you two talked."

Nick stifled a groan. In other words, she was only giving information in pieces and still holding some of her cards close to the vest, using communicating with him as a bargaining chip to share more intel.

"Man, you know the job. Things are busy." Inwardly he groaned. He didn't want to help that woman. If he didn't talk with her, his job could be on the line. But if he talked to her, his job might be on the line too. Nick nearly growled at the no-win situation.

"I know. I just need your permission to play a game with her."

"Uh . . ." His brain went into overdrive trying to decode the spook lingo Jake seemed to be feeding him. But whatever it was, he didn't care. He didn't want any part of it. "Listen. You do your job. I'll do mine. We'll call it good."

"That's all I needed. Take care, Nick, and tell that bride of yours I'll see her at the wedding. I might even bring a date."

The call ended. Nick sat stock still, his heart racing, remembering a few months earlier when he had discovered that a wanted terrorist was his mother. And that same mother had cost Logan his leg and kidnapped Kaylan and Megan. In the aftermath, he'd undergone questioning and an investigation. He'd worried he would lose his job. The job he loved. The job that made him what he was—a United States Navy SEAL.

He smacked his palm against the steering wheel. If she was asking for him, then it couldn't be good. She'd confessed that she didn't have a motherly bone in her body, and he wasn't about to think she had changed after a short time in jail. If anything, she wanted to get back to her life of luxury.

And then there was that little bomb Pap had dropped. A sister. Natalie Grace. Somewhere in California. He shook his head. Too much. It was all too much. All he cared about right now was working with his team to catch Janus's boss and marrying the girl of his dreams. Everything else could wait.

Slowly he unfolded himself from his Jeep, slammed the door behind him, and crossed the parking lot. He stopped at the restaurant door, his eyes drifting to the scene on the other side of the window. Kaylan's head tipped back in laughter. Her cheeks flushed pink in the dim lighting. He knew that sound, melodic, comforting. A loose bun held her wavy, auburn hair at the back of her head. She leaned toward Seth, grinning from ear to ear before laughing again. Micah, David, and Melody sat across from them, snacking on peanuts and joining in the joke. As the waiter approached the table, Kaylan came alert, her eyes roaming in a quick study of the restaurant.

Looking for him.

He reached for the brass door handle on the big wooden door and stepped into the din. His girl waited for him. Tomorrow could wait. As he crossed under lingering Christmas lights to join their table, he muttered a mantra all SEALs knew by heart: "The only easy day was yesterday."

CHAPTER THREE

The evening hours arrived before Kaylan could fully prepare—the time to remember Sarah Beth's homegoing. All day, Kaylan had fought the desire to snap at her brothers or respond sarcastically to Megan. In truth, she had failed in both departments. It wasn't until she finally retreated to the solace of her room and grabbed an old photo album that she allowed herself to feel. When would the grief lessen? Some days, Kaylan forgot to hurt, forgot to feel sad. She would pick up the phone to tell her best friend about her day, only to feel the distant weight of rubble settle on top of her.

Truth be told, she didn't think there would come a day when she didn't miss Sarah Beth Tucker. If that day came, Kaylan feared it would mean she'd forgotten. Forgotten the hard lessons learned in Haiti, forgotten Sarah Beth's bubbly personality, forgotten how she made Kaylan love deeper, laugh harder, and live in the here and now.

Her ringing phone jarred her reverie. Pap. How did he always know when she needed him?

"Sugar, it's your Pap." She couldn't help but smile. He'd long since ignored the fact she had caller ID. Said it made it more personal when a person declared themselves.

"Sugar?"

At the sound of his voice, her emotions caved. Tears coursed down her cheeks as she held back her sobs. She clutched the photo album to her chest and leaned back against her headboard.

"Ah, baby. Micah told me what you were going to do tonight. So I knew it would be a tough day. Wish your parents, Gran, and I were there. We're telling our own stories here. Talk to me, sugar."

Kaylan sniffed. A tear dripped off her face and landed on her arm. More followed its silent trek. "She should be here, Pap. I don't want to do this. She should be here."

Her gaze drifted to the album and a picture of Sarah Beth and Kaylan on her parents' lake house dock. The sun cast a translucent glow on Sarah Beth's blonde curls as they posed in their chairs, soaking up the summer sun. Sunglasses on and skin lathered with tanning lotion, they'd thought they were too cool to be fourteen, despite their telling braces and acne. The camera had captured Micah and Seth creeping up behind them. The next photo caught their unwilling dunk into the lake. A smile broke through her tears.

"Remember that winter Sarah Beth broke her arm, Sugar? You two stayed inside for weeks."

Kaylan blinked back another wave of tears. "I don't know how many Doris Day movies we watched then. She was fifteen but still went for that hot pink cast. She wanted everyone to sign it. So of course everyone did." Kaylan clutched at her shirt right above her heart, as if reaching for it could somehow numb the pain. Her chest ached with the loss. "Everyone always loved her. Why, Pap? I still don't understand why."

"Ah, sugar. No backtracking now. You've asked your whys and hows and how comes. It doesn't change the fact that God is God, and we're just not going to get it this side of heaven."

"But I want to understand. I want her back." Kaylan reached for a tissue on her nightstand and dabbed at her nose. "She should be in my wedding, Pap. I never bought into that whole notion of romantic soul mates. But friends? Sarah Beth was my soul mate, my heart friend. What if you only get one of those? I grew up with her. What if no one else can measure up? What if I don't want someone else? What if I just want her back?"

"Now, Sugar, I need you to snap out of it." Pap's strong, smooth voice anchored her harried emotions. "I need you to remember the sweet moments. The reason you two went to Haiti. I need you to remember what Sarah Beth told you in her last minutes before the good Lord took her home. She was ready. You got that, sugar? No regret. No wishing for more time. She was ready."

Kaylan remembered those last moments all too well. They haunted her dreams. But rarely did she remember the words associated with the broken, dusty, bloody image. She sniffed and took a breath. The tears eased a bit. Peace. That's what she'd seen on her friend's face. Excitement to be with her heavenly Father. And her last words to Kaylan were to count it all joy.

"She reminded me to be happy."

"You do not have to mourn your best friend forever. I loved that little girl like a granddaughter, and I know she would want to stand next to you at your wedding."

The waterworks resumed, and Kaylan groaned. She squeezed her eyes shut. "Pap, you're supposed to help me stop crying."

"Now hang on there, sugar. Hear me out. She would want to be right next to you in your wedding if she were still here. But I guarantee, she doesn't want to come back down from glory to stand next to you on some hot, sandy beach."

Kaylan laughed at the image. In that light, it did look ridiculous. Why would she want to come back? Why would Kaylan want her to?

"I just miss her, Pap."

"And you probably always will. There won't come a day when you won't want her by your side. But the perspective will grow, and the years will pass. Before you know it, you'll be up there with her, and all this time spent missing her will seem pointless." Silence stretched over the phone. Then Pap cleared his throat. "Sugar." His voice grew husky, and Kaylan knew he cried for the girl they'd both loved and for Kaylan and for a thousand tomorrows, but neither of them cried because of her residence. "She wanted you to live."

A knock sounded on Kaylan's bedroom door and the noisy hinge groaned in protest as Megan pushed it wider. "Kayles, are you ready?"

She heard the hesitation in Megan's voice, the silent questions she refused to ask. Kaylan didn't meet her roommate's gaze. She swiped at her splotchy face. "Pap, Megan just got here. We need to go meet the guys. Thanks for calling."

"Anytime, Sugar. You call if you want to talk again. I love you."

"Love you, too. Bye, Pap."

"Hold on, hun."

Kaylan waited, her emotions ebbing a bit as she met her roommate's eyes and tried to offer a small smile. Pap continued, "You tell Megan I said hello, and you let that young woman in now, ya hear?"

Kaylan picked at her bedspread. "I have, Pap."

"I know you have, but I think you could do so a little more. She isn't Sarah Beth, but that girl makes you a stronger person."

Kaylan glanced back up at Megan. Her black three-quarter-length-sleeve shirt with a muted rose print and holey jeans made her look like a rocker. Add to that her dark brown pixie cut and cartilage piercing in her right ear, and Megan couldn't be more opposite from Kaylan. "You're right, Pap. She is pretty tough."

Megan grinned and flexed her arm muscle, her smile setting her cinnamon eyes sparkling. "Gotta go, Pap. Love you." She tossed the phone on her pillow as Megan sank down on Kaylan's lavender comforter.

"You know"—she traced a pattern on the pillowy top—"Nick will never let you have a lavender bed when you two move in together."

Laughter broke through the tears. "Oh, yeah?" Kaylan grabbed a pillow and whacked Megan over the head.

Megan jumped off the bed and leapt for a pillow on the floor, holding it in front of her like a shield. She paced, looking for the best place to pounce. "Don't dish it if you can't take it."

"Oh, I can take it." Kaylan rose up on her knees, her pillow at the ready. She struck again, barely missing. The draft worked to dry the tear tracks on her face. "And let's just say Nick wasn't around when I worked on the registry. He might have a few surprises."

"That's what returns are for." Megan lunged and tackled Kaylan, beating her with the pillow until Kaylan rolled with laughter. "I give. I give. I give."

Megan rose from the bed and brushed her bangs from her face, grinning in victory. "Like I said, don't dish it if you can't take it." She held out her hand to pull Kaylan up. "Now, are you ready to go?"

Pain descended again, though not quite as heavy this time. She didn't want to cry anymore. January 12 was three days away—the official anniversary. But it would be good to talk and laugh with her brothers and Nick and Megan tonight.

Kaylan glanced down at her own clothes, a cream off-the-shoulder shirt with a tank top underneath and jeans. She'd asked to celebrate Sarah Beth in an unusual location, and casual worked just fine.

The tires crunched over gravel as Nick pulled the car into the parking lot of their favorite frozen yogurt place. The neon pink and green sign complete with dripping yogurt for the O brightened the dark night. Nick killed the engine and they sat for a moment, Kaylan noting more cars than usual in the small lot. A group of people huddled close inside. Kaylan didn't think she could handle strangers watching her fight tears.

"Maybe we should go somewhere else." After minutes in silence her voice sounded loud to her own ears.

"Why?" Nick reached for her hand. The glow of the digital clock highlighted their laced fingers. His thumb traced circles on her wrist, sending goosebumps dancing down her arms.

"Too many people. Let's just go back to your place and turn on a movie, maybe play Monopoly with my brothers before they leave in the morning." She turned pleading eyes on his handsome face. "Please, let's just forget it."

Panic built in her chest, clawing its way up her throat. She'd thought long and hard about where to celebrate Sarah Beth, some place happy, relaxed, some place with memories, some place where tears wouldn't emerge unbidden. But sometimes the grief didn't obey her command. She'd moved past anger. She'd accepted. But a life well lived begged to be celebrated, and with that realization came the sorrow that the time appointed for Sarah Beth's life felt too short to Kaylan.

Her mind retreated back to a night in Alabama after finals. Summer lingered on the horizon, teasing them as they waited for grades and freedom. Kaylan and Sarah Beth had landed in a frozen yogurt shop after ten, strung out on coffee and ecstatic about the end of their sophomore year.

"Can you believe my French professor wanted me to read that whole page in front of the class? I swear he fakes that nasal accent. He's from Kansas, for goodness sake. And I froze, Kayles. I totally froze. Do you know how long I practiced reading that?"

Kaylan rolled her eyes and laughed as they each chose their poison—creamy goodness twirling from the machines and into their waiting cups. "Actually, yes. You were up at five-thirty this morning practicing in the mirror."

Sarah Beth winced. "You heard that?"

"*Je m'appelle* Sarah Beth. *Je viens de* Tuscaloosa. Blah blah blah."

"See, even you remember it!" She smacked her forehead with her free hand, her curls bouncing. "I mean, how do you forget your own name and where you're from?"

"In your defense, there was a lot more to that verbal exam. And you have never been great with a script in front of people."

"I know, right?" They moved to the toppings. Sarah Beth began to scoop every bright-flavored candy available onto her yogurt. "Especially a script in another language. Geez, people really need to just go with the flow. He should have just let me go up there and say whatever I could. Then he would see how much I had learned."

Kaylan chuckled. "At least you didn't have to remember how to spell every muscle in the human body." Kaylan spooned chocolate chunks on her yogurt before paying.

"You're right. You're right." Sarah Beth chose a bright pink plastic spoon and slid into a booth. "We both failed in the foreign language department today." She scooped a heaping bite of yogurt dripping with Sour Patch Kids, sprinkles, and Skittles into her mouth.

Kaylan winced. "That is way too much sugar in one bite."

"Kaylan, Kaylan, have I taught you nothing?" Sarah Beth rolled her eyes and sighed. "It's not about the sugar. It's about the color. It makes me happy. Happy mouth, happy belly, happy brain." She dumped the spoonful in her mouth and talked around the goodness. "And a very happy Sarah Beth Tucker."

"Whatever you say, Bubbles."

They stayed until close, exhaustion and sugar pushing them to the point of delirium. By the time the manager kicked them out, Kaylan's stomach ached from laughing so hard, and Sarah Beth's tongue had turned a dark brown from all the dyed candy. Swearing to the manager that they weren't drunk, they left the shop giggling uncontrollably, arms around one another, celebrating the perfect end to an imperfect day.

"Kayles? Come back to me."

She blinked as Nick's deep voice tugged her back to the present. She swallowed back sadness at the memory. Sadness and the urge to laugh uncontrollably.

"It will just be hard to celebrate with that huge group of strangers in there."

"Well ..." Nick cleared his throat just as a blonde-headed child skipped from the middle of the group. Kaylan recognized Molly Carpenter, Logan and Kim's little girl, and the apple of Nick's eye.

"Nick Carmichael, why are the Carpenters here?"

He rubbed his hand over his hair and just looked at her.

"Nick," she warned.

"They wanted to come, Kaylan." He shrugged. "The guys heard what we were doing tonight, and they wanted to be here for you."

"But they didn't know her. Why would they possibly want to come?"

His finger traced a trail down her cheek, his feather light touch awakening every nerve in her body. He leaned forward and placed a kiss on her lips. His face a breath away, he whispered, "Kaylan, when are you going to accept that there are people who love you? They want to support you."

For the last few months, Kaylan had locked away her sadness about Sarah Beth, only sharing it when necessary, never allowing the ache to control her life, not after the darkness that had swept through her in the immediate months after the earthquake. She'd fought a depression that dragged her so far down that she couldn't love, couldn't accept love, and couldn't even acknowledge her loving Father.

It had taken an act of God to break that nightmare. An act of God and Nick Carmichael. Still, during the times she remembered the death of her best friend and the destruction of a nation, she wished she could switch her emotions off. But she knew strong emotion often came with a soft heart. And to let others love her in her darkest moments meant freedom.

Nick's Team didn't look at her and see an earthquake survivor or the victim of a kidnapping or even the girl who lost her best friend. They saw Kaylan.

Like her, they had lived through suffering. They had walked through the loss of Logan's leg, the time away from loved ones and family, and the sacrifice of fighting. And yet, they still showed up for one another.

A car door slammed next to them. Kaylan jumped at the tap on her window. Micah stood there, a sad smile on his face, with Seth, David, Melody, and Megan right behind him. She turned to look at the yogurt shop and noticed that the Carpenters, Titus and Liza, Jay, and Colt all stood at the window waiting for her. Tears welled in her eyes, and one trickled down her cheek.

"No tears, Kayles." Nick brushed it away with his calloused thumb, kissing her cheek in its wake. "It's time to celebrate the life of someone you loved with others who love you." He nodded at Micah, who opened her door and pulled her from the car.

"You ready to do this?" He placed his arm around her shoulders as Nick rounded the car to join them.

Kaylan could only nod as she wound her fingers with Nick's and leaned into her brother. Her feet dragged on the gravel as they approached the brightly lit shop.

A bell jingled above the door as David held it open for the group. With a deep breath, Kaylan stepped into warmth, brightness, and an immediate party.

"Hey! She's here." Colt gave Kaylan a hug.

"'Bout time." Jay grinned. "We thought we were going to have to come out there and carry you in."

"I know how you accomplish jobs. There is no way you are carrying me anywhere."

Jay laughed. "Stubborn little fireball you got there, Hawk."

Nick punched Jay's arm. "That she is."

Kim Carpenter fought through the mass of hellos to wrap her arms around Kaylan. Despite her small frame, her hug was fierce. "I can't believe you didn't tell us."

"Yeah, girl." Liza sidled up, her fluffy black hair drifting into Kaylan's face. "What were you thinking?"

"I was thinking you wouldn't want to come."

Megan hip-bumped Kaylan as she joined in. "See what I have to deal with?" she told Liza and Kim.

"Girl, we wouldn't miss it," Liza said as they ushered Kaylan to the cups. The kids started filing through the line under Logan's supervision, with Colt, Jay, and Seth close behind.

"Aunt Kaylan, Aunt Kaylan!" Molly came running up. She wore a headband with a pink rose that sat mussed to one side.

"Hey, ladybug," Kaylan said, using Nick's nickname for her. She bent down and straightened the headband. "What's up?"

"Do you like my headband? Uncle Nick said your friend loved pink." She leaned close, her sticky hand drawing strands of Kaylan's hair as she whispered, "Just like me. I love pink everything."

Kaylan's heart jumped a bit at Nick's thoughtfulness and Molly's care. She tapped the little girl on the nose. "I love it. And Sarah Beth would have, too. Thank you."

Molly smiled shyly. "You're welcome. Will you help me pick the stuff to go on top?"

Kaylan chuckled at Molly's already melting chocolate yogurt. "Sure thing, ladybug. Let me just get mine real quick."

"Hurry, Aunt Kaylan. Before everything melts."

Kaylan bit back her laugh at Molly's drama as she grabbed a cup and filled it with plain yogurt, perfect for the toppings she had in mind.

"Aunt Kaylan, you move too slow." Molly grabbed Kaylan's free hand and tugged her in front of the guys, drawing a few laughs and complaints. A hand settled on her waist, and she leaned back against the man behind her. She'd know his touch anywhere, and she knew Nick would have her back tonight. And every step of the way.

"Now what should I get?" Molly wondered, her eyes bright and fixed on the sugar at eye level to her four-year-old height.

"What do you like?"

"Sprinkles and chocolate."

"You got it." Kaylan spooned the toppings onto Molly's yogurt as the little girl held the cup high.

"Kaylan, if you put her in a sugar coma, you get to take her home tonight," Logan warned from a few people back.

"Oh, can we have a sleepover?" Molly did a little jig, and a few sprinkles tumbled to the floor.

"Not today, munchkin." She surveyed her selections, but she didn't have to think too hard before she began shoveling ingredients into her cup.

"Sprinkles, Sour Patch Kids, and Skittles? You aren't normally a candy girl, babe."

She met Nick's eyes, drawing strength from the depth she found there. "It's not for me." She caught Micah's knowing smile as they turned to pay.

If this night was a celebration, then she was going to do her best to remember everything about Sarah Beth that once made her smile. The sweet memories didn't have to fade.

While Nick paid for their treats, Kaylan slipped a spoonful into her mouth, her tongue protesting at the instant tang of yogurt and sour candy. She smiled. She loved it. She slipped into a blue plastic chair, the din of her friends' conversation overpowering the steady hum of the yogurt machines lining the wall.

Oh, how life had changed in just a year. She missed a lot of things, had experienced the worst pain of her life, but oddly enough, she wouldn't change any of it, except losing Sarah Beth. She took another bite. But this. This night made her realize goodness didn't live in the past. It existed now, ready to be seized in the present.

Molly squirmed into Kaylan's lap. Her cup began to tip, and Nick threw out his hand to steady her.

"I got it, Uncle Nick."

"Molly, baby, Aunt Kaylan probably doesn't want you in her lap."

"It's okay, Kim." She smiled at her friend, who was feeding three-month-old Nadia a bottle. "I promise."

Truth be told, Molly was therapeutic, a taste of sunshine and sweetness. Bubbly and joyful, she was a little Sarah Beth in the making. Despite her dad's frequent deployments and the recent loss of his leg, Molly's spirit remained unbridled. Kaylan intended to enjoy that for as long as Molly was part of her life.

"Aunt Kaylan, why did you get so much candy?"

"Because my friend Sarah Beth fixed her yogurt like this."

"Do you still miss her?"

"Molly Carpenter," Logan's voice boomed, and everyone at the table stilled.

Kaylan swallowed and summoned a smile, a smile she felt in her heart a bit more every time she used it. "It's okay, Logan."

Kaylan felt the weight of their eyes, the calculated gazes of the SEALs, familiar with life lost. Compassion danced across the faces of Megan, Kim, Melody, and Liza, mixed with a regret that she now had to respond. But on the faces of her brothers and Nick, she saw reassurance and an encouragement to accept, to share, to let people in, to reclaim a little of the girl she used to be.

She turned to Molly. "Yes, I still miss her. She was my best friend ever, and I met her when I was about your age." She squeezed Molly, eliciting a musical giggle. "She had curly blonde hair, just like you. She smiled and laughed all the time."

"Just like me?" Molly pointed at her chest with her dripping spoon.

"Yep, munchkin, just like you." Kaylan's heart constricted. Nick slipped his arm around her shoulders, his fingers drifting up and down her arm.

"Daddy says she's in heaven. Is that right, Aunt Kaylan?"

Kaylan cleared her throat, ignoring the eyes focused on her. "Yes, last year about this time she went to heaven to be with Jesus. I'll see her again someday. And today I wanted to celebrate her."

"Since she went to heaven, that means I'll get to meet her someday, too."

Kaylan leaned down and touched her nose to Molly's, grinning at her giggle. "You bet, munchkin."

Molly leaned forward and looked in Kaylan's cup, the yogurt gathering in a growing liquid pool and bleeding with color. "She sure liked a lot of candy. Look at all those colors, Aunt Kaylan! They're everywhere."

Kaylan grinned. "Don't they make you happy?"

Molly's blue eyes met hers. "I like lots of colors. Like a rainbow. They just make me smile."

Kaylan looked at her brothers, knowing they remembered Sarah Beth's candy fetish.

"Happy mouth," Micah grinned, a knowing look in his eyes. She knew he was remembering similar moments with the girl they had once known and loved.

Her heart constricted, joy and overwhelming nostalgia jockeying for prominence. But the tears were gone. At least for now. Nick wound his fingers in her hair, giving her enough strength to remember to choose joy. "And a very happy Kaylan," she whispered with a smile.

CHAPTER FOUR

Janus had made a deal with the devil, and she would have to pay. If there was one lesson she'd learned over the years it was that no good deed went unpunished. No bad deed did either, but somehow she'd managed to outrun the consequences. Until now. She should have known that someday they would come back to bite her.

A knock broke her reverie and she looked up. A man she only knew by Jake entered the interrogation room where she'd been escorted moments before. His dark hair fell above dark eyes that held a thousand secrets. She could only hope his expertise and government didn't wind up getting her killed. So far the plan had worked. Play regretful mother and sell some intel to the Americans, all for a lighter sentence, and, at the very least, a temporary reprieve from whatever demon stalked her in prison.

Unlike others she had already talked to, Jake never wore a suit when coming to see her. Today, he wore a white V-neck shirt beneath a brown leather jacket and jeans rolled up slightly over plain-toe, leather boots. His gaze and demeanor told her he would play fair, but he meant business.

He slouched against the wall, crossing his arms as he faced her where she sat perched on the edge of the seat. "Well, Anya, we have a plan."

She flinched as he said her name. No one had called her by her given name in years, but his tenor voice reminded her too much of her brother Andrei. Only he had called her "Annie."

"We will fly out of here and meet with a joint task force to pass on what you know. You so much as try to get off that base, and I will sanction anyone who sees you to use you as target practice. Are we clear?"

Anya refrained from smirking. His threats held little terror for her. She'd survived the Iron Curtain, the assassination of her beloved brother, the loss of her own children. And now the silent killer, cancer, threatened to take away what little time she had left. What more could they do to her?

The guilt snaked its way through her heart again and she bit down, squelching the pain. Andrei had always fought for the underdogs, those who just wanted a better life in the West. He rejected the confines of the Wall. He'd fought the Soviets and smuggled many to freedom. Then he'd come for her. He always came for her.

She was a rising star, poised to take a position in the East German secret police, despite her Soviet background.

So she'd watched his work from afar, even covering for him at times. It amazed her that someone could believe in something so fully that they would give their life for it, for strangers. She wouldn't do that for her country. To hades with the USSR, the German Democratic Republic, and their ideals. She believed in one thing: survival. But her brother had made her hope, made her wonder. Until someone betrayed him, and she was forced to watch as he was executed, shot pointblank for rebelling against his rulers. Their father stood without blinking, firmly trusting Andrei had been a traitor.

"Anya, are you with me?"

She schooled her features against the sudden urge to cry. With a curt nod, she muttered, "*Da.*"

"Good. And English, please." Jake came to sit at the table with her, his confident stance reminiscent of Nikolai. And Andrei. She knew their kind. The call to sacrifice won out over the instinct to survive, and their heroics could cost her. She would need to be careful.

"Nick and his team will be present at the briefing. You will not engage with him in any way. You are there only to relay intel. At the point you are no longer of use, we will ship you right back to the hell hole you are living in. Understood?"

Anya smirked and leaned forward, intertwining her hands on the table in front of her. "It would be wise for you to hold your tongue, American." She tipped her head, studying his guarded expression. "You do not know the secrets I possess."

Across the table, Jake mirrored her actions, his face coming within a foot of hers. His amused smile rankled her. "I work for the United States Central Intelligence Agency, Ms. Petrov. You do not know the secrets that I possess." His voice lowered to a whisper that chilled the air around Anya. "You are expendable."

Desperate to maintain the upper hand, she masked a wince as she leaned back in her chair. "We shall see." But inside, she feared she would never taste freedom from captivity again.

Once more, she might be forced to sell her soul. She didn't have much left to give. Wounded animals did not do well when cornered. If she went out, she planned to take people with her.

CHAPTER FIVE

Nick and Micah received the call at five in the morning on Monday. With hurried goodbyes to a groggy David and Seth, they slipped from their house and headed to the War Room on base in Coronado.

"Kaylan is going to kill me if I miss helping with the last-minute details for this wedding." Nick groaned, rubbing the sleep from his eyes as Micah drove his Mustang. Street lights cast an orange glow on the pavement as they covered the short distance.

"I told you that y'all should have taken care of every bit of it before Christmas."

"I just thought we were done with all of the short, unplanned deployments until we deploy with the Team next year. But when duty calls, we go."

Micah spun into the parking lot and crawled from the car. The two nodded at others entering the building. "Not a decision to make right now, Hawk. You've had a lot happen in the last few months. Let's just focus on the task at hand and make big decisions after the wedding."

"You better pray we make it back before the wedding."

"You have about nine weeks until March 12, man. Plenty of time. Now snap out of it."

"You really are a bulldog in the morning," Nick grumbled.

"Get me some coffee, and we'll call it good."

Rounding a corner, they entered into controlled chaos. Quiet chatter filled the room. A pump pot full of steaming black coffee with Styrofoam cups off to the side beckoned Nick and Micah. Several men with bags under their eyes eagerly filled the tiny cups. Nick always thought of the cups as a tease. They gave him just enough for a taste and an increased craving for more black fluid.

At the front of the room, their boss took the floor. "All right, ladies. Grab a cup of coffee and let's get to it," Senior Chief X shouted in his gravelly voice. His red hair stuck out at odd angles, indicating he too was a victim of an early morning wakeup call.

Titus passed Nick and Micah small Styrofoam cups filled with rich, black brew. One sip sent his brain spinning into gear. They had a full team gathered. He searched the crew and moved to join Colt and Jay, already seated on fold-out chairs in the front row. An ache filled him at Logan's absence, but he shoved it away. Logan wasn't feeling sorry for himself, so Nick wouldn't either.

"Morning, sunshines. Time to get to work. Tonight, we leave for Afghanistan for a capture-kill operation. We will join with others from SEAL Team 2 that are already deployed in the area as well as their Afghani counterparts. We will be fully briefed upon arrival. We leave tonight at twenty-three hundred hours. Let's take care of business, ladies. You know what to do."

"Radio prep at eleven hundred hours. Anyone having comms issues, come see me," newcomer Bates shouted over the noise.

"Organize and load weapons in two hours. Hawk, you're with me on that." Colt slapped him on the back as they hustled to pack up the gear.

The room broke into a flurry of activity, guys preparing for an op without specifics. But right now, they didn't need any. They were ready, come what may.

"Looks like we're going to need more coffee," Titus said, staring into his already empty cup.

Jay slapped him on the back as he stood. "You're always on top of it, my man. Good lookin' out."

Titus rolled his eyes. "You ever gonna grow up and be responsible?"

Colt dropped his arm around Jay's neck. "If he grew up, he wouldn't be the J-Man we all know and love." Jay elbowed Colt in the gut. Colt jumped back and blocked his ribs. "Easy there, brah. I was paying you a compliment."

"Logan's not here to wrangle the children. So I guess that job falls to me." Micah grinned, the coffee clearly doing its job.

"Man, please." Jay threw his head back in a laugh and jerked free of Colt. "We all know T-Brown or Hawk will have to fill those shoes now."

"Now look here, Jay . . ."

"Ladies . . ."

Nick stood and stretched, his eyes drifting to the coffee station. "Looks like X is running this ship. Let's get busy."

As Nick and Micah moved to get more coffee, Micah said, "Did you hear Logan may be able to get fitted with a prosthetic soon?"

Nick froze, his hand hovering over the pump pot. "Seriously? That's awesome! I wonder what he could do in the Teams."

Micah shrugged, dark circles evident on his tan skin. "You know him. God, family, and country. He'd jump back in in a heartbeat, and

Kim would stand by his side the whole way." Micah shook his head. "Now, that's love."

Nick filled his cup again, inhaling the steaming brew as he nodded. Since his engagement, his fear had sky-rocketed for Kaylan, for himself, for their relationship. He no longer could look out for just himself and his team. He had to consider her, too. But he knew she wouldn't ask him to do anything else with his life. Still, his heart pounded a little harder as he prepared to leave. How could he reassure her during his absence?

After prepping his gear and helping take inventory with Colt, Nick slipped away to meet Megan at four o'clock. He had only an hour and a half to take care of what he needed to before Kaylan got off work. He would stop by and see her and then head back to base to prepare for departure. Once again, he didn't know how long he would be gone, but he hoped it would be brief. The wedding approached, and Kaylan would want him nearby for all the last-minute details and preparations.

Megan stepped from her car, ripped jeans, thin black shirt, and wet hair telling Nick she had rushed her from her job at the aquatic center. While all outward appearances indicated that Megan preferred marine animals to people, Nick surmised that she really craved a deep friendship and didn't quite know how to get there. Since being taken hostage months before, she'd stopped her serial dating and one-night stands and started asking more about God. She'd softened a bit, and Nick could see Kaylan's influence in that.

Nick smiled. Kaylan couldn't help but nurture others. Her patience and sweet spirit made her a lighthouse that consistently called him to love others the way she did—with compassion and a firm hand. Man, he loved that girl.

"You rang, soldier boy?" Megan stopped in front of him and he caught the faint scent of the sea. "Don't you have other people you could call?"

He crossed his arms and leaned back against his Jeep. "Question. Do you always smell like fish?"

She rolled her eyes and turned around. "I'm outta here."

Pushing off the car, he sidestepped and cut her off. "Kidding, Meg." He chuckled and held up his hands in surrender. "Will you help me, please? It's for Kaylan."

Her eyes softened just a bit, but she huffed. "Yeah, okay, fine. What are we doing at an apartment complex in Imperial Beach?"

Nick turned her toward the front office and began to walk. "Like I said on the phone, I have to leave town for a little while. I don't want Kaylan to feel alone when deciding things that have to do with our life together, so I decided to go ahead and rent an apartment for the two of us for after the wedding. I need you to keep it our secret until she needs to know."

"And how will I know when she needs to know?"

Nick grimaced, figuring Kaylan would hit a point where she got frustrated with the ill-timed deployment and grow overwhelmed. "Trust me. You'll know."

They entered the front office and Nick signed the paperwork, paid the deposit, and grabbed the keys offered to him. He motioned to Megan. "This way. We're on the first floor."

Nick walked them to a unit in the second building. The blue-gray exterior appeared muted against the apartment's attempts to create an oasis. Brightly colored flowers and palm trees adorned the grounds, and a pool sat in the middle of the complex. Nick thought it a poor substitute for the beach only miles away.

Shoving the key in the lock, he turned the doorknob and stepped inside the home he would share with Kaylan. Megan stepped in by his side. She paced the small living and kitchen area and then headed back to the two bedrooms, one decidedly larger than the other. "What do you think? I know it's not much." But he could picture it becoming a cozy home. It was close to Titus and Liza. Close to Micah, Colt, and Jay. Close enough to the Carpenters, and countless other families in the SEAL community.

Megan came to stand before him, her brown eyes calculating. "I think she'll love it. My turn for the question. Why'd you bring me?"

"She trusts you. She needs you, Megan. You're strong, and she'll need your grit to help her stay strong and positive."

"I'm sorry, she needs me?" Megan threw up her hands, exaggerated shock written all over her face. "Soldier boy, have you met Kaylan?"

Nick nodded, the seriousness of his face telling her it was no joke. "When I'm away, it's hard on Kaylan."

"Because of losing Sarah Beth. Because of the earthquake."

"Even without that it would be hard, Meg." He walked to the window and stared at the palm tree growing just outside. Its rough, layered bark made it seem like a tall sentry, standing watch. "She's adjusting. But I think having this apartment will make it easier for her. She can even start moving our stuff in and decorating when she's ready."

Megan joined him at the window, and he held up the key. "Will you hold onto this until she needs a reminder that she isn't in this by herself? I'm leaving her some other surprises while I'm gone, and I'll need your help with those, too."

He glanced at his watch. Almost out of time.

Megan took hold of the key. "No one's ever asked me to be part of something like this before." Her brown eyes filled with awe and a hint of confusion.

"Hey, you're family to Kaylan now. You're in the wedding. We want you to be a part."

She dropped her gaze, her hands toying with the key. "Family. I never really knew what that was like." When she looked up, he saw anger brewing. Her mouth stretched in a taut line, a storm gathering behind those guarded dark eyes.

"Why do you do it? Why do you fight for your country and leave your family?" Her voice dropped to a deadly whisper. "Is it worth it?"

Nick leaned against the windowsill, wondering how to answer her question. He had asked himself the same thing recently. Given everything she'd gone through in Haiti, why ask Kaylan to endure the hardship of military life? Deep in his heart he knew the answer wasn't that simple. He also knew he was inviting her to be part of something bigger than themselves—to fight on behalf of others like God called him to. He was inviting Kaylan to be part of the incredible pride, the honor, and the camaraderie that came from belonging in this community.

But Megan's question gnawed at him daily. What if he died and left Kaylan alone? What if he wasn't there for his kids? Despite his questions, Nick kept coming to the same conclusion, and then peace flooded his soul, despite the fear. He could only tell Megan what he reminded himself every day.

"The way I see it, I have two options. I can stay at home, find a good job, raise a family, and pretend like nothing is going on. Or I can fight, whether here or abroad. I chose to fight abroad so that something like 9/11 doesn't happen again."

"But why? Why do you care when your family will pay the price for it?"

He met her gaze, understanding the pain behind her questions. She'd grown up an Army brat, her mom left the family, and her dad was either deployed or drinking. Either way, she'd been shoved off onto relatives until she'd been old enough to take care of herself. "Megan, have I ever done anything to demonstrate I'm like your dad?"

He watched her wrestle with his question. In Nick's opinion, Megan's dad had missed the best years of raising a pretty tough daughter, one who would have given him her whole-hearted support if he'd only shown her a little love.

Slowly she shook her head. Her shoulders deflated a fraction. "No."

He nodded. "I go into harm's way to fight for Kaylan and for you because I believe I'm doing something that matters, something that not everyone can do."

"Even when no one else knows what you do? What you sacrifice?"

"If I did it for the glory, I wouldn't be a SEAL. I do it because it's right. I'm fighting for good in a world full of evil, protecting and fighting against injustice."

A shadow drifted across her face as the palm leaves outside danced in the breeze. "And how do you handle all the evil? You believe in God and yet look at all you've seen. How do you see the good?"

"Are you thinking of what happened to you and Kaylan last year?"

"And Kaylan in the earthquake and what you see on every deployment that you can't tell her about. How do you see the good?"

Nick took in the apartment around him, imagining it to be a safe haven, peaceful. A place for good memories. Home. None of that was possible if men like him refused to do the hard jobs. "All I can tell you is that when bullets are flying, it's love for and trust in the men by my side that keeps me going. It's the victory in knowing that I've stopped a terrorist or freed a people from a tyrannical government. It's the freedom I witness in women and children being liberated from oppression." He gripped her shoulders and met her eyes. "Megan, it's because I believe victory belongs to God. God already won. And I'm just one man that He chooses to use to fight for others until He comes back. If I can be just a small part of that grand design, then this is all worth it. And Kaylan believes that, too."

Megan studied him, searching for sincerity. Her features were so different from Kaylan's, beautiful but darker, marked by past pain and questions. He offered her a small smile as he crossed his arms and leaned against the window frame, fighting the urge to look at his watch. "Just say what you want to say."

Whatever she'd been holding back exploded from her. "Bullets? Bullets, you idiot."

"What did you think we were shooting with? Paintballs?"

"You could get killed. You could hurt Kaylan all over again. Doesn't that freak you out?"

Nick straightened, an uncomfortable twinge coursing through him at the reminder of the fear he kept locked in the deepest recesses of his heart. It would cripple him if he allowed it to gain any ground.

"Megan, I don't want to hurt Kayles. That's not what I want . . . ever."

"Then how do you live so unafraid?" She flexed her arms. "Muscles only get you so far, soldier boy. And we all know your brains aren't keeping you going." She slumped against the wall, her voice falling to a mere whisper. "So how do you do it? How do you live so"—she searched for the right word—"brave?"

"You think I'm not scared? Everything that has happened lately terrifies me."

Meg rolled her eyes. "Please. You are as cool as a cucumber."

Nick chuckled at her theatrics. Little did she know. Never had he feared anyone or anything so much as Janus. His mother had the ability to hurt the ones he loved the most. He met Megan's brown eyes. "I trust that God is sovereign. He knows my days and this job He called me to. I can enter every situation with confidence because He goes before me, and He has given me the men that go into battle by my side. There's an inherent trust, an unspoken knowing that while I'm looking after them, they're looking after me."

"And how do you get that brave? How do you get that selfless? I would turn tail and run while firing over my shoulder."

He grinned. "Maybe just avoid the military."

"Nick, I'm not joking. How can I be brave?"

He heard the vulnerability in her tone and gentled. "Bravery is simply facing each fear and refusing to back down, even when it seems that fear has the upper hand. Fear can't stand in the face of courage. It only holds as much power as you grant it."

Megan's eyes drifted down. "I'm tired of living scared of what happened a few months ago. I'm tired of looking over my shoulder, of not letting people in because they might hurt me." Her voice faded to a mumble.

Nick squeezed her shoulder. "Then fight it, Meg. Every day. Do it with Kaylan. Do it for one another. Lean into the strength the Lord gives freely to all who ask. You can be brave."

Megan stepped back from him, breaking the weight of the moment. A small smile cracked her tough veneer. She jangled the key and moved to the door. "You SEALs are a special breed. You're pretty smart. Maybe you do have a brain in that head of yours, Scarecrow."

He laughed and ruffled her hair. "And maybe you have the courage of a lion after all. Who knew an annoying goth girl would turn out to be cool?"

"I am not goth. I just like black and dark colors."

He crossed his arms and smirked. "Whatever you say."

She returned his smirk. "The love of your life is waiting and you have a job to do." She grinned as she opened the door. "I'll help Kaylan hold down the fort while you're gone."

"Avoid psychos this time, will ya?"

Nick could have sworn her eyes rolled into her brain on that one.

He took one more look around the small living area and then joined Megan at the door as she locked up. They walked to the parking lot, Nick giving her instructions while she jotted notes on her phone. He only hoped the apartment would help Kaylan. He knew this assignment had come at a bad time for her.

As he opened the door to his Jeep, Megan's hand stopped him. "Soldier boy, thanks. For what you do out there. And for trusting me with this." She nodded back to the building. "Home. Family. That's a new thing for me. I won't let you down."

He pulled her into a hug and held her until she relaxed. She felt like a sister to him, and she loved his girl. "You won't let me down, Megan. Family isn't about performing. It's about loving. It's why I do what I do, and it's what Christ did for me." She pulled back and offered a tentative smile. "The greatest love is demonstrated in someone who is willing to give his life for his friend."

She took a step backwards, a mischievous grin lighting her face. "Just don't ask me to shoot anyone. I don't love you that much."

He chuckled. "You got it, soldier."

She opened her door. "And maybe don't call me that either."

He grinned. "Don't worry. You'll grow into it."

She rolled her eyes. "Be safe, soldier boy," she said as she crawled into her car.

"Hey, Meg," he called just before she closed her door. "Welcome to our family."

She nodded, and he could have sworn her eyes glistened. Waving, he watched as she started up the car and sped off.

Nick returned to his own car, thanking God for the friend Kaylan had found in Megan, even if Megan didn't realize her own value yet. She was different from Sarah Beth, but she was loyal and passionate and just needed someone to love her enough to bring out those qualities in her. If anyone could do it, Kaylan could. And already, Megan was blossoming. Witnessing that made him love Kaylan even more. His little warrior. She fought for people's hearts, making her own all the more beautiful.

He pointed his car toward their special meeting place. He had an hour before he needed to be back, and he needed to see his girl before then, his little taste of home before making war.

CHAPTER SIX

Sunset Park held a special place in Nick's heart. In his time separated from Kaylan, he had come here to spend some of his evenings. He'd brought his Bible, books, and note pads and read and scribbled until the orange light of the setting sun had receded into twilight. Even then, sometimes he just used the flashlight on his phone and kept working. It's how he had disciplined himself to learn and grow in a faith that Micah had been privileged to experience his whole life. During his deployment, the discipline had served him well.

And now, Kaylan waited for him in the same place. Children played on the colorful jungle gym on one side. A grassy knoll occupied another side of the park. He spotted her before she saw him, stretched out on a polka-dot blanket in her work clothes and light jacket, a book held above her face.

The soft grass muffled his footsteps, and the nippy sixty-degree air tugged at his thin long sleeves. It would be dark soon. Dark and chilly. He studied the position of the sun through several trees on the horizon. Funny how California was able to intermix the tall, slightly awkward-looking palm tree with the full grace of the shade tree.

He stopped on the edge of the blanket, grabbing the foot Kaylan bounced on her knee in midair.

"Haven't I told you it isn't nice to sneak up on people?" she said, a smile in her voice. Her gaze never left the book still suspended above her head.

He crawled next to her and lay down on his back. Angling his head toward hers, he said, "At least you are getting used to it. What are you reading?"

"*Romeo and Juliet.*"

His head came off the blanket. "Seriously?"

She closed the book and rolled onto her stomach, her green eyes drawing him in like the trees on the edge of the park—free, strong, beautiful. "I'm brushing up on some nutrition research. Do you even know who wrote *Romeo and Juliet*?"

Nick scrunched his forehead and tapped a finger to his chin. "Bill Wakespear or something like that." He fought to keep a straight face.

She giggled and swatted his arm. "You're hopeless."

He wound his fingers around the back of her neck and into her hair, memorizing the silky feel. "You're right, Kayles. Hopelessly in love with you."

He lifted his head and his lips met hers, heating his blood, his mouth moving in rhythm with hers. He could feel her smile.

She pulled back. "What a line."

He let his head fall back to the blanket as he stared into her face, memorizing every angle and light freckle. "But a romantic one."

A cloud drifted over the sun, and she dropped her gaze. "The call. The request to leave work a little early and meet you. You're leaving. Dave and Seth said you left the house early this morning."

He nodded. "Did they make it to the airport okay?"

"Megan and I took care of it." She shivered. He sat up and tugged the excess blanket around them, then slipped his arm around her shoulders. She curled into his chest. Her body tucked against his almost made him question his orders. Almost.

"Nick, I really need you here. There's so many little details to finish. I need you to help make decisions."

"I can't help it, Kaylan."

"Can't they send someone else?" She pulled away from him, but this time he didn't like what he saw brewing in her gaze. Shadows had descended and darkened their deep green hue.

"That's not how it works, Kayles, and you know it." He moved his arm and wrapped it around his knee. "Besides, I wouldn't want anyone else to take my place out there." He reached for her hand. "I want to go."

"And I want you to stay. We are about to get married, Nick. I want to be selfish. I deserve to be selfish right now. They can have you on the next deployment. But I need you right now."

Nick's patience bled to frustration. "Kaylan, it's just wedding plans. You'll be fine without me."

"I don't want to do this by myself! You're always leaving when I need you most."

"A little exaggerated, don't you think?" He threw the blanket off his shoulders, his tone matching hers and escalating quickly. He couldn't help it. She should know better. How many times were they going to have a different version of the same conversation? But a small part of him remembered leaving a broken version of her after the quake and a haunted version of her last fall. He knew it was part of the job. Knew she wasn't broken or haunted anymore, just struggling with the normal ache that came with a deployment. He took all of it as part of the job. He took the good with the bad in this calling, and he needed her to do the same.

He forced his voice to a deadly calm, but emotion still poured from every word. "Kaylan, do you want to marry me?"

She rolled her eyes and tossed her hand in the air, light glinting off her ring. "I think we've covered this. And by the way, I liked the way you asked me more the first time."

Her sarcasm shoved him over the edge and any hint of compassion fled. "Well, you better suck it up and deal because you don't get to be selfish in my line of work, Kaylan. You don't get to pick and choose when I leave. If you can't deal with it, tell me now." He rose to a crouch, his gaze locked with hers. "Otherwise, get over it."

He stood and took a step towards his car, his boots sinking in the grass and anger seeping through him like steam. He paused, refusing to turn and look at her. "You have until I get back to decide if this is what you really want. This is the direction I'm going. Decide if you want to walk it with me."

Without another word he strode to his Jeep and spun out of the parking lot, too hurt and angry to continue the discussion. He'd never envisioned this type of goodbye, but if Kaylan couldn't handle the military life, he was better off knowing now. All the love in the world could never make up for the times his job, or he, would hurt her. Would she give him that power, a power to love her fully? With it came the ability to hurt her more than anyone else. He knew that vulnerability, because he'd already handed that power to her along with his heart. And he was suffering for it now.

With that thought, he shut out the ache threatening to tear him apart, telling him to go back and fix it. No more thinking. No more feeling. Only duty. He just didn't know whether the job now came as a welcome escape or whether this conversation would haunt him until his return.

He ground his teeth. One thing was certain. It was time to focus, time to leave. And time for Kaylan to be left on her own—to decide.

CHAPTER SEVEN

Kaylan's eyes flew open. She sucked in a deep breath and sat up, rubbing away the lingering effects of another nightmare. Sarah Beth, screaming. Nick, appearing, but then walking away, oblivious to her cries. Nothing like the guy she knew. She hated dreaming about him that way.

Shaking it off, she stretched, the muscles in her back so rigid she ached. Red numbers glowing from the clock next to her bed provided the only light in the dark room. 4:07 a.m.

Scowling at the covers, she tossed them back, then stumbled to the kitchen in the dark. The small light over the sink shattered the gloominess of the dark house. Kaylan groped for a glass, filled it with water, and drank, her eyes squinting in the light. She groaned. He couldn't control his schedule, but sometimes military life was so frustrating, so inconvenient. She set her cup on the counter and stumbled back to her room, crawled into bed, and pulled the pillow over her head. Stupid dream.

Kaylan knew she never should have let Nick leave like that, never should have let him walk away. She thought back to the moment she'd seen him leaning against a truck the morning of her graduation. He'd done so many little things to let her know he was there for her—showing up in the dance studio after Pap's hospitalization and giving her a box of letters he'd written to her on his deployment, even when they weren't a couple anymore.

She remembered his face in Haiti glowing like an angel come to rescue her from the darkest night, the strength of his arms as he carried her wilted body away from the rubble. He'd pulled her from the water, chased after her when a trafficker kidnapped her and Megan.

Nick pursued relentlessly. Yet, this time, he'd walked away.

And he hadn't looked back.

A faint knock sounded on the door, and Kaylan tensed. She inched the pillow off her face to stare in the direction of the tapping.

"Kayles?"

Breath left her in a whoosh. "Come in, Meg."

Megan opened the door and shuffled into the room. Kaylan could only see her outline, swaddled in flannel pajamas. "I heard you get up. Are you okay?"

"Just a nightmare."

Megan curled up on the end of her bed, reminding Kaylan of so many nights with Sarah Beth. Her heart felt a familiar ache, and she longed for that kind of friendship again. She patted the pillow next to her.

"Seriously?"

"Seriously. It's late, or early. I don't want to get up yet, and you're making me tired just sitting there like that."

"Don't have to tell me twice." Megan crawled to the head of the bed and burrowed under the covers. Kaylan liked seeing her like this with her walls down.

"Tell me about the dream."

"It's nothing."

"Kayles, you sleep like a rock unless you have a bad dream. Now spit it out."

"It's not really about the dream. More about the fact that I let Nick leave while we were both angry. I let him walk away, and I didn't go after him."

She remembered sitting bundled in the blanket, watching him hustle to the car. She noted the tension in his shoulders, the resolve in his step, the confidence in his life calling. He gave her a choice. He'd always given her a choice. Sometimes she just handled it better than other times.

"Megan, how do you handle this military life? Does it ever get any easier?"

Megan froze. Her life as a military brat always touched a painful chord. "It's always hard, Kayles. It's hard on families. It's hard on marriages. If you aren't committed come hell or high water, you'll do exactly what my mom did and bail." She molded the pillow into a ball under her head.

"I love Nick, so it doesn't make sense. Why am I having such a hard time with this?"

"Maybe"—her alto voice held a hint of warning—"because outside of Haiti, you never had to deal with heartbreak, or major change, or long-distance relationships. You lived in a bubble, and you were happy and safe there."

Kaylan flinched, her hackles rising. But she bit back her response, chewing on Megan's words, thinking back to her childhood. Back to her relationships and life in Alabama. Her parents, brothers, and grandparents had always been a constant. She'd never spent more than two weeks away from Sarah Beth. She'd gone to college close by.

Megan was right. With the exception of the Haiti earthquake and her near-death experience at the hands of a psycho a few months earlier, she'd never had to deal with loss, extreme hardship, change, or distance.

"Kayles?"

"So basically this fight was my fault."

"I'm not sure what your fight was about, Kayles, but I'm sure it wasn't all your fault."

Kaylan rolled on her back and stared at the ceiling. Moonlight drifted in from the curtains, casting weird shadows on the wall. "I asked him to stay. I got angry with him."

"Why did you ask him to stay?"

A tear slipped past her lashes. "I wanted him here to make last minute decisions with me, to be part of these last few weeks until the wedding. I just didn't want him to go. Then I accused him of wanting to leave me."

"Yikes. Kayles, call me stupid, but that man is crazy about you. I'm sure he wants to help with details, but in the grand scheme of things he could care less. Decide what you need to. He will only be looking at you at the wedding. Besides"—her voice grew shy—"I'm here to help you."

Kaylan rolled onto her side, noticing how young Megan looked, how innocent and vulnerable without her black clothes and dark makeup. She hid behind it. Kaylan liked this version better.

"You're not so tough."

Megan yawned and smiled a sleepy smile. "Don't take advantage of my mental state right now."

"I think this unchecked mental state is a very good version of you. You should let her out more often."

Megan's eyes closed. "We'll see."

Kaylan closed her eyes, praying for sleep and wishing she could call Nick. She didn't know when she would see him again or hear his voice. Her heart raced as different scenarios flashed through her mind. What if he got shot? What if he didn't come back? What if their last words were said in anger? What if . . .

"Kayles?" Megan mumbled against her pillow.

"He got mad because you asked him to change who he is. Would you be okay if he asked you to do that?"

Kaylan's heart sank at Megan's words. "He's never asked me to give up who I am or what I'm passionate about."

"Then figure out how to not question him when duty calls. One thing I learned from my dad is that being in this kind of life is hardwired into their very DNA. To ask them to change or do something different would destroy them. Just trust him, okay? And trust that God you keep telling me so much about. Nick will be," she yawned, "back before you know it." Her breathing deepened as sleep overtook her again.

But Kaylan was wide awake. What if he didn't come back?

What if she lost another best friend?

CHAPTER EIGHT

The roar of the engine muffled Nick's ears but did nothing to mute his thoughts. He'd left. Just left. Angry and hurt. That wasn't his MO. Not now, not ever.

If any other person had challenged him to defy orders or find a replacement, he would have laughed it off and ignored them. But somehow in the last few months, he'd given Kaylan the keys to his heart and with that, the ability to wound him more than any other person could. He'd given her the ability to crawl under the armor he'd so carefully worn for years. Someone should have told him that a diamond ring created a weak spot.

He knew she'd spoken out of fear, but her words messed with his head. He couldn't afford that on this op, and neither could she.

Micah sat to his right on the plane and leaned over to yell in his ear. "Did you get to see Kaylan before we left?"

"Briefly. Did you?"

He shook his head. "Called her right before you showed back up."

Nick studied his best friend. "Did she say anything?"

"It's what she didn't say, Hawk. She didn't say one word about you. What happened?"

Nick massaged his neck, the drone of the plane sounding louder all of a sudden, setting him more on edge. He searched his pocket for his favorite vice. He felt the crinkle of a wrapper in his pocket and pulled out the gum, his crutch when he needed and wanted to stay calm. He felt Micah's big brother mode rising to the forefront.

"Hawk, why is my sister upset?"

Nick popped the piece of Juicy Fruit in his mouth. The mindless motion and familiar flavor reminded him of nights at the ballpark and his dad cheering him on as he smacked the ball and ran the bases. It tasted like home.

"Hawk."

Hawk leveled Micah with one look. "Kaylan and I are going to get married. I need you to let us work out our arguments. She's a big girl, and she needs to learn how to deal with this."

For a moment, it looked like Micah might snap, but with a small nod, he leaned his head back and closed his eyes. "She's just scared, you know."

"Who's scared?" Jay shouted. "Ain't nobody got time for scared."

"Says the little man," Colt said, a lazy grin spreading across his face as he poked their resident tiger.

"Little? Who are you calling little? I am full of figure and tall enough to kick your butt all the way to Canada."

"I just call it like I see it, brah. I forgot to mention big mouth, though. You have no trouble keeping up there."

"Are you for real?" Jay looked like he was about to stand up and take Colt to the belly of the plane. Titus slapped a hand across his chest, pinning him in place.

"Man, why you gotta get him all riled up right before everyone tries to sleep?" Titus groaned at Colt. "You make my job a lot harder."

Colt pulled a pen out of his pocket and twirled it between his fingers. "Remember when I told Logan I could show him how to kill a man with a pen?"

"Yeah, and he showed you up, if I remember correctly," Micah challenged.

Colt studied the black ink pen. "Careful, Bulldog. Your mouth is almost as big as Jay's."

Micah's lazy smile matched Colt's beat for beat. "Don't start something you can't finish."

"I never do."

"Oh, man, this is about to get good." Newbie Bates rubbed his hands together in anticipation.

Colt fixed his eyes on Bates. "Why don't I demonstrate on Bates here?"

Bates's eyes grew wide in his baby face. "Now wait a minute."

Quick as lightning, the pen came to a halt at Bates's jugular. He swallowed, the pen making a black blot as his Adam's apple bobbed. Colt chuckled.

"Should have kept your mouth shut, Bates." Nick grinned from his seat across the aisle. "It is never smart to mess with Colt. He always means business."

"Noted."

With a sly grin, Colt capped the pen and settled back in his seat. "Wet your pants there, Bates?"

"Guys, bring it on down." Titus pulled out his headphones and plugged them into his phone.

"Ah, T-Brown, don't tell me you are taking old man Logan's job on this trip," Jay groaned.

"Someone has to corral the kids." He popped the buds in his ears and shut his eyes.

"How does he do that?" Micah asked.

"Must be some weird, get-in-the-zone thing that happens when you become team lead," Nick answered.

"Do you want to do that someday, Hawk?"

Nick's fight with Kaylan raced through his mind again. What would he do if she couldn't fully accept his job and let him go when duty called? He knew she loved him. So what held her back? And how could he move forward in his career without her support? Short answer . . . he couldn't. If she couldn't get on board, something would have to give. But as surely as he knew he loved Kaylan, he knew he was called to be a United States Navy SEAL. He would have to trust the Lord to calm her heart.

"Someday, yeah, I would. I was born to be in the Teams, man. I didn't even realize it until I finished BUD/S and it hit me that all the late nights, sore muscles, training, and yelling didn't kill me. Someday something will. But I would rather it come from doing this than anything else."

"And Kaylan? A family?"

"The Carpenters and tons of SEAL families do it. It's what we both want."

He would just have to trust the Lord to make it happen.

Their boots hit ground shortly after two in the afternoon in Afghanistan, and already the sun cast a sweltering glow. The country boasted desert landscape and harsh mountains, the difficult terrain a challenge for American military.

"Family chat in five, ladies. Lose your gear and hustle."

"Bates, on me," Nick shouted to the newbie. Talented in comms, the rookie exemplified the SEAL mantra of never quitting. After dropping out of BUD/S the first time due to an ankle injury, Bates hadn't hesitated to dive back in to the next class. His dedication and loyalty earned him the respect of many in his class. But on his first Support Activity 1 assignment with these experienced operators, he looked young and green.

They dropped their gear by bunks stacked in a row in a simple, long building. The floor, ceilings, and walls were all bare wood and plywood, with a fine layer of dust from the Afghani desert. It made Nick feel like he lived in a box. A couple of moth-eaten couches sat on one end of the long room surrounding a television and an old Nintendo 64, compliments of one of the other teams. Nick doubted they would be playing much. He hoped they wouldn't be here long, but he mentally buckled down for the duration. They wouldn't leave, wouldn't quit until the op was accomplished.

Nick snagged a top bunk and quickly pulled a photo of Kaylan out of his bag. He propped it against the windowsill next to his pillow. "You got a girl, Bates?" He turned to face the newbie who was eyeing Kaylan's picture. A couple years younger than Nick and Micah, Bates's eagerness and excitement for the job spoke volumes to the guys around him, but his large hazel eyes exuded a nervous energy that made Nick slightly uncomfortable. Nick wasn't worried about Bates's capability, but in certain moments, he worried about his immaturity. However, he knew SEAL training made men out of boys. Childhood got scrubbed out of you during long nights on the beach "getting sandy."

Bates tugged a picture from his pocket. A younger, prettier version of himself stared back at Nick. "I got a sister. She's my main girl."

"Good enough." Nick's mind roved to Natalie, the sister he'd never met. The sister he wondered if he ever would meet. He shook his head and moved to the door, hoping to leave all thoughts of home in the bunkroom.

Bates matched his stride. "Do you think we're here for that Kahuna guy everyone keeps talking about?"

"Maybe." Nick shrugged. "Looks like we are about to find out."

They entered a stark room with scratched walls and floor. Maps hung on several surfaces, and his team had spread out around a couple of white folding tables in one corner of the room. White. He still couldn't figure out why they tried to maintain the clean white in the desert. War made everything dirty, no matter how you dressed it up.

Several men shuffled, creating a clean path to the corner where a blonde woman with piercing, cold blue eyes took in the room. Eyes that immediately locked on Nick.

Nick swore.

Jake, Nick's CIA buddy, stood next to her. He lounged against the wall as if he didn't have a care in the world, but his alert gaze told a very different story.

"Relax, Hawk." Micah appeared at his side, his hand like iron restraining Nick. Nick took a deep breath, summoning a calm developed from years of discipline. No battles were won in the absence of cool emotions.

"I'm relaxed."

Nick didn't have to look at his best friend to know he was smirking. "Relax more. Your muscles are wound so tight, I could beat someone to death with your arm."

Nick took another deep breath, forcing every muscle in his body to release one by one. With each conscious choice to relax, tension fled, putting Nick firmly back in control. Micah removed his hand but stayed close.

Within seconds, Jake appeared at their side.

"A heads-up would have been nice," Nick greeted his friend.

"From murderous to bored in two minutes flat. Quite impressive."

"Don't play games with me, Jake."

The man's gaze drifted to Janus, his usually coifed hair falling limp in the heat. His white t-shirt clung to his skin and his thick gray pants prepared him for hiking in the desert if the situation called for it. "She's under strict orders not to speak with you."

She was nothing. No one. Just another informant. Just another criminal providing information in exchange for money or a lighter sentence. In her case, maybe a new yacht.

Nick knew he'd better keep his emotions in check. Micah and Jake watched him. He didn't need to look in X's direction to know Senior Chief's sharp eyes gauged every nuance. Nick knew how to get the job done. He knew how to engage an enemy without fear because he believed what he fought for carried more weight than fear. He could forget this woman.

His mother.

He *would* forget.

Nick nodded. "Let's get this over with and send her packing."

"Let's get started," X's voice boomed above the noise. The room descended into a restless quiet that came when adrenaline and focus kicked into full gear.

Jake took his place at the front of the room with X. Nick and Micah settled in near Titus, Colt, and Jay. Nick found an odd comfort in knowing they were aware of the full story and still trusted his loyalty, his capability, completely. He relaxed even more, his mind hanging on every detail.

"All right, listen up, ladies. This is Jake. He's going to share a bit of intel with us, then we'll dive into op specifics."

Jake clasped his hands behind his back, his alert gaze roaming over the group. "We recently received information that a known Russian businessman is selling weapons to our friends in the Taliban. As you know, they are always trying to reform and grow new cells. However, this time, we believe he may be about to make the biggest deal in years. Without his second in command"—Jake nodded to Janus—"he is vulnerable. We want to make him even more so. We have an informant that will tell us the location where the next meeting is to take place, but the informant will only speak with this woman. We call her Janus." A few eyes floated to Nick before landing back on Jake. "We need to meet with the informant, learn the location of the meeting, and take out this cell before they have the chance to get any more weapons. We will weaken his trade options and draw him out of hiding."

X took over and began to go over op specifics. They would leave first thing in the morning and travel with a Marine unit to a town about an hour away. Janus and Jake would accompany them.

Nick listened carefully, at the same time taking a personal inventory. To his relief he found that the more time he spent in the room with Janus, the greater his power to ignore her. She was a captive, incapable of hurting him or Kaylan.

Kaylan. A pang of regret sliced through him, more potent than any injury he had ever sustained.

Micah jabbed Nick in the side, and Nick snapped to attention, avoiding Micah's glare. He pulled another piece of gum out and popped it into his mouth. Enough of the distractions. Enough thinking about Kaylan, or Janus for that matter. Women complicated his life, and he didn't need to think about either one of them on this op.

His life and the lives of his teammates depended on it. Out here in the middle of the desert, it was team and teammates over everything.

And for now, Nick liked it that way.

CHAPTER NINE

Wednesday arrived without Kaylan's bidding and with it, the memories of Haiti and Sarah Beth. A year had passed, but Kaylan knew she would feel every January 12 with extra weightiness for the rest of her life. Everything had changed—for Haiti, for Sarah Beth, for herself.

Now, with Nick deployed and their fight still lingering, she felt his absence weigh heavier by the hour. The grief of the day increased her fear that she would never see him again. She fought the ache, but it was tough to keep it at bay.

Her only distractions came in the form of her patients as she planned meals and focused on the diet of each individual. Back home after work, she cleaned the house and whipped up a meal. By the time Megan walked in the door smelling like the ocean, dinner was ready and the house sparkled. She'd lugged her tired body to bed shortly after, praying for dreamless sleep.

Thursday dawned bright, and with the new day, Kaylan's spirits rose. For the past couple of months, she'd taken to going over to the Carpenters house to give them a date night while she played with the kids. They brought her joy unlike anything else. Tonight was no different. With these kids, she surrounded herself with laughter and chaos. The living room looked like a tornado of toys and dishes had swept through, but she didn't care.

"Aunt Kaylan, I want you to play with my dolls now. Please?" Molly looked up from her spot on the floor surrounded by dolls, a tea set, and stuffed animals.

"Just one second, ladybug." Kaylan's tongue hung out of her mouth as her little car raced around the track. Playing *Mario Cart* with Tanner and Conner reminded her of years playing with David, Micah, and Seth. Only those games usually ended in a fight over who cheated and who really won until Mom took away the controller and sent them all outside to play. "Almost there . . ."

"Kaylan, you bumped me. No fair."

"You bump people all the time, Conner. Don't use that on me when you are losing."

"Ha. She told you." Tanner taunted Conner.

"Shut up."

"Yes!" Kaylan threw her hands in the air and stood, doing a happy dance in front of the boys. "Victory for me. And that was not nice to say, Conner." She pointed at him. "Your parents don't let you talk to one another like that, and you aren't going to do it on my watch."

Conner mumbled a "sorry" to his older brother while Kaylan smothered her smile.

"Close enough." Too much like the Richards' kids growing up. She couldn't wait to be an aunt for real, but in the meantime, she loved these kids with her whole heart.

"Aunt Kaylan," Molly called again.

"All right, ladybug. It's your turn." The boys resumed their game with just two players while Kaylan sat down on the floor with Molly. The four-year-old had spread out several dolls in various stages of donning princess dresses.

Kaylan snuck a quick glance at baby Nadia in her swing. She hadn't dosed off yet, but she would soon.

"Aunt Kaylan, pay attention."

"Sorry. All about you now, munchkin." Kaylan chuckled at the little girl in front of her. A tiara sat on mussed blonde curls and big blue eyes stared intently at the dolls around her.

"We are missing a prince."

"Why do we need a prince?"

"The prince always rescues the princess, Aunt Kaylan."

"What does he rescue her from?"

"Whatever isn't happy in life."

Kaylan picked up a beautiful, brown-haired doll and a red-head doll that resembled Arial from *The Little Mermaid.* "Maybe the princess doesn't need rescuing. Maybe she can be brave enough on her own."

Molly made a face at Kaylan. "Maybe. But isn't it always better when there's a prince?"

"Sure, baby girl."

"Mommy has Daddy. You have Uncle Nick. Aunt Liza has Uncle Titus. I don't know who Uncle Jay, Uncle Micah, or Uncle Colt are rescuing."

"Maybe they haven't found their princesses yet."

Molly put her hands on her hips. "They better hurry up."

Kaylan laughed. "I'm sure they will someday." She ran her fingers through Molly's tangled curls. "And who do you have, baby girl?"

Molly crawled into Kaylan's lap, bringing her dolls with her. She searched through the mess on the floor to find a crown for the doll in her hand. "That's easy. I have Daddy and Jesus. And Daddy says my other prince will come someday, but as long as I have Daddy and Jesus,

I'm just fine." She flashed her bright blue eyes in Kaylan's direction and smiled.

Kaylan's spirit crashed. She'd begged Nick to stay home because she needed him, and somewhere along the way, she had forgotten that she didn't. She wanted him. Wanted him more than anything in life. But she *needed* only one thing. Jesus. He never left her alone.

Kaylan held Molly while she played, basking in the childlike trust of a little girl in her father. How much more should Kaylan trust her heavenly Father? All her life, she'd learned that God was a loving Father who desired to give her good things. Her dad had been an excellent example of that. After Haiti, she had learned that God wasn't good just because good things happened, but that goodness itself was intrinsically part of His character. So if He was a loving Father who desired to give her good things and didn't withhold any good thing from her, then it made sense that even His "no's" and redirects were an act of love on her behalf. Didn't it?

Her mind flew back to Thanksgiving when she was ten. She'd gone Black Friday shopping with her family and found a new bike. It had been shiny and sleek with a horn on the handle, and it had been on sale. But her dad said no. She'd thrown a fit, causing her parents to drop her off at her grandparents before continuing their Black Friday shopping.

Then on Christmas day, she'd understood. Her dad had bought her an even better, prettier bike. Her dad wanted to give her the best. He knew she wanted something in a moment that would fade. He knew what she really wanted is what he finally gave her—the best kid's bike on the market. Oh, for trust like Molly had, to trust Nick, to trust her Father, to trust His care for her, even in seasons when emotions overwhelmed good sense.

She checked her watch. Right on schedule. "Ten minutes before we need to start getting ready for bed."

"How about an hour?" Conner bartered.

"Twenty minutes and a bedtime story." Kaylan picked up another doll and began to dress her in a sunny yellow dress.

Tanner groaned. "Bedtime stories are for babies."

"I'm not a baby," Molly piped in, "and I still love bedtime stories."

"Just proves my point," Tanner sighed, his eyes still glued to the television. Within minutes Conner cheered while Tanner swatted him with a pillow.

Conner dodged his brother and ran around to kneel by Kaylan. "I have to wait to go to bed until my dad gets home."

"And why is that?"

"He promised to give me his Trident to take to show-and-tell tomorrow."

Kaylan ruffled his hair. "I'm sure he can give it to you in the morning."

"He has a doctor's appointment in the morning, and someone is coming to pick him up and take him so Mom can take us to school. Please, Kaylan, I need to wait."

She leaned in close so Molly wouldn't hear. "Let's go ahead and get ready for bed and be quiet about it. Then you and I can wait for your dad. Deal?"

Conner fist-bumped Kaylan. "You get the award for coolest babysitter ever."

"How about you get me a medal for that, and we'll call it even?"

His grin looked so much like Logan's. "Deal."

The next twenty minutes turned into a whirlwind of pajamas, toothbrushes, quiet protests, a quick bedtime story for Molly, and finally lights out.

Conner and Kaylan tiptoed back into the living room and sat down for another game of Mario Cart. They had been playing only a half hour when the key scratched in the lock.

"Dad's here!" Conner dropped the controller and jumped up to greet Kim and Logan as Logan wheeled his chair through the door.

"Hey, champ, what are you still doing up?"

Conner's gaze filled with admiration as he greeted his dad. "You promised I could take your Trident with me to school tomorrow."

Logan grinned at his son. "I did, didn't I? It's in the velvet box in my top dresser drawer. Why don't you go get it out and bring it here?"

Conner raced off. "Conner, do not wake your siblings," Kim called after him. In their small house, it wouldn't be hard to do.

"How was the movie?" Kaylan asked.

Kim placed her hand on Logan's shoulder. Kaylan admired their synchronicity, never more than a few feet apart, normally touching in some way, united, together. Would she and Nick reach that stage of oneness? She hoped to someday.

"It was good. Thank you so much for watching the kids. With four of them now, it's hard to get moments to ourselves."

Logan covered Kim's hand with his own as Conner hurried back into the room, a small velvet box in his hand.

"You found it." Logan wheeled to the couch and Conner sank into the seat next to the armrest, as close as he could get to his dad. Kim and Kaylan smiled, watching the scene. Would she have a son who looked up to Nick that much? Kaylan didn't doubt it. Nick was as strong as he was gentle, and if the way he treated the Carpenter kids was any indication, he would make a great dad.

Another pang stabbed through her heart. How could she have been so ugly to him before he left?

"Dad, will you tell me the story again?"

"Sure thing, champ. Do you want to hold it?"

"Yeah!" Conner held out his hands as Logan placed the gold Trident pin on his son's palms. Conner stared at it in awe.

Kaylan and Kim looked over the couch as Logan talked to Conner. "I had finished all of my SEAL training except one last part."

"The Trident swim?"

Logan grinned at his son's familiarity with the story. "You got it. The Trident swim. We had to wear our cammies and drag a rucksack with a bunch of clothes."

"Was it heavy?"

"You bet. The water made the clothes even heavier, but we took turns swimming with it held between us and a buddy."

"And someone else swam with a sledgehammer, right?"

Logan nodded. "Yep. A guy named Cameron was the strongest swimmer in our class and carried the hammer the whole way."

"But you're pretty strong, too, right, Dad?"

Logan chuckled. "I can hold my own. But when we work as a team, we all take turns carrying the load, and each man uses his strengths to help the team."

"What's your strength, Dad?"

"I have the biggest mouth."

"Dad . . ." Conner laughed. "You do not."

"All right. All right. So after we finished this really long swim in the ocean, we stood in a line in the surf at attention. We were soaking wet, and our commander came around and pinned each of us with our Tridents."

"Did you bleed?"

Logan looked up at Kim and Kaylan with a knowing grin. Kaylan knew that after the official ceremony, often the true initiation came when new team members had their pins punched into their chest. They bled together and now could fight together. Or at least, that's how Nick explained it.

"SEALs can handle a little blood." Logan grinned at his son. "Now why don't you tell me about the pin. Do you remember?"

Light filled Conner's eyes as he began to point to each element on the pin. "The anchor represents the Navy. The gun . . . "

"What kind of gun?" Logan prompted.

Conner's forehead crinkled in thought. "It's a . . . flintlock. A cocked flintlock, right, Dad?"

"You got it. Why is that important?"

Conner's face glowed and Kaylan wondered if they had another little SEAL in the making. With his dad teaching him, Conner would learn from the best the Teams had to offer. "It means SEALs fight on sea, air, and land. The pistol stands for land, and it also means SEALs are always ready to fight the bad guys."

Logan chuckled at his son. "Something like that. You skipped one."

"Oops. The Trident represents the ocean. They call you frogmen because you like the water, right?"

"SEALs love the water. What else do ya got?"

"The eagle. It represents air. And doesn't it mean freedom, too?"

"Yes, eagles are a symbol of freedom in the United States."

Kaylan bent over the back of the couch, taking a closer look at the bird. "I always wondered why its head is bowed. I always picture eagles as proud and regal."

Logan turned to Conner. "Do you want to explain it to her, champ?"

Conner twisted on the couch to look at Kaylan as he pointed to the eagle. "His head is bent to show people that a warrior's strength comes from humility. Doesn't the Bible say pride comes before a fall? I guess the SEALs believe that, too, Aunt Kaylan."

Kaylan smiled at the little SEAL aficionado while Logan and Kim beamed with pride for their son and the lessons he understood at a young age.

"Thanks for teaching me a thing or two, Conner."

Conner puffed his chest. "I can teach you a lot of things, Aunt Kaylan. Want to know more?"

Kim laughed and ruffled her son's hair. "We are still teaching him what it looks like to *act* with humility, but at least he understands the concept. All right, Conner, it sounds like you know how to talk to your class now. Time for bed."

"Ah, Mom."

"No, ah Mom. Hop to, mister."

"Okay." He stood from the couch and reverently placed the Trident back in its case.

"Don't lose it, champ," Logan said as he passed the box off to his son.

Conner held the box tightly, his knuckles turning white. "Never."

With goodnights all around, Kim ushered him off to bed.

"You don't have to rush off, Kayles. Sit down, stay awhile," Logan offered.

"You sure?" She wasn't sure when her heart made the transition between Alabama and California. Maybe when Nick said those three little words that made her head spin. Maybe when he proposed or when guys from his Team showed up to both celebrate and grieve with her over Sarah Beth. But in this moment, her heart knew the familiarity of home with this family and this husband and dad who reminded her so much of Nick. California and Nick suddenly felt more permanent, more appealing than Alabama ever had.

She sank into the brown suede couch in the Carpenter's living room, her eyes flitting from photo to photo of the Carpenter family and landing on the newest with Logan's leg absent, but a beautiful new baby girl completing the scene.

"How are you doing with the separation? Any easier than last time?"

Kaylan shook her head. "I think it's harder now."

Logan tipped his head to the side, his kind eyes absorbing her internal struggle. "Why is that?"

She shrugged, not sure where to begin. "Have you and Kim ever fought before a deployment?" Kaylan already suspected the answer. Kim was a saint, the perfect SEAL wife.

"Yes, we did. Hardest deployment of all time because of that disagreement. He never left with things unsettled like that again," Kim answered before Logan could as she reentered the room. "Every deployment is difficult, even more so depending on the season—pregnancy, a move, family illness. Life happens. But we determined after that deployment that we would never part with things that unsettled again, no matter what's going on. It just isn't worth it." Instead of sitting by Kaylan on the couch, she perched on Logan's good leg, wrapping her arm around his neck.

"How did y'all deal with that first disagreement?"

Logan and Kim shared a knowing smile. "I waited until he finally called me and then begged and pleaded for forgiveness and then made it up to him when he got home."

Kaylan nodded, not feeling any better. She wanted to fix things now. Wanted to wrap her arms around Nick's neck and kiss him until everything went back to the way it should be.

"Kayles, I promise Hawk won't hold onto it for long. Don't beat yourself up over it."

Kaylan couldn't meet Logan's eyes. "You don't understand. I accused him of wanting to leave me. Then he gave me an ultimatum."

"Oh, one of those." Kim reached for Kaylan's hand and squeezed. "Hawk loves you. It isn't the end of the world."

"Kayles, look at me." Logan waited until Kaylan raised her head. She saw that his compassion for her was edged with a silent challenge. "Hawk never wants to leave you, but he will always want to go. It's the dichotomy of a fighter. You are marrying a warrior who doesn't know how not to fight or answer the call of duty."

"Trust me," Kim chimed in. "It will always be hard." She squeezed Logan's neck. "But loving a warrior is always worth it."

"And why is that?"

Kim slipped next to Kaylan on the couch and squeezed her knee. "Because even when he leaves you, he's always fighting for you."

At Kim's words, Kaylan's heart swelled with love and pride for her warrior.

Logan continued. "Tell him you love him, reassure him that you are here. Life will go on at home, and the separation will end. But don't make it harder for him to leave, Kayles. It will create a rift between the two of you and distract him while he's gone. A SEAL who is mentally distracted isn't good to anyone, and guys on the team will blame you for that. Love him by letting him leave well. And then show him how much you missed him when he's back. You will treasure the time home even more. Besides, coming home after a long absence keeps life new and exciting." Logan winked at Kim, who turned a deep crimson.

"On that note," Kaylan chuckled, "Conner said you have a doctor's appointment in the morning."

"He does." The excitement in Kim's voice charged Kaylan. "He might qualify for a prosthetic."

"Logan, that's great!" Kaylan squeezed Kim's hand.

"Here's what's even better." He lowered his voice but nothing could squash the hope emanating from every syllable. "They've asked me to be an instructor at BUD/S. Kayles, I would get to be the gatekeeper of the community training of our future ranks."

Kaylan squealed. "That is the best news I've heard all year! Have you told anyone else yet?"

Logan shook his head. "They know about the possibility, but not that it might be a reality. Keep it quiet for now. I want to make sure the doctor is on board and I take the necessary time to heal and adjust. I'll tell my team, but I want to wait and tell the guys when they get back. They don't need anything to distract them while they are gone."

"They won't hear it from me, then. Let me know how it goes." Kaylan stifled a yawn. "Time to go. Thanks for letting me hang out with the kids tonight."

"Anytime you want to give us a break, you just let us know," Kim chuckled.

"Will do." Kaylan waved before Kim closed the door behind her. As she headed for her car, she stole another look at the house. She couldn't help but think that this breed of warrior couldn't be defeated, in death or injury. Their courageous spirit remained unshakeable.

CHAPTER TEN

Kaylan found the first note attached to her wedding dress bag hanging in her closet. It was a sunny Saturday. Nick had been gone for five days. Five long days. Her only contact had been a couple hurried emails saying he was fine, Micah was as annoying as ever, and he would call her soon. The rift between them still weighed heavy.

Final wedding details were coming together. She'd asked for her girls' sizes, ordered dresses, and now was on her way to a fitting and to pick up the dresses at the boutique she had found an hour and a half away near Los Angeles. But the note gave her pause. He must have written it before their big fight.

She fought back the "what ifs" that threatened to cloud her mind in a hazy fog of emotion and irrational thinking. Life was too short for "what ifs." To be the epitome of a SEAL wife, she better grow a backbone and quit panicking every time she thought about Nick not coming back. He was coming back until she got word that he wasn't. No need to entertain nightmares any further.

She laid the garment bag on her bed and sank into the pillow-top mattress. "To my girl" stretched on the front in his strong but hurried writing. Kaylan pulled a letter out of the envelope and smiled as she remembered the letters Nick had once written to her while in Haiti. She'd loved every one, her very own love language that Nick spoke all too well. It made her miss him even more.

Hey, babe,

Don't worry, I didn't take a peek at the dress. Megan was hovering like a buzzard, so there was no chance anyway.

Kaylan laughed, biting her nail as she fell into his prose.

I knew I wouldn't be here to talk through decisions with you, and I know how much you love that, so this was the next best thing. If you are looking at your dress, you are either one of those girls that needs to try it on every day to make sure you haven't gained weight (you haven't, by the way), or it is time for a fitting, which also means you are going to get the bridesmaids' dresses.

So here's my two cents on those. Don't get the pink if you don't want it. Sarah Beth wouldn't care. Her memory will be with you that day, even if her favorite color isn't. Be free to choose what YOU want. However, if you want pink, I'm all for it. Just figure out a manly way to incorporate it, and maybe don't make the guys wear it? I may veto you when I get back, or we will have a full-fledged groomsmen mutiny on our hands. SEALs don't wear pink and neither do your brothers. Well, maybe Seth from time to time. And maybe Jay and Colt. Okay, forget I said that. I don't want to wear pink. Period. But I GUESS I will for you if there are no other options.

Kaylan laughed out loud. What a guy to think she could change the color after she had ordered the dresses.

Wherever I am, know that I'm thinking of you. Know that I love you. Know that I can't wait to spend a lifetime picking out colors for things. Please never doubt any of that.

Nick

Guilt weighed as heavy as a rock in the pit of her stomach. He'd known it would be hard, known her desire to have him with her every step of the way, and he'd done this for her. She suspected she would find more letters as the days passed, but even the thought couldn't erase the burgeoning desire she had to apologize, to take back her accusations and scathing words. She'd lashed out in fear and insecurity, and now she just wanted everything back to normal. She would send him another email when she got back home.

Kaylan still didn't know how to cope with his absence in big moments. The surprise letter still couldn't make up for the fact that he wasn't here, making plans for the future with her.

Nor could it dispel a deeper fear: that she'd lose him forever.

Just like she'd lost Sarah Beth.

Her heart in turmoil, she knelt beside the bed and pulled the box Nick had made her. In it she kept all the letters he had written her after their first breakup and during his first deployment as a SEAL. On top of that sat letters from Haiti, and a strand of a tassel he had tied around her ring finger the first time they took her ring to get cleaned and she felt naked without it. Photos rested haphazardly on top of the letters, and a Ziploc bag contained dried petals from numerous bouquets. On top of all that she placed his most recent letter to be read over and over again until his return. Then she closed the box and slid it back into place under her bed.

With new resolve, Kaylan grabbed the dress and snagged a white piece of paper with an address scribbled in blue ink from her dresser. A pang of guilt shot through her at the thought of what she was about to do, but she had decided it was for Nick's own good. He had so much to think about. She would help him with this, and he would thank her later. But guilt stung as she remembered his words to leave it alone.

With a final glance at the paper in her hand she left the house for a fitting and the unknown.

The coffee shop beckoned with the earthy smell of beans and the crunching whir of a grinder. Brick comprised one wall of the room, with antique mirrors and frames decorating the rest. Vintage couches formed intimate corners in the back, and mismatched circular tables and chairs were scattered around the distressed hardwood floors. The room was a cozy kind of cluttered.

A few people worked or read while others sipped coffee and talked. Mostly a hipster crowd, a few young couples and a group of girls sat on one side of the room. A balding man with a sharp gray suit sat in the corner sipping coffee from a white mug with black script that read "My mom says I'm a superstar." Kaylan smothered a smile at the irony of the stiff businessman trying to look cool in the quaint coffee shop.

Kaylan ordered coffee in a carry-out cup in case things didn't go well with Natalie. She accepted the warm cup from the barista. Turning to find a seat, she nearly bowled over the businessman, who stood behind her waiting for a refill.

"I am so sorry. I didn't see you there." The man stood several inches shorter than her willowy height. He seemed easily amused or nervous, possibly both.

"It's quite all right. I'm happy to see you didn't spill."

His slight nasal tone and Eastern European accent sent a chill through her. He sounded just like . . . She shook her head. No. She wouldn't go there. He wasn't Dmitri. No use dwelling on past horrors.

Kaylan managed a smile. "Nope, nothing escaped." She held up her cup to show him. "Sorry again. Have a good day."

He nodded and stepped around her to request a refill. Dispelling the mood that threatened to descend along with past memories,

Kaylan grabbed a high wingback arm chair in the back corner and began flipping through a wedding magazine, paying more attention to the customers entering the shop. She glanced at the large clock hanging near the coffee bar. 3:30 p.m. Natalie should be here any moment.

As if on cue, the door opened, and Nick's sister, Natalie Grace McMurray, waltzed into Kaylan's life.

The woman searched the dimly lit room, and Kaylan lifted a tentative hand. Her light blonde hair hung right above her shoulders and flipped out. Her flannel shirt, jeans, and Converse shoes spoke of a girl who knew how to dress cute and comfortable—a girl who knew who she was and didn't need to apologize for it or dress to impress anyone else. She was related to Nick, all right. Kaylan liked her already. But what if Natalie didn't like *her*?

Natalie smiled and held up a finger as she placed an order. Kaylan ran her hands over her jeans to alleviate the sweat. What was she thinking? She finally understood why Nick hadn't wanted to do this, hadn't known how. How could she disrupt this girl's life? How could she disrupt Nick's? Nick had walked around in shock for weeks after finding out he had a blood sister, a twin. Family that he had always wanted. But how could she spring this news on this unsuspecting woman?

Grabbing her magazine, she stuffed it into her oversized purse and prepared to bolt. Light blue Converse stopped at her bag. Slowly she looked up at a friendly smile and eyes as blue as cornflowers.

"You must be Kaylan. I'm Natalie." She held out her hand.

Too late to back out now. Kaylan stood and returned her handshake. "Hey! Thanks for meeting me. I hope it didn't put you out any."

"Not at all. In fact, you saved me from doing laundry." Natalie sank into the plush armchair across from Kaylan and curled her feet under her. She took a sip of coffee and grimaced. "Whew, too hot."

Kaylan laughed. "What'd you get?"

"That caramel, mocha macchiato thing-a-ma-jig they have up there. I don't know." She took another tiny sip and wiped foam off her lip. "All I know is that it's amazing."

Now Kaylan really liked her.

"What did you get?"

"Their signature coffee. I'm not sure what country it's from, but I want to hop on a plane and go there right now."

"Girl, take me with you. Although I might pass on the coffee and try some of the local cuisine instead." Natalie took another sip.

"Not a big coffee fan?"

"Only the flavored stuff. And only when I meet people like this. Otherwise I stick to tea or water."

"Noted for next time."

Natalie unfolded from her chair and reached into her bag. "Your email said you were interested in the Air Force." She dropped a thin folder on the small table between them. "Here's some info. By the way, how did you say you came across my name again?"

Kaylan swallowed coffee, the sip scalding her throat and warming her belly. "I don't think I did. It was just a friend of a friend. Anyway, they said you'd grown up in the culture and worked at a base now and could tell me a bit about it."

Natalie's light blue eyes sharpened as she studied Kaylan. "Uh-huh. Let me know if you have any questions. I'm not actually in the Air Force, I just help out around the base, so I may not be the best one to ask." Her eyes drifted over Kaylan from head to toe. "You interested in joining up?"

Kaylan shook her head, struggling with the lies that kept piling up. Well, half-truths, anyway. But there wasn't really a difference no matter what she told herself. "No, just research. After hearing a little about you, I thought it would be cool to meet you in person." That was true.

Natalie nodded, her gaze growing more reserved but her friendly smile still in place. "So tell me a little about yourself, Kaylan. You don't sound like you're from around here."

Now this was safe territory. At least most of it. Kaylan relaxed into her chair. "Is my accent bleeding through?"

"More like gushing."

Kaylan laughed. "My momma would be proud. I grew up in Alabama. After college, I applied for internships all over the country and landed in California."

Surprise laced her face. "That's a long way from home."

"Some days it's farther than others."

Her sad smile spoke of one who understood the pain of absence. "Do you see them often?"

"Well, I have a brother that lives out here, too." Dangerous territory. Kaylan sped on, "And we try to go home as often as possible."

"What does your brother do?"

Kaylan paused and shifted in her seat, wondering how far to take this conversation. Should she just dive in and talk about Nick? "He and my fiancé are both SEALs."

"Ah, some of those." Natalie grinned and took a sip. "It's hard to handle one of those guys, let alone two."

Kaylan chuckled, thinking of all their bonfires, dinners, and parties. "You get used to it."

Natalie set her cup on the table and leaned forward, her elbows on her knees. Her eyes met Kaylan's and demanded connection. "I grew up in an Air Force family, moving from place to place. My dad's in Washington, D.C., now. He didn't want me to have that kind of nomadic life, so he begged me not to join. That's about the only thing I listened to. Still, I couldn't escape the tug of that community, so I work at the base as a civilian in public relations. It's as close as I can get to the sky and still honor my dad's wishes."

"Sounds like you have a pretty good dad." Kaylan tensed under Natalie's relentless gaze. Her baby steps had been too much, too fast.

"He's pretty great. He and Mom used to say I have x-ray vision."

Kaylan's laugh sounded nervous, even to herself. Natalie's face had lost every hint of a smile. Curiosity, defensiveness, and a quiet strength radiated from her in waves. How many more traits would remind Kaylan of Nick? "Why did they say that?"

"It means I've always been good at reading people, knowing if they are telling the truth, and you, Kaylan, have been hiding something since I walked in that door." She leaned back in her chair and pulled a knee up to her chest, once again completely comfortable and in control in her environment. "Now, how about telling me why you really contacted me?"

Kaylan gripped her cup. It was now or never.

CHAPTER ELEVEN

Natalie demanded the truth, but the truth could destroy what she knew to be true of her world. Regret coursed through Kaylan. She shouldn't have gone against Nick's wishes. But as she studied the woman sitting across from her, she sensed Natalie came from warrior's blood, just like her brother. Somehow, Kaylan knew she could handle it.

"Natalie, I'm sorry you feel manipulated right now." She waited for Natalie's acknowledgment and received a nod to continue. "I didn't lie about who I am or how I got to California or about my family. I got your name from my fiancé."

"Do I know your frogman?"

"No, you've never met. And he actually doesn't know that I'm here. Nick grew up in a loving home here in California. His parents adopted him as an infant, but both of them have since passed away. For the past couple of years, Nick has been looking for his birth parents off and on, just to see what he could find."

Kaylan stopped, unsure of how to continue. Across from her, Natalie went rigid for the first time since entering the coffee shop.

"Did he find them?"

Kaylan shook her head. "Not exactly."

"What does that mean?"

Kaylan knew she couldn't say a word about Janus, couldn't even mention that Nick had found his mother. It was bigger than a family issue. It was a national security issue. She was a protector of that secret now, but it didn't mean she couldn't share the rest of what she knew about Natalie's birth family.

"My grandfather used some of his connections to help locate information and found a death certificate for his dad. And he also found . . ."

Natalie had moved to the edge of her seat, and Kaylan wondered if the twins had both been searching for one another the whole time.

"He found a sister."

Natalie went as still as stone. Kaylan waited for her to connect the dots. When she finally spoke, her voice came out as a husky whisper. "And you think I'm his sister?"

Kaylan nodded, silently apologizing and steadying herself to comfort the girl across from her if she fell apart or panicked. "That's what the records say."

"Why?" Her voice rose an octave. "Why are you telling me this? How can you even be sure? And why isn't he with you?" She cast a darting glance around the room.

Out of the corner of her eye, Kaylan saw heads turn their direction at Natalie's elevated tone. She leaned forward and placed a hand on Natalie's intertwined fingers, feeling her tension, seeing her knuckles whiten.

"He didn't want to disrupt your life, and he didn't know how to tell you." Kaylan offered a gentle smile, beckoning Natalie to look at her again. "He's a guy, Natalie. He's a SEAL. When he couldn't figure out how to deal with it, he compartmentalized it and focused on other things. There's been a lot going on." Deep water again.

Natalie leaned back in the chair and hugged both knees to her chest. Her high-back chair swallowed her slender frame like a doll. Calm stole across her face. "I knew I was adopted. But I have a great family. Awesome parents, a sister. I always wondered about my birth family, but just didn't care enough to actually find out, because what could possibly be better than the family I had?"

Kaylan nodded. She understood having a tight family unit and the weight of what she'd always known being shattered. She thanked God Nick had grown up with loving parents, but her heart ached a little that he had been lonely since their death.

She pulled out a file she had prepared with condensed info from what Pap had given Nick. She had removed anything that might trace back to Janus. "Here." She waited for Natalie to take the file. As she flipped it open, Kaylan saw the photo of herself and Nick that she had paper-clipped to the top. "That's Nick. Listen." She sat on the edge of her seat and leaned closer to Natalie, desperate to be heard, to bring home the sister Nick had always wanted. "Don't take my word for it. My phone number is in there. This is the info Pap gave to Nick that led him to you. I included a couple of photos and a little about Nick. I figure it's only right that his privacy is a little invaded since yours has been."

That drew a small smile. "Thank you." But the expression on her face told Kaylan that Natalie needed time alone to absorb the shock.

"Look, I don't want to overwhelm you with everything all at once. I know how long it took Nick to process all this. So take a look at the file, then call me if you have any questions or want to talk or maybe even want to set something up to meet Nick. No pressure. Like I said, he doesn't even know."

Kaylan stood and Natalie's gaze darted upward. "Will he be mad that you told me?"

Kaylan wondered, but it was too late now. "Probably at first. But I wanted to give both of you the choice."

Her tortured blue eyes met Kaylan's. "And what if I decide not to pursue this, that the family I have is all I need?"

Kaylan's heart sank a little at her words. "Nick will deal and be fine. But whether bound by choice or bound by blood, family is too precious a gift to ignore forever. I promise you will be better for being in one another's lives. But it's up to you." She squeezed the girl's shoulder and offered a small smile, sensing it was time to go. "It was nice to meet you, Natalie. I hope we get to talk soon."

With a wave and a nod from Natalie, Kaylan walked from the coffee shop, releasing a deep breath as she pulled the door open, causing the brass bell to jingle.

CHAPTER TWELVE

Scruff covered Nick's face, causing it to itch in the heat. Between his uniform, gear, and the helmet that had become a necessity, he felt like he might melt. Pockets. Pockets everywhere on this uniform. He felt hot and bulky.

What he wouldn't give for an ice cream cone and a good dip in the ocean. SEALs weren't meant to be this far from water. At least he wasn't. But SEALs trained to operate in all environments—sea, air, and land, including desert. This was just his least favorite of the three.

They'd spent the last few days chasing false leads and acclimating to the environment. Nick hoped today was it—the day they finally connected with their informant.

Their ground assault convoy followed a well-traveled Marine unit as they led the way into a mystery town. Janus rode in another vehicle, Jake no doubt glued to her side. Nick's vehicle consisted of a driver and radio guy in the front seat, a gunner, Nick, Micah, Bates, and Colt. The going was slow. More time to be patient, more time to mentally prepare, more time to plan and focus. As a sniper, he knew how to be still under a hide for hours at a time. It was less a physical discipline and more a mental one. As they wound through rocky, desert terrain, Nick prayed they didn't hit an IED.

It had taken a couple days away and back in his element to cool Nick's mind enough to see reality, the reality that he loved Kaylan, that he had been too harsh with his words, and that she had a tough job, too. He owed her more than a few short emails. Despite his bruised ego, he owed her an apology. But the biggest realization was that he was scared he would hurt her in a way she could never recover from. Her fear had shone a light on a vulnerability in him better ignored. His inability to stuff it down ticked him off.

"Nothing but sand, rock, and guys with funny toboggans for miles," Micah shouted over the sound of wheels crunching the road beneath them.

"Get used to it. They'll probably send us here on deployment early this time next year."

"Yippee kay-yay."

"How cool would it be if they let us pick where we deployed?" Bates mused.

"I think that's called a vacation, brah." Colt sounded bored. "I must be hallucinating because those rocky hills look like killer waves to me."

"You and I both wish." Nick grinned at his surfing buddy. The child of surfing hippies, Colt had taught Nick a thing or two in their time in Coronado. Nick wanted to take leave and hit a good beach with Colt to ride some of the waves he'd heard so much about, but he wasn't sure that would fit into the life he planned to make with Kaylan. Still, that kind of settling down didn't sound so bad.

They rode in silence for the next hour, stopping only once for a herd of goats and their owners, two teenage boys and a one-eyed man. Nick tried not to see every man as a potential threat. He tried not to imagine those boys growing up to hate America. On his last deployment, he loved playing with the kids and interacting with the teens. The teens were often forgotten in favor of the cute kids, but the teens were the next generation, and they needed to know they were valued. Unfortunately, out here all too frequently someone who looked harmless wouldn't hesitate to take an American life, especially as they entered a village known to be a meeting place for remnants of the Taliban, so he stayed alert, watching.

They left the vehicles outside of town and split up to hike in, their footfalls sending up puffs of dust beneath them. Bates stayed near Nick, and Nick found the kid growing on him. Bates seemed eager to prove himself, and he exuded a quiet strength and determination that impressed Nick.

"So about this girl you left behind," Bates said as they walked. "She got any hot younger sisters?"

Nick laughed. "She's got three big brothers, and one of them is walking right in front of you."

Micah coughed in acknowledgment but continued to scan the area around them as they entered the outskirts of the town. Nick switched into sniper mode, becoming the eyes of his team as he scanned rooftops and darkened doorways.

Janus walked a few paces behind him, Jake towering over her slight frame. Prison had aged her, but despite himself, he glimpsed what she could have been lurking deep beneath years of hard living.

"How about any cousins?"

"Shut it, Bates."

They came to a halt and scattered, taking up defensive positions as Janus, Jake, and X neared the door of a house on the edge of town. The door opened and a man with shifty eyes, black hair, and a black mustache stuck his head out. With a quick jerk of his hand, he ushered the three into the dark recesses of his hovel. Nick chomped down on his gum, now more gritty than flavorful. The town seemed pretty quiet, but looks could be deceiving.

Sun bore down on them from the desert sky. Sweat dribbled down the back of Nick's neck as he kept his eyes glued to the rooftops and the people milling about the streets. After ten minutes, the door opened and Janus, Jake, and X stepped out. Janus nodded at the informant, and Nick heard the low tones of another language drift on the breeze as the man responded.

"How about friends? Hook your man up."

Nick grinned, thinking about sicking Megan on this kid for one date. He would probably never act the same way again after she gave him the what-for.

A flash on top of a building several houses down caught Nick's attention.

"Sniper!" he yelled, but it was too late. The man talking to Janus fell backward, a bullet hole in his head. Nick hit his knee, steadied his breathing, and searched for the concealed man. He was trained. Few desert Bedouins could have made a shot like that. He prayed they had gotten the intel. Another movement and he fired.

"We've got another shooter at five o'clock," Bulldog spat over the radio, chatter filling Nick's ear as the team coordinated and communicated in sync with their movements. Bates crouched close to a building, filling in command over satellite radio. Nick turned long enough to see Janus and Jake in full retreat to the convoy as X and Colt covered them. If they could get away from the buildings, they would have a clear shot back to the vehicles. The town would rise up and make setting up a quick sniper position difficult for all but the most skilled and determined.

Gunfire peppered the air as a few untrained townsmen joined the fray, firing at the highly trained SEALs. Nick inwardly cringed as the locals fell one by one. "Second shooter down." Titus relayed. That meant only one sniper left. "Hawk, you got eyes on the first shooter?"

"Negative. Still looking."

"Hawk, get eyes on that package. Bulldog, close up the back door," Titus instructed over the radio.

Nick tapped Bates's shoulder and began to move, his gun poised as he slipped away to get a better view. "Hawk, shooter at two o'clock," Bates called. Before Nick could turn Bates had fired. Nick spun, trying to find their sniper, when he heard a thud and intake of breath. Bates went down on his knees, a red stain growing under his armpit beneath his armor.

"Down man. Down man." Nick ran back to his side and crouched. Shock stole across Bates's face, but Nick still saw fight in him. "We gotta get out of here. Suck it up and let's move. Now!"

Despite the glazed look in his eye, Bates lugged his gun into his left hand and began to fire as Nick ran by his side. Micah and Jay brought up the rear. Bates stumbled. "Keep moving, Bates," Nick yelled, fighting the urge to help him as he kept his eyes peeled.

Titus appeared at Bates's side. "Hawk, take care of that sniper."

Without another word, Nick searched for a clean shot. A staircase wound towards the roof on the side of a cracked two-story building. If Nick could get high enough without cresting the roof, he could take a shot and still maintain cover. "Bulldog, cover me." Micah immediately ran toward the stairs and took up post as Nick climbed. The street had gone quiet, local residents scurrying into homes when the gunfire started.

Whoever the sniper worked for, he'd accomplished his goal in shooting the informant. But then he'd stuck around to have target practice with Nick's team. Nick didn't have much patience for that. He crouched low on the stairs just before reaching the flat roof. He scanned the rooftops, easily locating where the sniper waited in the wide open desert air. The man's eyes were fixed in the direction Nick's team had disappeared, his gun still trained at the ready.

Nick aimed his weapon. The man's eyes appeared in all their detail in his scope. He forced his mind not to remember the man's features as he fired. With a small jerk, the man's head smacked the rooftop. He didn't move. Nick counted the seconds as he scanned the rooftop with micro movements through his optic, centering on his eliminated threat. After he hit thirty, he inched his way backward down the stairs.

"He's down. Contact clear, X."

Without a word to Micah, they took off in the direction of the team, praying Bates made it through with only a flesh wound and hoping against hope they captured the necessary intel before the informant's untimely demise.

CHAPTER THIRTEEN

"Kayles, slow down. I can't run as fast as you this early in the morning."

"Megan, speed up. Just tell your mind to tell your body you can do it. Running is good for you."

Megan stopped several feet behind Kaylan, clutching her side. "I may have better luck telepathically communicating to your brain that you are psychotic."

Kaylan burst into laughter and paced back to where Megan stood hunched over her knees. "You are a grouch in the morning."

"No one in their right mind should be up this early in the morning without a caffeine drip. You are killing me."

"I'm making you stronger." Kaylan slipped an arm around Megan and led her down the beach. "And you can't complain too much. Look at this view."

The sky and sea blurred together on the horizon. Color broke in the dawning Sunday morning and the ocean shimmered like dark glass. Kaylan's feet met the packed tide-kissed sand where the waves had recently changed the color from gold to brown.

"Kaylan, it's the weekend. This is ridiculous."

"You'll thank me later when you have energy to keep you going all day long." Kaylan began to run, pulling Megan with her. "C'mon. We've got one more mile."

Megan struggled to keep pace with her. Snatches of muttering and words that sounded close to "crazy, health nut, drill sergeant" floated to Kaylan's ears before the breeze pulled them out to sea.

On mornings like this, Kaylan felt closer to Nick. It had been almost a week since he left, a week since their fight. She knew the assignment was likely to be brief. Several wives and girlfriends had heard that they might be back soon. She'd only received short, vague emails from Nick. Nothing that addressed the hurt that had sprung up between them. She was beginning to see that his emotional energy had to be directed to his mission, but she longed for the chance to reconnect with him fully.

Her only phone call came from Micah saying he loved her and would see her soon. "Give him time, sis. I think he regrets the way he left and the idiot is too prideful to put that aside and call you. We're working on him. Just hang tight. He's miserable. And he loves you."

His words didn't bring Kaylan much comfort. Nick could call but chose not to. It hurt. She was miserable, too, but on mornings like this, she imagined him now running slightly ahead as she followed in his steady footsteps, his breath even as he cut a path for them down the beach. She knew the strength in his shoulders and the extra energy he mustered when they reached their last half mile. He added a burst of speed and finished with everything he had. He pushed her and she followed him into the finish line every time, using his strength to bolster her own.

Only this morning, she heard Megan's unsteady breaths and shaky footsteps as she followed in Kaylan's wake, straining to keep up. Kaylan slowed down a little. "Almost there, Meg."

They finished at the pier where Kaylan had been lured into a kidnapping only months before. A chill raced down her spine as she remembered the sweet smell of a drug and then nothing before waking up in a boat shed. She and Megan had barely escaped with their lives, but Nick and the team had come for her. He always came for her.

"You're thinking about it, aren't you?" Megan rubbed a spot on her head, probably remembering where she'd been hit.

"It's hard not to when I see this pier."

Megan shuddered. "Scariest moment of my life, but we made it."

"Do you still have nightmares?"

"Sometimes." Megan shrugged. "But they aren't coming as much now."

"That's great. What helped?"

Megan turned bright red and looked out to sea. "You and all that Jesus talk. I read a chapter in Psalms every night before I go to bed. It's hard to go to bed scared or with negative thoughts after reading that stuff. Not to mention it's got a nice ring to it."

"My roommate, the closet poet." Kaylan laughed and wrapped her arm around Megan's shoulders. "Watch out, Meg. You may end up becoming a Jesus-lover after all."

"It might not be the worst thing ever."

"Glad you think so."

As they began walking back to the car, a high-pitched yelp filtered through the breeze.

Kaylan stopped. "Did you hear that?"

Megan paused as the sound echoed again. Kaylan physically ached at the pain she heard slicing through the air. She turned, searching the beach for the source of the sound.

"Kayles, it sounds like an animal or something." She tugged on Kaylan's arm. "Let's just go."

"It sounds hurt. We need to find it."

"Kaylan . . ." A sharp bark followed by yelping sent Kaylan running under the pier, Megan scrambling to follow in her wake.

Sand kicked up behind her, stinging her bare calves. Her muscles ached with exertion from her run and now a sprint down the beach. As they neared one of the pier beams, Kaylan spotted a shaggy dog sprawled in the sand. His white and black fur hung in matted knots. He lay on his side in the sand, struggling to get on his feet. Every time he succeeded, a yelp cut through the air and he crumpled back to the sand to begin the fight once more.

"Kaylan, stop, you don't know where he's been or if he's friendly."

But Kaylan couldn't help herself. She approached him slowly. "Hey fella, it's okay. Let me help you." His tail flopped in response to her voice, sending sand grains airborne. His skinny belly rose and fell in sync with his frenzied panting. As Kaylan knelt next to him, she held out her hand to let him sniff.

"Look, he's hurt." She pointed at his back left paw. "It's still bleeding. I wonder if he stepped on a broken seashell or piece of glass or something." She looked around the area in search of the object in question.

"Kaylan, just leave him. Someone else will help. Maybe his family will find him."

"Who will help him if we don't, Meg? He looks like a stray. He doesn't have a collar, and he's hurt."

"Kaylan, don't you even . . ."

"We're taking him home."

". . . say that," Megan finished and groaned.

"Hey, boy, can I pet you?" Kaylan stretched out her hand to his head. When he didn't react, she slipped her hand behind his ear and scratched. She received a slobbery kiss in response.

"You've been slimed."

Kaylan chuckled and wiped her hand on her shorts. "I've been approved."

"How do you know it's a boy?" Megan questioned as she kept her distance.

Kaylan circled behind him and wedged her arms beneath his belly. He whined and struggled. She whispered, trying to soothe him as she lifted him.

"Yep, he's a boy." Megan confirmed as Kaylan moved past her, a furry mass in her arms.

"Hurry. He's kind of heavy." Megan ran ahead and grabbed an old sandy towel that Kaylan kept in her trunk for beach visits. She spread it across the back seat. Kaylan did her best to slip the dog in without bumping his leg, then slid into the front seat.

"He smells like wet dog," Megan muttered on the short drive back to their house.

"Did you expect him to smell like roses?"

"I didn't expect to smell wet dog, period."

"Can't be much worse than fish smell."

"I'll give you that."

Kaylan smiled and shook her head, her gaze alternating from the road to the mangy dog in the back seat. "Tell you what, while I give him a bath, why don't you start the coffee and get a dose of happy in your system."

"We're keeping this dog, aren't we?"

Kaylan didn't respond.

"What is it with you and adopting strays?"

Again Kaylan kept silent, basking in Megan's frustration. Her roommate was too much of a softy to resist long. Once Kaylan had him cleaned up and smelling nice, Megan would melt.

They pulled in front of the house and Kaylan gently maneuvered the dog from the back seat. "He needs a name."

"He probably has a disease."

Again, Kaylan smothered a smile as her roommate opened the front door. "Coffee, Megan."

"No need to tell me that again." She cut a straight path to the kitchen. "Soldier boy protects and you rescue. You really do make the perfect martyr couple," Megan shouted as Kaylan marched the dog back to the bathroom and plopped him in the tub.

When Megan put it like that, Nick and Kaylan really did sound like the perfect team, and both in the perfect places to fulfill their roles. One on the front protecting the lives of Americans, and one at home rescuing one puppy and surly roommate at a time.

It took an hour to clean the sand and blood from the dog's foot and wash and comb through all his knots. She'd even taken scissors to some. Megan finally appeared with a mug of coffee and sat on the toilet lid watching while Kaylan worked.

"Now he looks like a drowned rat."

Kaylan chuckled as the dog licked her. "He is pretty skinny."

"I put some food and water down for him in the kitchen."

"What are we feeding him?"

When Megan didn't answer, Kaylan turned to face her, a cup of water at the ready to force an answer from Megan.

"I may have run to the store real quick and grabbed food, a bed, and a collar. And if you pour that on me, I will take it all back and then kill you slowly."

"You old softy."

The chugging of the drain filled the bathroom as the dog slipped and tried to back away from the offensive sound. Kaylan reached for an old towel and began to dry him, avoiding the wound on his paw and leg.

"Sandy," Megan said over the growling drain.

"I know. I'll clean it up after I get him out of here."

"No, I mean his name. Sandy."

"That sounds a little too orphan Annie to me."

"Orphan who?"

"You were a deprived child, weren't you? What did you watch growing up?"

Megan's lip curled. "Nothing with singing in it."

Kaylan tried to help the dog from the tub as he slipped and slid and landed in a furry pile on his belly at their feet. Both of them laughed.

"Well, Sandy fits with how he looked when we found him, and I don't want to keep calling him 'dog.'"

Kaylan sank down on her knees in front of him and began cleaning and bandaging his paw with supplies she had laid out on the bathroom rug. He whimpered but held still, covering her hand and the bandage with kisses.

"He seems pretty nice."

"You could pet him, Meg."

Megan's grimace sent Kaylan into a fit of giggles. "Or not. You forget I prefer marine animals to the furry sort."

"He may change your mind." Kaylan finished the bandage and helped the dog to his feet. He limped a bit but found his footing as she led him to the kitchen and the bowl of food and water Megan had laid out for him. Megan followed and jumped up on the counter, watching him eat.

"He really does have a pretty coat now," Megan murmured. "He's too skinny though."

"We can fatten him up. We'll take him to the vet and see how old he is and get them to check his health, but he looks okay to me, just underfed."

"Maybe he got in a fight with a crab or something."

"Maybe." Kaylan watched Sandy. His white and black patchy coat shone after the bath and smelled infinitely better than he had an hour before. He seemed friendly and gentle, just in desperate need of affection and care.

"Are you okay with us keeping him?"

Megan smiled. "You are moving out in the next few months anyway, so I can handle him for a while."

"You're going to fall in love with him and not want either one of us to leave by the time this is all said and done."

Megan jumped off the counter and ran her fingers through Sandy's wagging tail. "All this sweet stuff is hurting my tough image."

Kaylan slugged Megan's arm. "Maybe it's time for a new image," she shouted after her as she went to her room.

Sandy walked to the bed Megan had laid out next to his bowls and collapsed. Kaylan bent to pet his still-wet fur, wondering if she had just found a companion for Nick's long absences. "Maybe it's time for an attitude change for both of us," she muttered.

CHAPTER FOURTEEN

Smelling of crayons and chocolate chip cookies, Timothy snuggled into Kaylan as she read a Bible story to her Sunday kindergarten class.

"How did the donkey talk, Mrs. Kaylan?"

She kissed his forehead and smiled at the other children gathered in her circle. "God told him to because Balaam was being stubborn."

Abigail, a little girl in purple and pigtails, raised her hand. "Can all donkeys talk?"

"Only if Jesus tells them to, Abby," Jason answered matter-of-factly.

Timothy turned his big eyes to look up at Kaylan, his black skin and curly short hair reminding her all too much of baby Kenny in Haiti. A wave of nostalgia washed over her, before she pushed back its tide. "If I'm stubborn like that, will God make a donkey talk at me?"

Kaylan gave him a squeeze, sending him into a fit of giggles and making the other children giggle with him. "I think what we can learn from this is that God wants us to be obedient, but he can use anything to make us listen if we choose to run from him or disobey him. So how can we be obedient?"

"Do what Mommy says."

"What does she tell you to do?"

"Don't push friends at school."

"Share my toys."

"Feed my dog."

"Those are all good things to do. Jesus loves it when we are obedient. But he wants us to obey Him because we love Him."

"I love Jesus this much, Miss Kaylan," Timothy said, stretching his arms out wide and leaning back into Kaylan's chest.

"I hope you love Him more and more." Kaylan saw several parents standing at the door ready to pick the kids up for the service. "Let's pray and meet your parents."

Timothy prayed quickly and then bounced from her lap to meet his mom at the door. As the other children followed suit, Kaylan rose to help clean up.

"Kayles?" Kaylan dropped what she was doing and turned to find Megan dressed in her ripped jeans and a nice black sweater wearing a terrified expression.

Kaylan schooled her shock. Megan had never come to church. "Hey, I didn't know you were coming today."

"Neither did I. Someone I met said I could find you in here. Does everyone know you?"

Kaylan finished putting the last block in the bucket and stood. "Not hardly. You just happened to run into the right person. You ready for service?"

"Is that a rhetorical question?"

"C'mon. No one will bite."

"I'm more worried about the lightning."

"Nothing has struck the building yet, so I'm pretty sure you're fine."

Kaylan navigated through the building, greeting a few people as she went and acknowledging several SEAL families who asked if she'd heard from Nick. With each "no," a part of her darkened more and more. She missed him. They needed to talk. And she needed to let go.

She just didn't know how. Pinning a smile on her face, she went through the motions during the music and pulled out a notebook and Bible to take notes during the message. But everything fell flat.

Where are you, Lord? Why does everything feel off?

"I want everyone to make a fist," the pastor said. His request caught Kaylan's attention.

"Is he about to encourage an all-out brawl in church? No one's drunk enough for that," Megan whispered, eliciting a smirk from Kaylan.

"I'm serious, make a fist," the pastor said as a few people cast bewildered looks at their neighbors. Kaylan formed a fist with her left hand, her heart wound more tightly than her knuckles.

"Now I want you to think of something that's hurt you deeply. Maybe it's something you are struggling with or someone that you are angry at. Maybe a husband left you or a child won't behave or your boss doesn't respect you or a friend won't speak with you. Now close your eyes, and I want you to give that pain to your Father in heaven who made you and loves you."

The medium-sized worship center felt small all of a sudden, like the walls were closing in and everyone was staring at her. She squeezed her eyes shut, blocking out the people, the room, and the hipster pastor on stage dressed in trendy plaid and asking her to relive her pain. But the pain she desperately desired to hold at bay shoved through her defenses. Her argument with Nick reared its ugly head.

Kaylan's last words with Nick stabbed through her mind, searing like a red-hot poker. Her hands trembled, and Kaylan squeezed her fist tighter. She was angry. Angry at the Lord for taking those she loved, for isolating her, for the pain she couldn't seem to release from losing loved ones. She was angry that the world was hard, angry that it could cost Nick and her new family their lives, and angry that he just accepted it, that at times it ranked higher than her.

But most of all Kaylan was angry at herself for not being able to move past it, for understanding why Nick wanted to go and yet holding it against him in her heart. She was angry that she couldn't be the perfect fiancée or perfect wife. That she would always struggle because nothing in the world terrified her more than losing her loved ones, than being alone. Nick was a liability to both of those fears, yet he'd chosen her, and she'd chosen him. Now he was asking her to be braver than her fears and trust him on the journey God had called him to travel.

"One last step. I want you to tell the Lord you are going to trust Him to heal that pain and commit to stop trying to fix it in your own strength." The pastor's voice sliced through Kaylan's battle. "Now open your fist and surrender your fears and your pain to Him."

But Kaylan couldn't release. Her fingers ached as she squeezed tighter. She wanted to. God, she wanted to let go of the pain, of the fear, of the desire to control and keep Nick close. She wanted to release all the tension and for the first time in a year experience the sweet sensation of relief.

As music began to play, Kaylan opened her eyes. The first thing she noticed was an atmosphere of peace, of free people who had relinquished control. Megan sang with everyone else, a single tear running down her cheek.

But that wasn't the problem. The second thing Kaylan noticed was her still-clenched fist trembling on her lap.

CHAPTER FIFTEEN

"Kayles, wait, I need to talk to you," Megan called from behind her.

As soon as the service ended, Kaylan made a beeline to the parking lot, forgetting Megan and ignoring the looks of friends and acquaintances on her way. She didn't know where to go, only that she needed to go figure things out.

"Kaylan, stop." Running footsteps and Megan's nearing voice brought Kaylan to a halt. She turned to meet her roommate, forcing her emotions to cool and her mind to stop racing.

"Are you okay?" Megan asked as she approached.

"It just got really hot in there, and I needed to get outside."

Megan nodded but Kaylan could tell she didn't really believe her. "Can we go somewhere and talk? Please?"

Kaylan fought the urge to say no but knew she would only go home and collapse on her bed in frustration until she figured everything out. "Sure. Coffee or lunch?"

"Tacos?"

"Tacos it is. The cart on the beach or Tank's Tacos?"

"Tank's. I want to sit."

"Meet you there." Kaylan hightailed it to her car, desperate for escape, but her solitude was short-lived. Within fifteen minutes, she pulled into the parking lot of Tank's Tacos.

A former boxer, Tank quit the sport to open his own restaurant armed with his mom's and grandmother's best family recipes. Despite his intimidating stocky, boxy frame, Tank acted like a lovable teddy bear, greeting every customer that walked through the doors. Nick and Micah had introduced Kaylan and Megan to the place. As Kaylan walked through the doors and into a large square room decorated with black-and-white boxing photos, she couldn't help but think the place felt empty without them.

"Kaylan, long time no see, *chica.* What brings you to my fine establishment?" Tank said in greeting as he gave her a quick squeeze.

Kaylan mustered a smile she didn't feel. "Hey, Tank. Good to see you. Megan and I had a hankering for your tacos." The door behind her opened and Megan waltzed in.

"For two of my favorite ladies, anything," he said as Megan joined him and smiled a greeting. "What'll you have?"

They took turns rattling off their orders and then settled into a booth next to big windows overlooking the parking lot.

"So," Megan started while twirling a fork in her hand. "Church was good."

"Was that your first time ever?" Kaylan nodded in thanks as Tank brought them water. She took a sip. The icy liquid cooled her nerves. What she wouldn't do for a glass of Gran's sweet iced tea.

"I mean a couple people took me here and there as a kid. But never to a church like that before. That pastor was so . . ."

"Hipster?"

"Yes! But that's not what I was going for. He was so real. I mean at first I thought that whole fist thing was totally lame, but then, I don't know, everything clicked and I understood what he was saying."

Kaylan sank back in the booth and crossed her arms, her mind and emotions churning as she remembered the pastor's analogy. But Megan didn't seem to notice Kaylan's response. In fact, she didn't seem to notice much of anything. Kaylan had never seen her so excited. Despite her own frustration, her curiosity was piqued.

"I mean I've been trying to talk to God like you've told me. But I always end up staring at the ceiling feeling stupid or let down. But today was different."

Megan continued. "There I was with my fist clenched, looking at everyone else and feeling like an idiot. Then I figured, why not try what the pastor's suggesting? So I closed my eyes and just talked to God like I would talk to you. Kaylan, I talked to him about my dad." Her hands moved with excitement and the fork bounced up and down in her fingers.

Kaylan noticed something different about her friend. The eyes that held the weight of the world had lost their dark cloud and sun peeked from their depths. "I told God I was angry at my dad and angry that he allowed what happened to me as a kid. I thought it would be pointless. But, Kayles, I felt this crazy pressure release. Right here." She placed her hand over her heart. "And then when we stood to sing, the lyrics really meant something to me. They were more than words. They were . . . real."

"Then in the car on the way over here, I talked to God some more and just told him I didn't want to feel the way I have felt my whole life anymore. I want what you and Nick and your whole family have." Megan reached across the table for Kaylan's hand, startling her with her intensity. "Can I really have a relationship with God?"

With rising excitement, Kaylan turned her hand in Megan's and returned her grip. "Sure you can. When Jesus died, it provided a way for sinful people to have a relationship with a perfect God because his death covered every sin we have ever committed and every one we will ever make."

"But I'll never be perfect."

"That's the beautiful thing about grace. You can't earn it. It's given. But it also has to be received. It's a commitment to follow the God Who gave His life for you. When you follow Him, you want to do more things that please Him because you see how much He loves you."

Tank brought their tacos on colorful plates that he placed in front of them. "Enjoy, ladies."

"Thanks, Tank."

Megan turned her eyes back to Kaylan. "So it's as easy as telling God I want a relationship with Him."

"Yep. And then comes the hard part. You have to work at the relationship every day."

Megan nodded. "Okay. I'll do it."

"Now?"

Megan smirked. "I'm going to wait until I get back in the car and can do it by myself. Baby steps, Kayles."

Kaylan chuckled and took a bite. The flavor of lime, avocado, barbacoa, and a hint of dressing made her taste buds sing.

"Just make sure you do it."

"I released my fist. No going back."

Kaylan swallowed hard as Megan mentioned the analogy once again. Shame like she'd never felt before filled her. She'd just shared the gospel with her roommate, the story of a loving Father who reached down from heaven to save a sinful world. A God big enough to do that, and she was angry because she felt alone.

"Kayles?" Megan chewed slowly, her eyes shifting between Kaylan and her food. "Is there a reason you couldn't open your fist or why you took off so quickly?"

Kaylan didn't move. How did she tell her roommate she was angry? With God, with Nick, but mostly with herself. Even after having a relationship with the Lord for years, she still didn't know how to let go of her fear.

"Just processing and dealing with a lot, Megan."

They ate in silence, but Kaylan could tell Megan struggled to sit still. As they paid the bill and rose to leave, Megan grabbed her arm with a viselike grip. "Kaylan, take it from me. Those things you told me about God, they helped me be free. Freer than I've ever felt. Whatever it is and whatever it takes, just loosen your grip. Let God handle it." She let go, but her dark eyes studied Kaylan. "I have a surprise. I've been waiting for the perfect time, and this is definitely it." She took a step toward her car. "Follow me."

"Meg, I'm not in the mood for a surprise," she groaned.

Her roommate only opened her door and fixed Kaylan with a stubborn stare. "Trust me. You'll be in the mood for this." Without another word, she slipped in her seat and started the engine.

Kaylan crawled into her car, wishing she could crawl under a rock. Fear bound her, and now failure crippled her. She wanted to pull the covers over her head and start the day over. But running away wouldn't solve anything.

Kaylan stepped from the car into the parking lot of an unfamiliar complex. The short drive helped to calm her, but she still just wanted to go home.

"Meg, where are we? Who are we visiting?"

Fingers slipped over her eyes, and Kaylan jerked. "Not funny." She tried to pull her roommate's hands away, but Megan only dug into her cheeks.

"Stop fighting and walk."

Kaylan sighed and took a step, knowing this was a battle she would lose. "You better not let me fall."

"It would serve you right for being a brat. Why did I agree to do this?" she mumbled.

"Agree to do what?"

Only silence greeted her. After what felt like an eternity of awkward maneuvers and a few scary moments, they stopped.

"If I move my hands, will you keep your eyes closed?"

"Well, that depends. Will you tell me where we are?"

"So nosy. I'm starting to understand your issue with your fist."

Kaylan stiffened. "Low blow, Meg. Fine. I'll keep my eyes closed." She crossed her arms and stood still as Megan moved her hands. She heard what sounded like a key in a lock before the squeal of hinges.

"You can open your eyes."

Kaylan opened first one, then the other and stood looking past Megan into an empty room. A short hallway branched off and ended with three doors.

"Don't just stand there."

She stepped inside, her flats sinking into carpet. "Care to explain?"

Megan dropped the key in her hand. "Welcome to your new home. Soldier Boy took care of all the details before he left. He didn't want you to worry about it."

Kaylan gasped and turned slowly, envisioning decorations, a place to build memories. She pictured a life. A home. She pictured Nick.

Kaylan's eyes swam. "This is the sweetest thing he has ever done for me," she croaked.

Megan tugged a packet of tissues from her back pocket and tossed them to Kaylan with a smirk. "I thought his proposal was swoon worthy, but your man knows how to take care of you."

Kaylan laughed through the tears. "Yes, he does. Even when he's not here." She pulled Megan in for a hug. "Thanks for bringing me today."

Megan pulled back enough to look at Kaylan. "Kayles, you need to remember distance doesn't determine love. Duty doesn't define it either. That man is loyal to you. He would do anything for you." She smiled and pulled away. "And so would I."

"Thanks, Meg."

Her roommate waved her off. "All right, all right, enough of the mushy stuff. How do you want to decorate?"

Kaylan's grin turned devious. "I'm so glad you asked, because I'm going to keep you busy until he comes home."

"I was afraid of that." She chuckled. "Well, talk me through it and we'll go from there."

Kaylan let her mind roam with the possibilities, but inside she prayed Nick would call, and soon. In the meantime, she would create a safe haven for him to come home to.

CHAPTER SIXTEEN

Nick hadn't experienced a drive that excruciatingly long since his trip to find Kaylan in Haiti. The heat and dust and bumpy road made it near impossible to try and patch up Bates.

"I'm a little worried the bullet might've nicked his brachial artery and then embedded in his side close to his heart. He's losing a lot of blood," Kite Kelly muttered as he worked on Bates. The corpsman's steady hands moved quickly to lessen the blood flow. The bandana wrapped around his graying buzzed head did little to stop the sweat from dripping off his face in the sizzling metal cab. Despite Kite's calm exterior, Nick sensed his worry.

"So stupid. So stupid," Bates kept grumbling. "Fix me up and get me operational." His sheet-white face countered his command.

"Chill, Bates. We gotta get you to a doctor." Nick pinned his good shoulder back, forcing him to be still. Adrenaline, a SEAL used to action and unaccustomed to failure, and major blood loss made for a bad situation. After thirty minutes, Bates passed out. Nick had a sick feeling that the bullet had somehow pierced his heart.

Base doctors had Bates before Nick could crawl out of the convoy. Within seconds, he was out of sight.

"He didn't look good, brah." Colt shook his head.

"He saved me and I left him open."

"Shake it off, Hawk. He did exactly what you, or I, or anyone else on this team would have done. Watch each other's backs. He'll be okay." But the worried look Micah tossed in the direction of the infirmary only added weight to Nick's own assessment.

T-Brown nodded after X. "Let's go see what all this is about."

"Hustle up, hustle up," X shouted in his gravelly voice as they entered the room that felt more and more like a confinement area. His red hair stuck out at odd angles after its release from his helmet, making him look like a cartoon character who just stuck his finger in a live electric socket.

"The Taliban cell in question planned to meet in two days, but our informant overheard their contingency plan. The meeting goes down tonight in the home of one of the leaders, which means we will need to account for women and children. No friendlies dead on our watch. I mean it. Heads in the game, ladies."

He continued with op specifics. The meeting was farther away, so they would take choppers to the appropriate landing zone and contain the house, following up with an assault. The team scattered to reload ammo and prepare for the evening ahead. The cover of darkness would add an extra layer of protection and familiarity. Nick, like every SEAL, preferred operating in the dark.

The town they were traveling to had been known as a Taliban hot spot over the years. During the war, the Taliban had scattered, their familiar meeting places abandoned, but this group appeared to be just gutsy enough to revisit and reclaim their stomping grounds. If the team didn't handle things right, the night could turn into an all-out gun fight. Nick wouldn't allow that to happen.

At some point during the tactical planning, Janus and Jake slipped from the room. Her task accomplished, she didn't need to stick around. The tightness in Nick's chest released with her exit. Despite his calm demeanor since accepting her role and presence, she still made him uneasy. That woman didn't do anything for free, and he didn't feel like becoming a bargaining chip in her game.

If Nick had his way, they would go directly for the head of the snake, Janus's boss and Russian oil businessman, Sasha Baryshev. The man had the ear of many an influential man in the Russian government and many a shady individual in the black market where he specialized in weapons and ammunition. Until a few months ago, they hadn't known what name to put on one of the biggest weapons terrorists in the world. Now they just had to catch him. If they could execute tonight's objective, they may be able to smoke him out of hiding. As long as they kept a tight grip on Janus, they may just be able to put an end to his business. Nick just hoped Jake kept a close watch on her. She hadn't remained hidden for years without skill and the drive to do whatever was necessary.

"We'll reconvene at nineteen hundred for a final walk-through and briefing. We'll leave at twenty. Get some rest. Call your families. And let's take care of business."

"I'm going to catch a few Z's. You coming?" Micah slapped him on the back as guys began filing out of the room.

Nick grabbed his rifle. "I think I'm going for a workout. Blow off some steam. Prep for tonight."

Micah's gaze was as pointed as his rifle. "It's not your fault, man. Please, go call Kaylan. Everyone is getting really tired of the tortured thing."

"I am not acting tortured. I just need to keep my head in the game, and dealing with how I left things with Kaylan is a distraction right now."

"Dude." Colt slapped him on the back on his way out the door. "Call her. Or she'll have a whole new reason to be mad at you."

"Yeah, Hawk, call her, or I will strap you to a chair and make you call her."

"Don't make me shoot you, Bulldog." Nick brushed past him and his told-you-so smirk. Still, Micah's threat hung in the air between them. As much as his buddy loved to joke, Nick knew he meant it.

The bustle of the base in the desert reminded Nick of his first deployment to the Middle East only a couple of years before. Right before he and Kaylan got back together. "Hurry up, do your job, and then wait" was true then, and remained true now. Nick arrived in the makeshift gym and settled in with weights. With the holidays, wedding plans, and dealing with Kaylan and Janus, his mind split off in a thousand directions and his skills felt rusty. Usually the eyes of the team, he felt like he'd let everyone down today.

He lifted the bar, his shoulders screaming and brain racing as he imagined the head of the man who shot Bates. He dropped and lifted again, the burn intensifying. His muscles responded; if only his brain would cooperate. Again he lifted and imagined Janus's head, her smug smile and blue eyes that spoke of death. Again and again he lifted, his mind sharpening, eyes zeroing in. With each rep, he imagined firing his weapon, his mind's eye focusing in on his target. He wouldn't let his team down tonight. He would focus.

He lifted again, but this time Kaylan's sweet smile flashed in front of his eyes. He fought to maintain control of the bar as his muscles shook. He swore. She couldn't be a distraction. He wouldn't let her be. It was the only way he would make it home to her intact. He fought for control and shoved the bar up again, straight above his head.

But it was the lingering memory of their fight that penetrated his heart. He closed his eyes. Heat suffocated him. He needed a shower, a bed, time to prep for the night ahead. He needed to call Kaylan. He needed to get this right. A week without hearing her voice, her musical laugh, was long enough. He could be such a prideful jerk, but the silence, the time without even a small piece of her wasn't worth it. He needed to fix things. She would still need to decide if she could deal. He had full confidence she could, but she needed to realize that. But until then, he would be strong for both of them. He couldn't wait any longer to make things right. To lead her as much as he loved her.

He glanced at his watch. Three-thirty Monday afternoon in Afghanistan, which meant Kaylan might wake up if he sent her an email and maybe they could talk before she went to work. Without taking time to second guess, he rushed off to email her. He could shower, eat, and maybe even nap before their Skype date. Hopefully she checked her email.

His stomach turned. On second thought, maybe he would wait to eat. The thought of how he'd left her made him sick. He hoped she wasn't upset, that he hadn't hurt her too bad. He wanted things back to normal. In the week since they had seen one another, one thing had become abundantly clear: he was a better person with her in his life. He could swallow his pride to make sure things got back to the way they should be. Of this Nick was confident: they were better together.

CHAPTER SEVENTEEN

Kaylan was first-date kind of nervous and excited. Nick wanted to Skype with her. She had crawled out of bed at five on Monday planning to run before work. But when she discovered his email, she stayed home and spent an hour picking just the right top and fixing her hair and makeup. Then she waited.

"Your nails are going to disappear if you keep chewing them like that." Kaylan jumped at Megan's voice behind her. "You scare way too easily," she chuckled.

Kaylan grabbed a pillow off her bed and let it fly in Megan's direction. "I'm nervous. It's been a week! And what are you doing up?"

"It's my turn to feed Napoleon this morning," she said, referring to their newest humpback whale. "So are you going to spend the next hour making kissy faces and telling each other how much you love one another?"

Kaylan's face heated. "Maybe."

Sandy slipped from behind Megan's legs and padded into the room, heading straight for Kaylan.

"Well, hey there, where have you been?" She glanced up knowingly at Megan.

Meg tossed her hands in the air. "He wouldn't leave my room last night. Who am I to say no?"

Kaylan laughed as Sandy settled on her feet with a huff. "You're such a sucker."

"I'm sorry, what?"

The musical tone signifying an incoming call sang out in the room. "Finally," Kaylan squealed, waving off her roommate's protests.

"I'll see you after work. Have fun." Megan closed the door behind her as Kaylan answered the call. In the moments it took for the video to turn on, Kaylan's nerves kicked into high gear. What if he was still mad? What if he didn't want to marry her anymore? What if . . .

"Hey there, gorgeous." Nick's blue eyes and smile, the one he reserved just for her, filled the screen, and she relaxed.

"Hi back. I've missed you."

"Me too, baby." She sensed a hint of regret in his tone. "You look good. You didn't have to get dressed up just for me, though. I know this was a little unexpected."

"What are you talking about? I woke up like this."

Nick chuckled. "You mean you will wake up looking like a model every morning of our married lives? Man, did I luck out. Great genes, babe."

Kaylan's smile slipped a bit. "So you still want to marry me?"

"Oh, babe." Nick squirmed in his chair, the empty room behind him wiggling as the camera moved. "Please forgive me for how I handled that. I do need you to decide now if you can handle this, or our marriage is going to be tough. But I should never have left angry."

Kaylan still felt unsettled. She couldn't quite figure out her tight grip, her need to make sure nothing happened to him, but she knew it wasn't right. "Please forgive me, too. You had a right to be angry. I never should have put pressure on you like that. Logan and Kim helped me understand better, and Megan, too, ironically." She rolled her eyes.

"Sounds like a story there."

Kaylan shrugged. "She just reminded me that love doesn't expect of the other what they can't give. It accepts them for who they are and pushes them to be better. Love lets them go and waits for them to come home."

He whistled. "Megan said all that? It is surprisingly devoid of sarcasm."

"No." She laughed. "She brought me to our apartment when I needed it most and reminded me that you loved me. The rest of that realization spun from there." She went on to catch him up on wedding plans and Molly's latest obsession with trying to feed Nadia "big girl" food. She thought about mentioning her coffee date with Natalie, but decided to save it for later. One thing at a time.

"Sounds like things are going okay there."

"They are." As Kaylan recited the normal events of the past few week, she realized to her surprise that life continued and she was doing fine without him, even though she missed him terribly. Maybe she could do this SEAL life after all. "I found the 'present' you hid in my closet. The only person I've wanted to use it on is Megan when she ate the last chocolate chip cookie." Among the notes she had found scattered around the house and at different wedding specific locations since his departure was a note directing her to a black box he'd hidden at the back of her closet—the box housing the pistol he kept for his own personal use.

His face went blank and his posture stiffened. She knew his combat-ready mode, even on camera. "Remember the lessons I gave you? Don't hesitate if someone comes in your home again. You shoot first and ask questions later."

"Nick, what if I can't shoot? It's a person, not a deer."

"Babe, if I suspected a normal burglar, pointing that thing at them might scare them off, but the people we are dealing with won't scare that easily. They respect action over words. Just promise me you'll take care of yourself."

She nodded, knowing if it came down to the person or Megan, she wouldn't hesitate. "Did I mention we got a dog?"

His blue eyes doubled in size. "Seriously?"

"He was hurt and all alone at the beach."

"So naturally you adopted him." Nick smirked but Kaylan sensed a glint of admiration in his eyes.

She shrugged. "I couldn't help it."

A knock sounded on the door behind Nick. "Wrap it up, Hawk."

"Got it," he shouted. "Gorgeous, I've got to go. I love you."

Kaylan fought back tears, knowing he had probably called because it was time to walk into danger. "I love you, too. Please be safe and come home to me."

"I hear we have a pretty big shindig coming up. I wouldn't miss it for the world."

"Thanks for all my notes." The one on her dress had been only the beginning. He'd left one at the caterer, the tuxedo shop, and the florist. Each note affirmed the decisions she had made and shared what he liked most about them, as well. And in each one she felt more loved that he'd taken the time to plan ahead for what he must have known would be a challenging separation.

"My pleasure." She detected a glimmer of regret hiding in his eyes, but his smile made her question her observation. She loved that smile, the one he saved for her. "Are we okay?"

She hesitated. Was she okay? Not really, but it wasn't because of Nick. It was something in her. Something she needed to fight and deal with, but she would deal with it on her own. For her, for him.

"Kayles?"

She realized she'd been quiet too long. Worry now clouded his face. She couldn't, wouldn't be the source of his distraction. "Absolutely. Go take care of business."

He nodded, his shoulders relaxing for the first time during their conversation. "Love you." And with that, he signed off.

Kaylan wiped a rogue tear and began to get ready for work. He would fight and she would pray. Together, they would both make a difference. But inside, she still couldn't quite let go of the lingering remnants of anger at her own weakness.

"Lord, make me brave. Make me strong in this. I want to be a warrior like Nick," she silently prayed. The spoken words bolstered her courage, if only a little.

CHAPTER EIGHTEEN

Kaylan had started to live for the weekend. She went through the motions to complete her training and become a licensed dietician. The work kept her busy and distracted, but she longed for the weekends to rest from her racing mind. Yet, this weekend brought a reminder of the Sunday before.

She grew tired of the internal battle. As she walked to her car after church, Kaylan felt as if she had survived another Sunday, but it was the pastor's message from the Sunday before that still nagged her. Throughout worship and the message, she had made a fist and released it, hoping her feelings would match. In theory, it should be simple. But the reality kept her trapped in a prison of her own making.

During her solitary drive home, Kaylan chewed on Megan's words and advice from the previous week. She had to let go of her fear, her anger. She had to stop trying to control. She'd watched as Megan worshipped this morning for the first time as a follower of Christ. Her face glowed as she sang, the lyrics taking root more with each repetition. How was it that Megan, a girl who'd experienced more abandonment and abuse than Kaylan could fathom, could let it all go, and Kaylan, church girl and sheltered daughter, couldn't?

Her pride felt bruised, her relationships broken. Ironically her fear of being alone tended to isolate her from those she loved most—Nick, the Lord, even her family after Haiti. Though it hurt those around her, Kaylan bore the most pain from her actions.

She pulled into her driveway and parked, staring at the stucco structure and white garage door. Her neighborhood teemed with life outside her car doors, but inside, Kaylan still couldn't loosen her grip.

She leaned her forehead on the steering wheel, the cool rubber and gentle texture massaging her aching mind.

"God, I don't want to fight You. I don't want to control. And I don't want to be afraid anymore. It cripples me." A tear tracked down her face, landing on her clenched fingers. "You called me to love a warrior, and You call me to go deeper in my relationship with You, but both require a bravery I don't know that I have. What happens if I lose him? What happens when I don't feel You?"

A breeze whipped through the trees outside and with it came a gentle whisper over Kaylan's heart. *Give it to Me, sweet girl.*

Tears coursed down her face. Reflecting on that gentle admonition, Kaylan realized she didn't have to figure it out or understand. She just had to trust. Trust her fear to a loving Father and remember He was near even when she couldn't feel it. She was never alone.

One by one, she released each finger until her hand lay open on her knee. Fingernail indentions decorated her palm. Their impressions would fade, could fade now that she had relinquished her grip.

But better still, Kaylan felt the knot of shame, fear, regret, and anger begin to uncurl within her. As she opened the car door, she took a deep breath, tasting the cool air. The moisture on her cheeks dried.

And for the first time in months she felt light. She felt free.

She had surrendered.

After an emotional morning for Kaylan and a long, heartfelt conversation with Megan once they both arrived back at the house, the two of them had decided to spend the rest of their morning recharging. Sun drifted through their sheer curtains and a candle scented the room with the fragrance of sea and tropical flowers, Megan's favorite.

A sharp rap at the door shattered the silence, causing Kaylan and Megan to jump up from their nests on the couches. After their kidnappings months before, both of them were leery of strangers anywhere near their home.

"Are you expecting someone?" Megan asked from behind her copy of *Lord of the Rings.*

Kaylan shook her head, wondering whether to get Nick's pistol. "Sandy, come." The dog appeared at her side immediately. Someone had given up a well-trained and loyal companion. He never let Megan or Kaylan out of his sight for long.

The doorbell rang. Kaylan peered through the peephole, her breath catching when she saw Natalie on the other side of the door. She fumbled with the locks and pulled the door open, startling a retreating blonde.

"Hey, where are you going?"

The girl turned, her cheeks a faint pink. "I assumed no one was home."

"Sorry, no, just lazy today. Do you want to come in?" Kaylan stepped aside to allow her entry, but Natalie stood frozen on the porch. "Okay, how about some coffee? Tea? Hot chocolate?" Natalie perked up on the last one. "Right, chocolate lover. Come on in."

Sandy sniffed at her legs as she entered, and she absent-mindedly rubbed behind his ears before turning to Kaylan looking like a lost child. "I don't know what I'm doing here."

"I don't know what you're doing here either." Megan looked up from her book and grinned. "I'm Megan."

Megan's brashness drew a smile and a bit of the spunk Kaylan remembered from the coffee shop. "I'm Natalie."

"Nice to meet you, Nat. And how do you two know each other?"

Natalie's face drained of color, so Kaylan quickly replied, "I met her when I went to pick up the dresses in LA a few weeks back. We had been emailing about some research I'd been doing and met up at a coffee shop."

"Well, *mi casa et su casa*, but if you two can keep it down over there so I can finish this epic battle scene, I would really appreciate it." Her face disappeared behind her book again as she sank into the couch.

Natalie followed Kaylan into the kitchen. "Hot chocolate, huh?"

"Hey, it got you in the door." Kaylan began to pull down ingredients from the cabinets. "You've got to make it with milk though, or it's no good. My mom says the creamier, the better."

"I'm sold."

"So, I'm a little confused. I gave you my number, not my address."

Natalie winced. "Sorry. I know. I just figured I would lose my nerve if I could hang up, but I'm stuck once I'm here in person. I kind of used some connections to look up your address a week ago. For some reason, I just got in the car and drove this morning. I couldn't stop myself. And I wound up here. I just need to know." Her cool blue eyes drifted around the kitchen and into the open living room. "Is he . . . Is Nick around?"

Kaylan stirred chunks of chocolate into Natalie's mug and then handed the cup to her, avoiding eye contact. "Nick is out of the country right now." To a military brat, that statement said all that was necessary.

"Got it. I would ask when he would be back, but I know better."

"Soon."

"Guys, please, I'm at the part where Frodo tries to leave Sam and strike out on his own. You're messing up the mood," Megan said from the couch, her eyes never leaving the page.

"Want to sit on the porch?" Kaylan led the way without waiting for a response. "We have a couple of blankets."

Natalie nodded and followed Kaylan outside. They sank into the cushions on the wicker love seat and pulled a blanket over their laps. Sandy lay down on top of Kaylan's feet, keeping them warm. For a few minutes, they sat sipping their hot chocolate and watching the neighborhood action. Nina puttered in her yard next door, fighting with the garden hose as she watered her flowers. Kaylan felt the urge to tell the woman it was winter, but Nina had a thing for caring for her yard. It was her baby now that her children were grown and gone.

Jenna ran past them on her daily jog. To Kaylan's knowledge, her asthma was better, and they caught up every month at Nina's little get-together.

"Can you tell me about him?" Natalie asked, interrupting Kaylan's thoughts.

Kaylan smiled into her mug. Praising her guy was one of her favorite things to discuss, but she wasn't sure where to begin or how much to share.

"Well, he burns toast but makes a killer omelet. Likes his coffee to look and taste like jet fuel."

Natalie laughed and made a face. "Are you sure we're related?"

Kaylan squeezed Natalie's hand. "Trust me." Kaylan could see Nick in the shape of Natalie's eyes, in the way her mouth quirked to one side when she smiled. And in her pursuit of truth.

"Nick loves the water."

"Yet another thing we don't have in common."

"And he loves the Lord."

Natalie smiled big for the first time. "Now that we really have in common. One way or another he is my brother."

"I think that's the best thing to have in common." Kaylan grinned. "I'm so glad you decided to come."

"Me too. I have so many questions."

Kaylan nodded. "Shoot."

"Why did we get split up? Who are our birth parents? I mean, don't get me wrong, I wouldn't trade my family for the world. It just makes me sad that we missed out on having a family together, you know?"

"I think he feels the same way."

A low growl interrupted their conversation. "Sandy?"

"Excuse me." A male voice spoke from the door to the screened-in porch. Kaylan stood and Sandy darted off Kaylan's feet, his bark vicious as the man backed up a few steps. His accent immediately sent a dart of terror through Kaylan, reminding her all too much of Dmitri and the damp smell of a confined boat shed.

But it wasn't Dmitri. His face was familiar. Confusion darted through her as she recognized the sharply dressed businessman she had bumped into at the coffee shop. "You. You were in the coffee shop." She remembered his accent and how out of place he had seemed in the casual environment.

Before the man could answer, the door to the house flew open and Megan stepped out. Kaylan recognized her own fear mirrored in Megan's pale face. "Kayles, why's Sandy . . ." Her eyes swung to the porch door and her voice grew sharp. "Who are you?"

"I'm here to see Miss Richards, and interestingly enough, I'm here to see you, too, Miss . . ." His gaze fixed on Natalie.

"Me?" Natalie's eyes grew big.

Kaylan's suspicions immediately tipped to high gear. No one knew of her connection to Natalie. No one but Nick. She studied the man's short, slight build. Round glasses perched on a nose between small eyes and a balding head. His suit spoke of money. He carried himself with an aloof confidence, hands clasped behind his back and an air of business about him.

"Megan, go call . . ."

"No need to call the authorities," he interrupted, his Russian accent bleeding through every syllable.

"Call Logan, Meg."

Megan immediately slipped inside, the door left open in the event retreat became necessary. Sandy continued his low growl, his body firmly planted between the girls and the door.

"Can you call off your canine so that we can talk like civilized human beings, please?"

Kaylan moved her body to block Natalie from the man's view, hoping to deter any more conversation in her direction. Her desire to protect overrode the fear that threatened to cloud her thinking. He wasn't like Dmitri. He would have done more than talk. She would keep him talking until the guys arrived. "The dog stays, and you'll stay right where you are. We haven't had the best experience with well-dressed men with Russian accents in the last few months. So I'll repeat my roommate's question. Who are you, and what are you doing here?"

The man sniffed and looked around the outside of the house. "My, my, what they say about American hospitality really is true. It is quickly disappearing. What a shame. Not to mention the fact that you are from the South, Miss Richards. I expected your Southern manners to rival those of Californians, but I see I was mistaken."

"You aren't helping yourself. Answer my questions or leave." Kaylan crossed her arms over her chest, refusing to cower. Megan quietly reappeared at the door, nodding in Kaylan's direction.

"I see. And I take it your roommate's reappearance means that several SEALs will be at your door within minutes, is that correct?"

"At least your powers of deduction are intact, even if your subtlety is not." She wielded her sarcasm like a shield and fought her body's desire to tremble.

"I don't believe in subtlety and neither does my employer. I came to give you a message."

Terror coursed through her, but she stood her ground. The guys would be here any minute. She just had to hold on. "Then shove it under the door."

"Oh no, no, no. No more notes, no more games. I know what you endured under my colleague, and I assure you we have no intention of repeating her mistakes."

Kaylan's senses kicked into high gear. She needed to get as much information as possible. "I'm not sure I've met your colleague."

"I believe you are familiar with her work and her relationship with your fiancé. Her games were mere child's play." Did he mean the mistakes she made in taunting and threatening Kaylan, or the mistake she made in not killing her the first time?

No apology rang from his eyes. No gentleness. He simply saw her as a business transaction.

"What's the message?"

"Let me put it this way. Your fiancé didn't stop when my colleague threatened your life last year. Whatever his reasons, clearly he loves his job more than you."

"Get to the point." Her heart raced. What was taking Logan and the guys so long?

"You are aware Nikolai is currently out of the country. His mission is to put my employer out of business. However, I can assure you, my employer is a Russian businessman with the highest credentials." His tone flat-lined. "If your fiancé continues his ridiculous task, he, your brother, and their friends will wind up on a permanent vacation in the water they love so much. Are we clear?"

Not trusting her voice, Kaylan remained silent, her hands now shaking. She clenched her fists and crossed her arms over her chest.

"Good. We wouldn't want another accident to befall you like the one last fall. And this time, Miss McMurray, is it?" He leaned to look around Kaylan and acknowledge Natalie. "You might be at risk, as well. Have a good afternoon."

He turned swiftly, slipped into the back of a black Mercedes, and sped off before Kaylan could get her thoughts straight.

"You have got to be kidding me. I don't want to do this again. I can't do this again, Kayles." Megan paced, running her fingers through her short, choppy hair. "I mean, is this normal for SEALs?"

"Not remotely." Kaylan chewed her lip, trying to remain outwardly calm for Natalie's sake. She kept her eyes glued to the street. "But the situation is complicated . . ." She slipped a look at Natalie, whose gaze flitted from Kaylan to Megan and back again.

"Yeah, yeah, I get it. Cone of silence and all that." Megan wrapped her arms around herself. "Do me a favor and tell soldier boy to finish this before we wind up dead this time," she spat.

"Who is that man, and what is going on?" Fear edged Natalie's voice.

To Kaylan's relief, at that moment Logan's car pulled up with Caveman and two others. She took Natalie's hand. "These are Nick's friends. I'll explain in a minute."

"Kayles, call off the dog so we can come in," Logan commanded from the sidewalk, immediately taking control of the situation. Two of the guys lifted his chair up the two stairs leading to their closed-in porch.

"Sandy, here, boy." Sandy immediately came to her side and sat, panting as if the shadows of a few minutes before had never existed.

"What happened? Are you all right?" Logan wheeled himself next to the loveseat while Caveman went to search the house. Javier and Gavin stood close by Logan's side, their eyes fixed on Natalie.

"I am really confused and would love an explanation right now. I'm Natalie. I'm an Air Force brat, so let's just get that out of the way for you macho SEALs."

Logan smirked. "I like your spunk, Natalie. Kaylan will explain as much as she can. But for now, I need to know if my guys overseas need to know anything."

"Logan, that guy just threatened the team. I'm scared they are walking into a trap." With her words, Kaylan's remaining energy left her body, and she slumped into the loveseat.

Anya Petrov, aka Janus, sat in the mess hall on a United States military base wondering how her life had taken such a drastic turn. A CIA agent sat across from her shoveling food into his mouth. Her lip curled over her teeth. Disgusting.

A clock hung on the wall. She swore the hands slowed more every minute. Somewhere Nick and his team prepared to board a helicopter and take care of the last Taliban remnant that served as a lynchpin for Sasha's black market arms dealing in the Middle East. If the team managed to eliminate them tonight, she would be one step closer to accomplishing her plan and one step closer to using the team to take care of her Sasha problem.

She stared at her plate. If everything worked well, she would be dining on finer fare soon. Her stomach rumbled and she forced herself to take a bite. She would need her strength and energy. Fortunately for her, sufficient willpower had never been her problem. She always got her way.

A memory of a stitched piece of fabric in a safety deposit box hidden with a colleague flashed through her mind, challenging her confidence. Well, she almost always got what she wanted.

CHAPTER NINETEEN

The *thowp, thowp, thowp* of the chopper blades sounded in Nick's ears as he chomped on a piece of gum and double-checked to make sure everything was ready. The sound of a bird beating its way through the night to an unsuspecting location got his adrenaline pumping.

Next to him, Micah strapped on his helmet and then turned to check Nick's gear. The rhythm of preparation readied him for when the command was given to repel down ropes and land where the bird hovered over the ground. They dropped outside of hearing range. Nick's wristwatch glowed twenty-three hundred as he surveyed the area. Quiet. The village would be asleep.

Mountains rose in the distance, dotted with snow on the highest peaks, but down in the valley, nothing but sand, dust, and desert spiders awaited. And a sleeping band of gathering Taliban wanna-be's.

They landed on the ground, silently checking the area. "We're one click out. Let's move." X's voice over the radio slipped through the chopper blades as they pulled away, probably moving to the rendezvous point. The team moved across the desert, the sandy stone walls of homes beckoning in the distance under a full moon. Nick glanced up at the sky. Not the best night to be out in the open while trying to maintain an element of surprise, but word had come that the meeting was going down now.

Within twelve minutes, they crouched near the home, prepped to invade. They knew each target's face and name. Nine in all would gather tonight. Nine men and a handful of women and children in a home surrounded by two others and a shared courtyard in the center. Lives depended on their focus and recognition. The men inside weren't afraid to die. They weren't afraid to take innocent lives or the lives of Americans. Nick wasn't afraid to take their lives either.

"One's set," came X's voice. "Waiting on two's."

"Two's, set," Titus confirmed. Nick prepared to breach. The men would be in one of the main rooms of the compound. Women and children would most likely be sleeping in the rooms. Nick wouldn't put it past some of the men to use the women and children for protection. While Nick and his team played by a certain moral code, these men didn't.

Jay popped smoke into an open window and noise exploded. Colt and Titus burst through the door, Nick and Micah close on their heels as yelling broke out throughout the three homes situated around an open courtyard. Nick hustled through the first open door with Titus and several others behind him. His quick scan of the room confirmed the frightened sleepy faces of two boys, no older than ten.

Titus spoke to them, motioning to sparse furniture in the corner of the room. Nick recognized the few tribal words. "We won't hurt you." They quickly secured the boys.

Shooting sounded from a distance. They finished clearing their building and rushed in the direction of the sound. Nick stayed alert. The longer this went, the more opportunity someone would have to set up in a room or . . .

The barrel of a gun flashed from an open window. Nick fired. A dull thud met his ears as he continued to search, his eyes on their six to make sure no one snuck up from behind.

"Three males down. One on the run," Micah said over the radio. Four down, five to go. Nick motioned to Titus and circled back to the window where he'd fired. One quick look told him they were looking for four more.

"One more down."

"Got the runner," Jay filled in.

Four more.

Nick, Titus, and two other men swept into the last building. Titus motioned for two of them to search downstairs while he and Nick took the upstairs. Nick led the way, silently slipping up the concrete steps. A bullet smashed into the wall next to his head. A man jerked back out of sight. Nick aimed just as another round whizzed past him, lighting his arm on fire.

He'd been hit.

Sucking in a sharp breath, he pounded up the last few steps, Titus firing all the way. As he landed on the last step, he fired at a man trying to slip through an open door. The man jerked and went down. Nick nodded at Titus and the two stepped over him and into the room. His gaze swept into the corners and landed on another man shielding himself behind a woman and child.

Nick recognized him as the leader of the group. He sneered, his black eyes full of malice. The little boy in front whimpered, trying to hide behind his mother's skirts. Tears streamed down her face, but it was clear she either couldn't move or wouldn't.

Titus began yelling instructions and warnings. The woman wept as she responded, her body shaking as the man behind her gripped her arm.

"You got a clear shot, Hawk?"

Barely. If the boy moved at all, Hawk would hit him. Somewhere in the back of his mind, pain screamed from his arm. He didn't know if he'd been shot or grazed but he feared the pain might affect his grip. He couldn't afford to slip or make a mistake.

Nick kept his voice calm and low. "T-Brown, can you tell the kid to stay still."

"If he ducks, can you get him?"

Over the radio, Nick was vaguely aware of "all clears" sounding from every other area of the compound. Pounding sounded from the staircase and Jay zipped into the room, swearing at the scene. In the dim light filtering into the room, Nick noticed a weapon pointed into the little boy's side.

Rage swept through him and Nick channeled every bit of it to his trigger finger to respond when he commanded. "Jay, you got a better angle?" Nick murmured. Titus spoke and the man began to yell. As the conversation escalated, Jay circled, trying to get a better shot. The man's fear got the best of him and he unfolded slightly from his crouched position. It was the opening Nick had been waiting for. Nick fired, hitting the man's toes, causing him to jerk. With a scream, the man popped tall and Nick fired again. The scream silenced to a gurgle and thud.

Titus rushed forward, catching the sobbing woman as she collapsed. He murmured instructions to her as he ushered her from the room with one arm, his other still holding his weapon at the ready. Jay hustled forward and checked the two men now laid out on the floor. "All clear, X."

Nick approached the little boy who stood looking at the fallen man, his eyes wide. He couldn't have been more than four. Nick crouched down and spoke the words Titus had taught him.

"It's all right. You're safe."

The boy's bottom lip began to quiver. Nick's heart crumbled. With a leap, the little boy fell into Nick's arms, wrapping scrawny limbs around Nick's neck. Jay nodded as Nick picked the boy up and followed Jay from the room.

Night cloaked the compound, and the sound of women crying bounced off the walls. Nick and Jay reached the open courtyard where the SEALs had gathered with the women and children and a man on his knees, his hands behind his head, heavily guarded by Micah and Colt.

A woman rushed forward. Her scarf slipped from her head and rich black hair tumbled loose. Sleep still clung to her eyes, but Nick saw fear edged with relief as she yanked the little boy from Nick's grip.

Nick tried to soothe her fears. He reached into his pocket and pulled out a few pieces of candy, offering them to the little boy as his mother nodded and scampered away.

"Let's move out," X said as the team began to slip from the compound, one detainee with them, as well as paperwork, electronics, maps, and other bits gathered from their sweep. Jake would pump the detainee for information and either try to flip him as an informant or lock him up where he couldn't do any more damage. The op had been a success.

They rendezvoused with the chopper and loaded their human cargo. As they sped off into the night, Nick looked in the direction of the compound one more time, his arm now stinging in earnest. He prayed the little boy would forget, but more than that, he prayed that little boy would never wind up on a list of men wanted for planning acts of terror on innocents.

"Hawk, let me take a look at that," Kite said as he maneuvered his way next to Nick. Blood coated a rip in the fabric on Nick's left arm. He fought back a wince as Kite moved the cloth out of the way.

"He zinged you. That's a pretty jagged gash. You may need stitches and some aspirin. Maybe a tetanus shot." He grimaced. "But no worse for the wear. One more battle scar to lie about to the kiddos someday."

Nick nodded, but the pain in his arm faded in comparison to the pain in the little boy's eyes and the desperation for safe arms to hold him, even if that meant a stranger.

"Kaylan's going to kill you, Hawk."

"No way. Your sister is going to be thankful we are both back in one piece." He nodded to his arm. "Just slightly scratched up." With the end of the op, it would be time to head home.

As they approached the lights of base, dread filled his stomach, overshadowing the night's victory. Would all of them be going home intact?

The birds touched down and SEALs unloaded. Nick's bed and a shower called his name. But the appearance of a doctor arriving to talk to X stopped him cold.

One by one, the team halted, watching the conversation. After what felt like hours, X hung his head and squeezed the doctor's arm. X turned and looked at the men gathered. Nick searched his face, praying he wouldn't find the answer he knew was coming.

With a shake of his head, X sighed. "Bates will get a hero's welcome home."

The picture of the young, shaved-head, eager SEAL flashed in front of Nick's eyes. The warrior who had braved hell week twice because he wanted to be a SEAL was gone. The kid with determined hazel eyes. Gone.

Nick squeezed his eyes shut to drown out the image of blood coating Bates's chest. All he wanted to do was sleep and forget the little boy used as a human shield and the heart of a SEAL who left this world too soon.

CHAPTER TWENTY

The creak of swings provided a familiar sound for Kaylan's frayed nerves. At the park, the innocence and joy of childhood collided with carefree moments spent with Nick. Megan dove into a book, Kaylan into her memories. She just wanted an escape. No, she just wanted Nick. *But You're here, Lord. You heard every word. You knew before they were said. And you love Nick more than I do. Keep him safe. Help me trust You with him.*

Every time she missed Nick and committed her relationship to the Lord another piece of armor fell from her heart. But now more than ever, she needed to talk to him, know he was okay. Even now, he could be headed into a snake pit, the kind you didn't walk away from unscathed. And she couldn't do a thing. It would almost be better if she didn't know when he would be in danger, although Nick seemed to attract it. For that matter so did she.

Logan and the guys had left and would take care of what was necessary on their end, and she could only wait and pray. She knew the SEALs would stick close to her until Nick came home. If the Russian approached her again, she was to leave wherever she was and call one of them. She wanted to be strong for Nick. She didn't want to live bound by the fear of her kidnapping months earlier. Truth be told, she was still quaking in her boots, but she just didn't want to respond in fear anymore. Kaylan knew her man. He wouldn't run from danger, didn't turn from fear. He would run toward it in pursuit of victory.

She would stand firm, too. But she would be smart about it. And that meant asking for help.

"So let me get this straight," Natalie said from the swing to Kaylan's right. Her feet traced patterns in the mulch. "A terrorist fixated on you, had you and Megan kidnapped, and Nick is now trying to catch that little weasel's boss?"

Kaylan had told her everything. Everything short of releasing a national security secret and revealing anything personal about Janus or her relationship to Nick and Natalie. But Natalie knew enough.

"You know about as much as I do now." If Kaylan had learned anything in the last hour, it was that Natalie didn't panic, another indication of her military background. She took in the facts, mulled them over, and then came to a conclusion.

"I've never really been around SEALs, but I know this isn't normal."

"Nope. This person made it personal." Because of biology. A genetic connection that Kaylan worried might now affect Natalie. The man had known.

"How did he even know I would be here? I didn't even know I was coming until I pulled up."

If Natalie kept asking questions, she would identify every hole Kaylan had desperately attempted to navigate around. "I don't think he knew you were here. Just knew who you were. I really can't answer how he knew." But she could use logic, and that logic scared her. He was either following her or had somehow gained access to the same file Nick had about his family.

"I don't even know what to do about this. How to think. How to feel. I mean, they are supposed to just deploy, fight over there, and come back, right?"

"Yep. The sooner Nick and the team catch whoever this is, the sooner this can all be over and we can go back to our regularly scheduled deployments and uncomfortably long absences with no terrorists threatening us here. I hope." Kaylan shoved off the ground, gaining a little air.

"Boy, what a mess."

Kaylan fought panic as she maintained an outward veneer of calm for Natalie. "I trust Logan. And I trust Nick and Micah and the guys they are with. I've seen them under pressure. They are warriors through and through."

"I still don't get how this involves me."

"I told you that you were related to a SEAL."

"A SEAL I've never met and didn't even know existed until a couple weeks ago. That man called him Nikolai."

Kaylan kept her gaze on the blue sky and white wispy clouds cutting horizontal lines across its expanse. "It's the name his biological mom gave him. He never used it."

"Is it Russian?"

Kaylan remained quiet.

"The name on my birth certificate is Natalia. I've never used it either. But that man and his accent and my br . . . Nick's name. Sounds Russian."

Kaylan was starting to appreciate Nick's ability to keep a secret with ease.

"You know more than you are telling me, but I know better than to ask."

Kaylan brought her swing to a halt, finally meeting Natalie's gaze. "It's a good thing you are familiar with the military then." She forced steel into her tone. "You know as much as I can tell you."

Natalie's eyes darted back and forth over Kaylan's face. She finally nodded. "Fine. I would still like to meet Nick, though."

Kaylan realized she'd been holding her breath. "I think he would like that. Growing up as an only child, he always wanted siblings. I can give him brothers in my family, but a sister"—Kaylan smiled, remembering Sarah Beth—"that's something special."

Natalie grinned. "True. And I wouldn't trade mine for the world. Call me when he gets back?"

They stood from the swings and began the short walk back to Kaylan's house and Natalie's car. "You bet. Thanks for coming. And I'm so sorry about today."

"I'll keep you posted if something happens, but maybe once I leave here, they will leave me alone and focus on you. No offense," she added quickly.

"None taken." Kaylan chuckled. "In fact, right now I would prefer that."

"I promise I'm not a coward or anything," she gushed, begging for Kaylan to understand.

"If you are anything like Nick, there isn't a cowardly bone in your body. This isn't your fight." They stopped at Natalie's car, and Kaylan pulled her into a hug, startling both of them.

"Maybe it will be." Natalie's eyes roved over Kaylan's face. "Some day."

"I'm hoping this is over sooner than some day. Go home. Stay alert, but don't worry about this. I'll talk to you soon. And don't hesitate to use my number this time, okay?"

As Natalie drove off, Kaylan waved, wondering if her prayers for a kindred spirit and a sister had been answered in both Natalie and

Megan, both women too tough and too loving to let Kaylan go it alone.

Nick settled heavy on her mind again. She wrapped her arms around herself, praying that Logan had been able to alert him in time.

CHAPTER TWENTY-ONE

Within thirty-six hours, the team exited the plane to a more somber homecoming. Bates had family on the east coast, so his funeral and memorial would be there. Nick heard a few guys might fly out for the funeral, but no details yet.

Nick always knew it could end this way, but never wanted it to. Bates knew the price he might pay, and when Nick hesitated, lost in the confusion of a gunfight, the kid, the SEAL from Virginia, didn't. Nick could wear the weight of that his whole life, or he could honor Bates's sacrifice every time he stepped on the field, letting go in order to function at full capacity.

Wives and families waited to welcome them home. Nick didn't know what to expect after his absence. The weeks had stretched without his girl. He scanned the gathering crowd and stopped on an auburn-haired beauty in an ivory and tan dress. She smiled and waved, unsure. Nick hated her hesitancy. Before he knew it he was jogging.

She darted from the crowd, running to meet him. His bag slid from his shoulder and hit the ground as she flew into his arms. He lifted her into his embrace and crushed her to him, ignoring the pain in his arm. The scent of lavender, of home, filled his senses. "I missed you so much." For the first time, he realized how close he had come to returning in that box instead of Bates. Kaylan would have been devastated.

He set her on her feet and met her anxious green eyes. "Are you okay? Did Logan talk to you in time?"

"Whoa, slow down, babe." He smoothed her hair back. "What are you talking about?"

"This man showed up at our place. Well, he showed up at the coffee house before then. And he threatened you and the team. He said you would end up in the ocean if you didn't stop chasing whoever you are chasing."

He squeezed her waist tighter. "What man, Kaylan? Did he mention a name? Anything?"

She shook her head, his grip tight on his arms. "No. Some Russian guy. Logan was going to try and contact the team."

"We were probably already finished and getting ready to head back so they didn't need to act on anything." He bent down to kiss her again, fear thrumming in his veins at the thought of her in danger again. Because of him. Because of his job. "If anything had happened to you ..."

"I'm okay. We're both okay. And you're home now. We can handle this together." Her eyes filled with hesitation that broke his heart. "I'm so sorry, Nick. So incredibly sorry. I want this, even if it means I have to wait months. I want you."

He groaned and crushed his lips over her own, tasting her lip gloss. His fingers found the gentle contours of her face and wound into her hair. A fire smoldered in his heart as she molded into him, responding to every touch.

At the sound of several wolf whistles, he broke away and rested his forehead on hers. "Kaylan, please forgive me for leaving like that. For not being the man who fights for us, even when it's hard. That always has to come first. I was a jerk. I am so sorry you were terrified and in danger again because of me. And I wasn't there. "

He kissed her again.

"We'll figure it out. I'm just so glad you're home," she murmured against his lips.

He grinned, feeling a little lighter. "You're going to have to help me learn how to balance all this, because with a welcome home like that, I may get court-martialed for ignoring my next deployment to stay home with you for an extended honeymoon."

Her laughter soothed the tattered places of his soul. He kissed her forehead and then rocked back on his feet as something collided with Kaylan and wrapped around his back.

"My turn," Micah mumbled as he sandwiched Kaylan between him and Nick.

"Micah," Kaylan giggled, trying to twist away from his bear hug.

"Seriously, we have got to get you a girl." Nick punched Micah's chest, eliciting a yelp. Micah let go and Kaylan turned around to hug her brother. Nick immediately missed the absence of her body curled into his.

"I haven't met a girl who could handle all of this just yet." Micah grinned and crossed his arms.

Colt came up and wrapped his arms around Micah from behind. "That's one fine specimen of a man."

"No doubt. But get off me or you're going to ruin my reputation."

Colt stepped back with his hands raised in surrender.

"There's someone out there, I just haven't found her yet," Kaylan informed her brother.

"*You* haven't found her?"

"Well, clearly *you* aren't trying very hard." Kaylan put her hands on her hips. Nick wrapped his arms around her waist and pulled her back into his chest as Kaylan began to hum.

"Kayles, don't you dare start humming that `Just haven't met you yet' Michael Bublé nonsense."

"Well, then stop messing with my mushy moments."

He tweaked her nose. "Quit having them in public, little sis. But don't you dare have them in private either. Just don't." Micah fixed Nick with a brotherly glare, but Nick only grinned in return.

"No promises, Bulldog."

Nick didn't have to see Kaylan's face to know she was beet red. He silently thanked God that he never had to guess when she was embarrassed or upset. God had seen fit to hardwire that response into her DNA.

"Go away, Micah." Kaylan shoved her brother.

"So it's come to this." Micah held out his arms in defeat as he backed away with Colt. "You've finally chosen him over me. I'm hurt, sis. Hurt."

"Well, when I find you a girl, you won't even notice."

A warning glint appeared in Micah's eye, and Nick chuckled. "Be careful, Kayles. Don't pick one that will result in payback."

With a wink, Micah jogged off.

Kaylan turned in Nick's arms and threw her arms around his neck. "I have to go back to work for a few hours, but I have a surprise for you tonight before we go to Logan and Kim's for a party."

"A surprise, huh? Does it include coffee and maybe cake?"

She stood on her tiptoes and placed a quick peck on his lips, leaving him wanting more. "I think we can arrange that. Go take care of business and maybe sleep a bit. Meet me at our new apartment at six."

"Now, Kayles, you know there's none of that until after the honeymoon."

She shoved him. "Don't get fresh, Hawk. You've been around the guys too much."

He snagged her hip and pulled her close again, stroking her back. "All right. I'll behave. See you there in a bit."

With a new energy to his step, he followed his team to close up remaining details of the op. With the wedding roughly six weeks away, he wondered when or if he would deploy again beforehand. He didn't have much control over it if they called his name, but he could always make an appeal. They'd wounded the snake, but the head still remained in place, and Nick wanted to be the one to sever it. He didn't want what haunted him on the battlefield to keep following him home. He needed to keep his girl safe while he was gone. It was time to call in reinforcements.

CHAPTER TWENTY-TWO

Kaylan fluffed up the throw pillow, put it in place, and then stepped back to survey her work. Everything needed to be perfect. Tonight, Nick would know she could and would take care of life without him when he was gone.

Organization had never been her strong suit, but with a mother who owned an interior decorating company, Kaylan knew how to make a home cozy. Thankfully, she knew what Nick liked. After Megan showed her the apartment, she'd found a faux brown leather sectional in January on clearance and had snapped up the deal. Logan and Kim had passed on their breakfast table that was now too small for their growing family. With distressed wood and four iron chairs with plush seat cushions, it gave the room a classy feel without being over the top. She'd spread a picnic on the living room floor, had Caveman install Nick's television in the living room, and had the furniture company deliver the mattress they'd picked out.

She ticked through a mental list. Everything was ready. She hoped. A key scratched in the lock, and she pivoted in the middle of the room, smoothing down the dress she'd never changed out of.

"Honey, I'm home." His voice tapered off as he stepped into the room and took in her handiwork. His jaw dropped. "Babe, this is incredible!"

"You like it? You can tell me if you don't. We can rearrange or take things back. Well, except the sectional since I got it on clearance.

It was such a good deal and—" She stopped talking when his finger rested on her lips.

"I love it."

She melted into him, relief mixing with a surge of pride. She could do this. No doubt. He trusted her. She'd begun to wake up every day and give Nick and her fear to the Lord. Slowly, the fear receded, leaving in its place a quiet confidence and resolve to put one foot in front of the other and just trust. Such an overly simplified concept. Trust held the weight of the world with a single decision.

"Can I see the rest?"

"Uh, maybe don't open the guest room." Over the last couple of months, wedding gifts had poured in from family and friends in Alabama, their friends in California, and from SEAL teams around the country, and even some of her dad's patients at the hospital. She'd stuffed the unopened gifts into that room.

He wound his fingers through hers and walked down the short hallway that ended in their bedroom. He grinned and placed a hand on the doorknob. "Will I get a taste of what our apartment will actually look like once we live here?"

"Hey, don't be mean." She moved in front of the door and blocked his entry. The rise and fall of his chest quickened at their nearness. "You will get a glimpse of the chaos of wedding planning. I left you some presents to open."

"All the good ones I hope."

"All the ones from REI."

"You do love me." He placed a quick kiss on her lips. "And the final door?"

"Um." She couldn't stop the blush that climbed up her neck and into her face. "That's our room. It still needs a bit of work, but . . ."

He opened the door and pulled her inside with him. "Kaylan Richards, look at you. You even made the bed."

A twinkle crept into his eyes, and she yanked her hands out of his, taking a step back. "Don't get any ideas, Nick Carmichael."

"Why not?" He took a step toward her, forcing her back into the wall. He encased her with his arms, both palms on the wall.

"Nick. Behave," Kaylan said but couldn't help but laugh at the passion she saw him holding at bay.

He leaned forward and kissed her nose, then her lips, pulling back to look in her eyes, before kissing her again. Teasing her. Her pulse rose as she ran her fingers down his strong jaw and fisted her hands in his shirt.

His lips explored hers, his hand drifting to her waist. "Nick," she murmured against his mouth, scared they would both be out of control if they kept going.

Nick pulled her from the room and closed the door behind him. "We are going to keep that door shut for another six weeks, and we probably shouldn't be here together too much. Or at all." He laughed, running a hand over the back of his head. When he finally looked at her again, he looked like a kid whose hand had been slapped.

"Sorry, babe. We might need to keep this lighter."

She chuckled. "Agreed."

He kissed her gently, the kind of kisses that made her want to marry him even more than the passionate ones. These were the kind that spoke of vulnerability, that he treasured her. "You got it. By the way ..." His grin made warmth spread through her body. "Loved the room. And the comforter you picked? It's perfect." He led her back to the living room and they sat on the blanket she had spread out on the floor.

"I'm glad you like it. Nick, I didn't handle it well when you left, and I . . ."

"Hey, hey, no more apologizing. Neither of us handled that well. I'm as guilty as you are. I need to know that you can let me go when I need to, though. Seriously, Kayles, I can't do that again. I can't have you fight me on timing I can't control."

"I know." She nodded at the room. "It took me some time to let go of my fear. To talk to the Lord about it. I was angry at you, at Him, but more at myself. But once I finally surrendered all that, I was able to look to what I could do to help and continue on with life, and I landed on all this. It's been fun." She shrugged. "It let me know that I can survive the absences. And now you have a place to come home to that is just ours."

"No more Bulldog, huh?"

"Well, I'm sure my brother will be over here quite a bit, but we have a Sandy now instead of a Bulldog."

"Yeah, about that . . ."

"Hey, you want me to cope with the deployments better, and now I have a companion. Did I mention he is very protective and well-behaved?"

"So he's better trained than Micah, then?"

"Nick . . ."

He chuckled and began to divvy up the food she'd prepared. "Kayles, thank you. For this. For making a home. For letting me go. It helps knowing you're here. I wouldn't handle the waiting and not knowing very well. I can't fault you for that. You have a tough job, too. I just want you to know that I appreciate it, and I couldn't do it without you."

His assurance healed all the sore spots of Kaylan's heart. More than anything, she wanted a companion, someone who didn't need her but wanted her and wanted to need her.

"You're welcome." She leaned forward and kissed his cheek. Candlelight danced off the walls as they talked about the plan for Logan and Kim's.

"How long do I have you home for?"

"Hopefully until the next deployment. But I don't know, Kayles." His voice held a warning, but she steeled herself against any other questions. "We may have one more op left to wrap up something big. If we time it right, though, it shouldn't take long. We'll see. Could be before the wedding." Her heart quickened a beat. "Could be after," he rushed on. "Could be while we are deployed next year, and you will never know about it. All just depends."

"I guess I will have to get used to not planning."

"Plan away, Kayles. Just be flexible when plans change." In the gathering silence and shadows, a distance crept into his eyes.

"You saw her again, didn't you?"

His gaze swerved to hers but he stayed silent.

"It's okay. I don't need to know. I can just . . . tell."

He set his glass down with a thunk. "Let's talk about your guest, Kayles, and what to do if he shows up again."

"You mean beyond calling the guys?"

"Yeah, beyond that. They are always an option and will always be here for you, but I think we need more than that now. I don't want a repeat of what happened last fall. I can't handle it, Kayles. I never want you to go through that again." He reached over and brushed a strand of hair behind her ear, his fingers trailing down her cheek before falling away.

"He threatened us, Nick. He threatened you. I was worried you were walking into a trap."

At that, Nick winced, his hand covering his left arm. She heard the faint sound of cloth rubbing against a bandage. "Nick Carmichael." She grabbed his arm and heard him bite back a curse. "What did you do?" She ran her hand up his arm until she felt a bandage wrapped around his bicep.

"I did my job and I came home."

"Nick, I'm serious."

"Kaylan." He stilled her hand with his. "I'm fine. I did my job, got a little scratched, and I came home to you. It will heal. I just have to keep it clean and keep applying fresh bandages now and then. I could have got scratched worse in a bike accident."

But Kaylan doubted that. "If only you had known in time. If only . . ."

"Kayles, we knew exactly what we needed to know. We went in prepared. Things happen. It was exactly as we suspected. No trap. But I need you to tell me what happened here."

Kaylan slipped away from him and onto the couch. She pulled her legs up to her chest. "Well, it was me, Megan, Sandy, and . . ." She stopped, her hands sweating. "Please don't get upset."

"You not answering is not helping me not get upset."

"That was a lot of *nots.*"

"Kayles," he warned.

"And Natalie, Nick. Natalie was there with us."

He was on his feet before she knew what happened, the candle-light making a giant of his shadow on the TV wall behind him. "I'm sorry, say that again, because I'm pretty sure I asked you not to involve my sister in this."

Kaylan was on her feet now, too. "Look here, buddy. You have searched for your biological family for years. I am not going to let your uncertainty and fear rob you of the option of having a sister. You got it? So, yes, I went to see her."

Silence engulfed them, his posture and the look firing from his eyes warning her, but she refused to back down. "I love you. I love you too much to let you hurt yourself more here. And I love you too much to allow you to live with regret. You wanted me to hold down the homefront, and I did. Only I expanded it a little, too. And guess what? She came to see me. She wants to meet you."

Shock fought anger and fear as she watched him process. He gripped her arms, his voice low, fear dripping from every syllable. "Kaylan, did it ever occur to you that I didn't want to draw any attention to her until I was absolutely certain this Janus stuff was over and done with?"

Kaylan's heart sank. She hadn't thought of that, but then again, she didn't know all of it, didn't know what fears he harbored. "I wish you would have told me that, but it doesn't matter now. The man knew who she was, Nick. It's better that she knows the truth, or at least as much as I could tell her," she finished quickly as his muscles tensed, "than to be out there with no clue and a man she doesn't know watching her."

Nick relaxed his grip on her arms, his fingers forming circles where moments before there'd been pressure. She felt his body relax, his forehead coming to rest on hers. She curled into his chest, knowing they both needed the comfort. "Thank you," he finally said, "for wanting to love me enough to give me what I've searched for. Can you do me a favor?"

"Anything."

He wrapped his arms around her and looked into her eyes. "Next time I ask you not to do something, can you trust me enough to know it's for your good or to protect someone else?"

She chose her words carefully. "I can do that. Next time, can you trust me enough to let me in on why you are asking me to do that if it is not job related? That way I can know whether or not I can ask questions that you can answer."

He nodded slowly.

"Nick, I trust you to protect and serve and love. But you can love to your own detriment. I need to know when something is job related and when something may be an area you just don't want to deal with, and I need to push. As your wife, that is the only way I can help you be better. And if we are both being honest, I think your request to not meet Natalie was as self-serving as it was job related."

She watched him process, watched the corner of his mouth twitch. Then she saw acceptance. "So what you're saying is we need a code word."

Kaylan laughed. "A what?"

"I mean when I ask you not to do something or to do something and I am not be able to talk about the details, we need a code word between the two of us so you will know why I am asking but know not to ask any more questions."

"That was a very long-winded and confusing explanation."

"Code word means job related. Don't ask anything else."

"Short and sweet. I like it. Now what's our word?"

He poked her side, causing a squeal as she twisted into him. He chuckled. "It has to be something that neither of us says on a consistent basis."

"How about pickles?"

"Pickles?" He laughed. "Where did that come from?"

"Well, I think they smell gross, and I don't buy them very often, and it's random enough to make us laugh when it is said."

He grinned. "Pickles it is. Now let's get out of here before we get ourselves in trouble and go celebrate with the team."

She kissed his cheek. "You got it."

"Kayles, one more thing." He reached in his wallet and pulled out two business cards. "If this guy shows back up or you feel unsafe around someone in any way while I'm gone, I need you to call this guy." He handed her the cards.

"Who's Caden Long?"

"He works for the Naval Criminal Investigative Service, NCIS. More importantly, he's here to make sure you are safe. Call him. He'll open an investigation, check this guy out, and arrange protection of some kind for you. One of us needs to give the other card to Natalie. She's part of this, too. We'll keep her out of it as much as possible, but she needs to know there is someone to call and someone who can look out for her from our community."

Kaylan stared up at him when he grew quiet. She silently willed him to fight against the shield he could so quickly wield to hide his feelings from her. She could see the emotions on his face. He was scared. Terrified. Giving her the card was for the best, but she knew a part of him felt like in doing so he couldn't take care of her in the way he wanted.

Kaylan rested her hand on his chest and stepped into his embrace, her nearness calming him. "I'll call him. I'll be okay." She smiled and felt his muscles relax. "What have you told me before? The Lord is my protector and defender. He just chose to use you to get the job done."

"That job is a privilege."

She giggled and pulled back, needing to lighten the mood. "By the way, you're going to give Natalie the card," she teased.

His brows raised, but he remained silent. He placed a feather light kiss on her lips. "C'mon, gorgeous. Let's go meet up with everyone." He ushered her to the door and pulled it open for her to walk in front of him. "But if you think we are finished talking about Natalie, you are sadly mistaken."

She met his eyes as he turned to lock the door. A fire simmered in their depths. "Oh, no, we aren't. In fact, we're just getting started."

Kaylan only grinned at his groan. He'd met his match.

CHAPTER TWENTY-THREE

The informant was dead and good riddance, the little rat. While Janus had always found him a valuable asset, she had a strong distaste for traitors. She caught a look at the reflection from the slender window near her bed in the cold cell. My, how the tables had turned.

Whispers had made their way to her in the prison. A bounty had been placed on her head. Sasha was running scared and playing dirty. He didn't tolerate loose ends. He didn't tolerate loose anything. She was a liability. She knew his secrets, his hiding places, his buyers, and his deals. She even knew a big one loomed, and now that the Taliban cell had been eliminated and she was in prison, his buyers were terrified and demanding a personal audience for guaranteed safe delivery. Sasha's presence at a deal meant the highest level of secrecy and security. Multiple bodyguards, all former KGB. All highly trained, deadly, and without morals.

She slammed her fist into the stone wall of her cell and plopped back against the thin mattress. She had to get out of here. Prison had become too dangerous. She would be dead within the week if Jake didn't make her another deal.

Anya could make him an offer he couldn't refuse, tell him about the coming deal that would force Sasha into a place where the team could capture or kill him and put an end to his weapons trade. Someone would rise up in his place. Someone always did. But it took time to gain a reputation in her business, one she still maintained with the right people. But sharing the intel would mean a larger bounty and more potential killers on her tail.

A clanging outside her cell sent her jerking upright. Anything would be better than dying like a rat in a cage. She'd rather be a rat on the run. She would call Jake. Set up to meet with another informant who held no love for Sasha, find out the details of the meet, get out of the cell they'd locked her in again.

But this time, she wanted to see Nikolai. And Natalia. She played with the strings on her jumpsuit, tying them in knots before loosening them and tying them again.

After all, children should see their mother on her deathbed. She had ways of making that happen, too. Threatening someone became all too easy when that person loved someone they were afraid to lose. She knew the weakness, she just had to find the scar and make it bleed. She smiled to herself.

She would be out of here again in a matter of days. She only had to stay alive until then.

"So then Micah goes to swat the spider off of Titus's stuff only to swat it onto Jay, who then freaks out and starts running through the bunks shrieking like a crazy man." Colt had the group rolling at Logan and Kim's as they swapped stories from the weeks they'd been apart. They squished together in Logan and Kim's small kitchen, drinks in hand and snacks spread out on the table. It was nearing midnight, but Nick could tell no one was ready to call it a night.

"I think we better let someone else tell the story. And I was not shrieking."

"Mhm." Micah took a sip of his root beer. "Pretty much like Molly when she thinks she sees a jelly fish. You stopped short of jumping into Hawk's arms and begging him to get it off."

"You ran around the entire room before you got still enough for Colt to get it off of you," Titus howled, his fingers threaded through Liza's as she grinned next to him.

"Man, that thing was big. I am deathly afraid of spiders. Isn't that like the most dangerous one in the world? You guys should really take this more seriously." He pointed at them before taking a swig of his drink.

Nick chuckled and swung his arm around Kaylan, not wanting to be farther than a few feet from her at all times. "Hey, Jay. Did Colt forget to mention the spider was fake?"

Jay's face flushed beet red and his gaze darted from face to face. Logan held his stomach, his laughter uncontained.

"Hon, keep your voice down," Kim snickered next to him. "The kids are asleep."

"It wasn't." Jay shook his head, still looking from one SEAL to another. "No, I saw it move."

Titus leaned into Liza, tears falling from his face. "That's because I made sure to jiggle my bag just enough before Micah sent it sailing onto you. We might have put some glue on it so it would stick to your shirt."

"Et tu, Brute?"

"You got schooled, brah," Colt howled.

Jay turned his chair backwards and plunked down on the seat. "Payback is going to be brutal." He scowled.

"It always is with you, but that makes these moments that much sweeter," Nick said, tousling Jay's hair.

"I'm so confused. I thought SEALs were supposed to be tough," Kaylan teased.

"Kayles, I promise you don't want to get in the middle of this."

"I grew up with three brothers. I think I can handle it."

"Oh, babe." He patted her head. "This would be ten times worse than anything your brothers threw at you. Trust me. Don't start."

Kaylan looked from Nick to Micah. "Trust me, Kayles. We were little lambs compared to what these guys dish out."

"Like what?"

Liza whistled. "Girl, please. Titus still won't tell me, and I finally stopped asking."

"Think of the worst pranks you could possibly play and then magnify it by their training and daredevil antics, and you have one gigantic recipe for disaster." Kim gathered a couple of dishes and plopped them in the sink. "Trust me. Logan isn't allowed to tell the boys any of these pranks until he is on his death bed."

Logan winced. "Maybe even then. We'd have to bail them out of jail if they didn't do some of it right."

"Well, you are vague with your work and vague with your play. Anything you can share in detail?"

Liza chuckled. "Just wait until you start dishing it back to them. 'Honey, what did you do while I was deployed?' 'Oh, not much. Just worked and hung out. You know, the usual.'" She tapped her hand on Kaylan's knee. "Drives Titus crazy." He nodded in affirmation. "Course I can't do it to him for too long." Her eyes found his and held. "I love him too much to be mean forever. But it's fun while it lasts."

Nick slipped his arm around Kaylan's neck, causing her to squeal. "Don't do that. I want details."

"No promises." She laughed. "I like Liza's idea. I might make you work for it."

Now Nick knew they shouldn't be alone much until the wedding. A few of the guys whistled as Kaylan turned crimson. "I didn't mean like that."

"Sure you didn't." Jay let loose a catcall.

"Geez, I'm going to have to cut my ears off. That's my baby sister. Shut it."

Nick leaned in and kissed Kaylan, the whistles growing louder before Kim shushed them.

"And now I'm going to gouge my eyes out, too."

Colt slapped Micah on the shoulder. "Cheer up, brah. We've got to find you a girl."

"So I've heard." Quieter conversations and laughter broke out around the table.

As the clock slipped past midnight, Logan finally cleared his throat. "So when is this memorial for Bates?" Silence entombed the room. Nick heard the drip of the faucet and a car backfire on the street before anyone spoke.

"X talked to the family. They set it for Thursday morning. Those who want to will fly out and fly back in," Titus informed him, his gaze focused on the flickering candle in the middle of the table.

Nick immediately knew he and Micah would be there. Bates had been a Petty Officer Third Class on SEAL Team 5, Nick and Micah's team. Nick couldn't imagine not attending the service, even if it meant a quick turnaround.

"We'll all be there," Colt answered for the group. Nick tightened his grip on his water glass, beads of perspiration slicking his palms. When he remembered Bates, he thought of Janus. It was her fault, after all. If she hadn't instigated this whole crazy op, maybe Bates would still be alive. Maybe Nick's dad would still be alive. Wherever she went, death followed. Nick's anger grew, and his hand began to shake. Why did she get to live, while an innocent man like Bates died?

"Babe." The gentle pressure of Kaylan's hand on his made him release his hold and reach for her fingers.

"I should have been paying more attention."

"I saw it go down, Hawk." Micah's gaze held a warning to keep the details and his mourning to a minimum. "You couldn't have done anything differently. It happened. Bates knew what he was getting into."

"He wouldn't have changed it, Hawk," Logan's booming voice commanded Nick's attention, his admission. Nick only nodded in response. But inside, he felt Janus had deprived the world of one more good soldier, just like her selfishness years ago had deprived the world of a young airman with eyes the same shade as Nick's.

CHAPTER TWENTY-FOUR

A light mist fell in Arlington, Virginia Thursday morning, threatening to turn into snowfall by afternoon. Dressed in his blues and white cover, Nick arrived at the cemetery with the rest of his team. He didn't know what he'd expected, but he thought it would be quieter than this since Bates's team was on the West Coast. But as a small-town kid from Virginia, Bates had had folks show up en masse.

Nick couldn't take his eyes from the flag-covered coffin, the red, white, and blue draping a soldier in glory. Nick hadn't wanted this. He never did. But he'd buried friends before and would again. It's what they did. Around the tent that had been erected stood older men and women in varying degrees of uniform. Some only wore hats that dated back to Vietnam. Some wore uniforms from the time of the Gulf War. But each stood solemnly, a flag in hand, in honor of a soldier who didn't make it home.

A lump formed in Nick's throat as he felt their pride ripple off them in waves. A young girl no more than twelve or thirteen sat next to a sniffling woman on the front row. Bates's sister. Nick recognized her from the photo he'd seen Bates carry. He'd left her behind. Nick stared at the photo of the young kid, ready to change the world. He hadn't believed in waiting until he was older. He'd believed he could make a difference now.

Men from Bates's BUD/S class and those he'd been close to on the team began to fold the flag, a memento now for his family. A symbol of freedom at the cost of sacrifice. Nick could think of no greater gift to give a loved one in the loss of their hero. He prayed Kaylan never had to experience it, but deep down he knew it might one day be a reality.

Bates's mother received the flag, steeling her bottom lip to thank the men. She made eye contact with each one. Bates had been raised by a fighter.

As X stood to say a few words, all heads turned toward him. "I've done this too many times. Saying 'I'm sorry' doesn't quite suffice. I've never been a man of many words. I've always thought I'd let my actions do the talking for me. It's one reason I joined the Teams. I could hate on politics or the events in the Middle East or the direction our country seems to be going, or I can do something about it.

"We say SEALs are a special breed of warrior, born of adversity. After we come through those fires, we've been refined into something stronger. And Bates, well, he believed in what he was doing. I want to read you something we found in his bag. Apparently Bates was a man of words and action." He reached into his pocket, his white gloves fumbling to unfold a single sheet of notebook paper with a dirty streak on the back side. He cleared his throat to read.

"I'm back in the desert and back to being hazed. But I don't mind so much. I'm here. I'm here where things are happening. I'm here where I can make a difference. I'm here. And I don't care how much razzing I have to endure. There's nothing I can imagine that would be better than being a SEAL or guarding my country with these men by my side. I never have to worry with them at my back."

Nick's arm throbbed from his injury as he listened to Bates's words. He hadn't had his back, but Bates had Nick's. To the end. And even then.

"I fight for something good knowing I go to something better if I die in this place. But if I die, it will be next to men I love for a country I love. I earned the title of SEAL, but in truth I wake up and earn it every day. Every day that role, that title makes me a better man, a better brother, a better soldier. One way or the other, even if this ends in death one day, I win. Becoming that man and protecting this country are worth fighting for. If death calls my name, I will be brave. I die a United States Navy SEAL. Some things are worth dying for."

X's voice never wavered, but Nick read the emotion that threatened to overtake him if he let it. "Your son, your brother, your friend," he addressed the crowd, "died a hero. He did not die in vain. He will not be forgotten. His example will keep us going and we will continue what he started." He nodded at the crowd and then approached Bates's family and knelt in front of his mother and sister.

Nick rose with Micah and his teammates for their final act. One by one, they filed past the mahogany coffin. With each man who stepped up, a dull thud sounded in his wake as he pounded a gold Trident into the lid. Man after man went before him until it was Nick's turn. He punched his pin through the wood and let his fist drop with all the anger and pain and grief he held. And he left it there. He leaned forward and touched his forehead to the shiny wood. "Thank you," he whispered. Without another look, he stood tall and fixed his eyes on the backs of his brothers in uniform who had gone before.

Nick never could visit Arlington without visiting the Tomb of the Unknown Soldier. He watched the changing of the guard, nodding at a few who stopped to thank him for his service. He appreciated their acknowledgment, but he would do what he did without it.

The white marble sarcophagus reminded him of his mortality. This whole place did, but lately he didn't need any more reminders. From dust he was made, and to dust he would return. Life was fleeting. While many lived for their names to be remembered, he lived much like the soldier buried in this tomb. He cared more about doing something worth remembering. He cared about making a difference. For years now, people had stopped by this tomb, watching the guards diligently and meticulously maintaining their post. No one could tell you the man's deeds, how he died, or his name. But they could tell you how he lived. Sacrificially. That's what Nick wanted. To be selfless.

"Makes you wonder, doesn't it?" X stopped next to him, startling Nick from his reverie.

"Makes you wonder what?"

"If it's worth it."

Nick shook his head. "It doesn't make me wonder that."

X chuckled. "Good. For a second, I thought you were getting all melancholy on me. But I guess a bit of that is allowed after a day like this. Leaving soon?"

Nick looked at his watch. "I've got a couple hours."

"Walk with me." X nodded to the sidewalk winding past rows of neatly placed tombstones. American flags waved in front of each on a well-manicured lot. Nick thought it might be one of the most beautiful sights he'd ever seen.

"Our friends in Langley made a deal with Janus to get more info."

Nick fought the urge to react. He clasped his hands behind his back, squeezing so tight his knuckles ached. "Are they stupid?"

"Just politicians."

Nick chuckled. "So why are you telling me?"

"You were part of the deal."

This time he couldn't help it. He stopped walking. "Me? And you're okay with this?"

"I'm okay with getting this Kahuna fellow behind bars, and I think you can handle this witch."

Nick nodded and resumed their walk. Snow began to fall, tickling Nick's neck where it drifted down his collar. "What does she want?"

"I think just to talk. Probably to try some psycho mumbo jumbo. Most likely just to say she can. The point is, if you can handle it, it may get us everything we need to finish this . . ." X came to a stop and fixed his beady eyes on Nick. ". . . once and for all."

"And how am I supposed to talk to her?"

X pointed ahead of him where a car waited on the street. "You can talk now and still make your flight. Not sure where they are taking you, but Langley is nearby, and I imagine she is, too."

Nick refused to take another step, only stared at the car. The last person he wanted to see on a day like today was her. He was tired of her invasion of his life, his emotions, and he didn't like playing games. He refused to play the minnow in her shrinking pond.

"Hawk, go. Get it over with. Keep your head on straight, and put this to bed so we can finish what we started."

"X, she's the reason Bates is dead. Forget it."

X made a sharp turn in front of Nick, his nose almost touching Nick's. "Then make her pay. Now go."

Nick squared his shoulders and walked to the car. He would treat her like any other informant, and he would make sure she was locked up for the rest of her life. And then some.

Nick crawled out of the car in front of a brownstone that looked more like the set of a quaint television show than a location for the right hand of one of the world's leading arms dealers. Nick grimaced. She'd talked herself into a sweet deal.

Jake opened the door before Nick could decide whether to approach or crawl back in the car. His friend wore a white sweater over blue jeans. His black hair fell in waves on his head, a look Kaylan would describe as "endearing." Nick preferred the tousled look himself. Nick tried to smile at his friend as he approached the door, but it fell flat.

"Hawk, good to see you."

"Jake."

"What, no love?"

"You're lucky I don't rescind the wedding invite."

"Ouch. Kaylan would not approve."

"Well, Kaylan would get over it."

All joking fell from Jake's tone. "How was the service?"

Nick only stared back. After seconds of silence, Jake nodded. "He died doing his job. He wouldn't have asked for more than that."

"No. He wouldn't have. But he might not have died at all if not for the woman you are now giving houses to." He looked around the nicely furnished if not rather sparse living area. "At least she didn't talk you into a yacht."

"She tried." The hint of a smile cracked his endearing bad boy look. "The house is merely a loaner." He gestured through a doorway. "She's right through here. Just keep her talking. We may be able to get more of what we need."

Nick bit back a retort. Personally, the last thing he wanted was to keep her talking. Professionally, he hoped she didn't shut up so he could finish this last part of the op. Failure wasn't an option.

"Shall we?" Jake led the way into a cozy but small kitchen that reminded Nick of a set out of *Leave It to Beaver.* The only thing missing was a woman walking around with an apron and a smile. What met him instead was a terrorist and his mother.

She sat at the kitchen table, her cold eyes studying him. A sneer stretched muscles on her face that Nick suspected she rarely used. Her once understated designer clothes and expensive makeup and hair had been traded in for a dash of lipstick and flat blonde and graying locks. Yet somehow she seemed more lethal, a caged animal examining every weakness for an avenue of escape.

Nick refused to be that avenue.

It took every bit of his discipline to take the seat in front of her. He laced his fingers together and leaned forward on the table, his gaze slamming into hers. Bates and his new-kid smile flashed in Nick's mind. He fought the urge to lean across the table and punch her.

"I'm here. Start talking."

"Uniform looks good on you. It looked good on your father, too." She sat back and crossed her legs, still maintaining an air of poise. But Nick had seen her fire a gun pointblank. The woman was no lady.

"You never knew my father. He was a good man. Taught me everything I knew growing up."

"He was merely a substitute."

Nick smiled and leaned back, his leg bouncing up and down beneath the table. "Well, your substitute could have won an award for best mother of all time."

"Now is that any way to talk to your mother?" She slipped into Russian as easily as Nick slipped into water.

"English, please," Nick responded. His parents had suggested he learn Russian in college, but he never expected to actually like it let alone use it. He silently thanked his schoolteacher mother who had held an affection for the language. He could never say no to her.

"Don't deny your heritage, my son," she fired back, again in Russian.

"I know whose son I am, Anya." She winced when he said her name. He filed it away to use later. "Your claim is in word only. Now, shall we get down to business?" He unbuttoned his coat, forcing his body to sprawl in the chair while his brain told him to run.

"It's your funeral."

"How about we start there?"

"Fine. Sasha Baryshev is a powerful man. For years, I did his dirty work and until only months ago, you did not know who either of us was. Now his entire operation is threatening to fall around him, and you are firing the weapon. I know his habits. I know his contacts. I know his secrets. I can help you put an end to him."

Nick glanced at Jake. His expression told him nothing. "In exchange for what, Anya?"

Her icy blue eyes fractured at her name again. What secrets did her name contain?

"My freedom. Or at least a measure of it." She glanced at Jake. "There are people who want me dead. Men I once provided weapons to who are willing to kill me for Sasha's favor. I can provide names, locations, and weapons sale information in exchange for my freedom. I will disappear and you will never hear from me again."

"Is that a promise?" Nick muttered.

A cruel smile spread across her face, causing wrinkles to crack over her pale skin. "I can give you the location, date, and time of the largest weapons shipment Sasha has sold in a while, and I can tell you that he will be there to ensure the transaction takes place."

Nick and Jake both came alert. "And how do you know these details haven't changed?" Jake questioned as he bent over the small circular table. The light fixture hanging above him caused his shadow to spread, darkening part of Janus's face.

"Because you just eliminated that Taliban cell. Because I am no longer in play. And because there is no one he trusts more than himself to get the job done now that I am gone."

"How big a shipment are we talking?"

"Enough to create another catastrophe the size of nine-eleven on American soil if executed correctly."

Adrenaline charged through Nick, the kind that made him ready to jump a plane to the Middle East or wherever this transaction would occur. The kind that made his trigger finger itch to hold his rifle. One last op. This could be it. This could eliminate a major terrorist and a plan to hurt America again.

Jake slipped into the chair next to Janus. Nick felt the controlled energy radiating off of him as he leveled his tone. "I'll ask again. How do you know all this?"

"Because I set up the buy months ago. And one of the informants trusts me more than Sasha."

Jake looked at Nick, who nodded. "If we can confirm your information, we'll talk terms. But we will need specifics."

The ball was in Jake's court now. Nick rose to leave, buttoning his jacket as he prepared to revisit the snowy environment outside the door. Cold, wet stuff should never be allowed to fall from the sky, but he'd rather be out there than spend another minute looking into the eyes of a woman who could get them all killed. "I'll see myself out. Keep me posted."

"We'll be in touch soon, I'm sure."

"Wait." Her sharp voice sliced through Nick. "I'm not finished with you yet."

Nick turned. "I think you've said all that needs to be said."

"Not quite. I have one more condition for my deal. I want to see Natalia."

He didn't need to step outside for his blood to freeze. He slumped against the wall and crossed his arms. "No."

"Then no deal."

"Then you're dead." With each passing moment, Nick found it harder to control the emotions. He'd never met his sister, but he didn't have to think at all to know he wouldn't allow this woman within a mile of her.

"Hawk," Jake warned.

"I'm not going to do that to her, Jake."

Jake only stared. "We'll talk about it."

Nick pushed off the wall but stopped as Janus stood, all five foot two inches of her focused on him. "If I do not see her, I will make sure it reaches Sasha's ears that I have two children I gave up at birth. Two children that I long to reconcile with before I meet my death." Her voice blackened with every word and her eyes held the threat of death. "I will make sure he knows exactly where to find both of you. And I believe that address will soon include a certain auburn-haired beauty, am I correct?"

It took every one of Nick's instincts to stay calm. Her decisions, her selfishness had resulted in the death of his biological father, Bates, and countless others. Kaylan and Natalie would not fall into that count. He didn't care if he died trying. He would not lose either one of them. This conversation was over.

"Jake, I trust you'll take care of this."

Jake's gaze traveled from Janus's poised stance to Nick and back. He nodded as Nick turned and made himself walk from the room. But with everything in him, he wanted to sprint back to California, lock Kaylan and Natalie away, and take this guy out with his team.

If he'd learned anything over the past few months, it was that Janus only looked out for herself. Nothing good could come of her meeting Natalie, and nothing good could come from this meeting. But he would rather go to his death than let her near the women he loved. His heart hardened within him as he stepped into the cold. Flurries floated through the air and landed on his face. Despite the freezing temperature, his blood boiled, heating every part of him. He couldn't let it go. He couldn't give the grace that he knew he should give to his enemy. She'd threatened him for the last time.

Anya Petrov was too far gone to forgive.

CHAPTER TWENTY-FIVE

Nick held Kaylan tighter than he'd intended on their Friday night date, but he didn't care. Dread still filled him at the thought of Janus's threats only twenty-four hours before. He hadn't been able to sit still during the plane ride this morning or during the car ride from the airport when they arrived this afternoon.

"Babe, you're hurting me."

"Sorry." He released her and stepped back but reached for her hand and wound his fingers through hers. Man, it felt good to touch her, to be near her.

They walked down the beach towards the traveling carnival where a Ferris wheel, games, and several other rides dominated the parking lot. Despite the chill of the night, his blood ran warm. He slung his arm over Kaylan's shoulders and kissed her hair.

"Want to tell me what has you upset?"

"Who says I'm upset?"

She wrapped her arm around his waist, their pace comfortable, in sync. "I know you. And you can't hide those raging emotions from me. You may be as cool as a block of ice in a fight, but y'all boil pretty hot the rest of the time. Even if you don't show it." She grinned at him. "At least my SEAL does."

"You think you're so smart." He couldn't resist kissing her cute grin. They came to a stop at the edge of the carnival, the night reserved for just the two of them. Lights glowed in the darkness, obscuring the stars Nick loved so much. The Ferris wheel lit up with hundreds of multicolored lights. Children squealed in delight from the tilt-a-whirl. The ringing of victory and games charged the air. Nick knew he should relax, but all his senses felt heightened, on alert at all times. He wanted to be here with Kaylan. But he also wanted to deploy and take care of business.

"Hey." She squeezed the hand hanging over her shoulder. "Be here with me, please."

He turned her to face him, squeezing her waist. "You and me, babe. What do you want to do?"

"Let's start with the Ferris wheel." They turned and walked toward the line. "And don't think I didn't notice that you avoided my question."

"Forget smart. You're brilliant. And a little too observant."

"You bug me about not paying enough attention. You bug me about paying too much attention. Pick one."

"I need you to not pay attention when I don't want you to poke."

She stood on her tip toes and kissed his cheek. "I think that's when I need to know the most."

"Maybe." He smiled.

They slipped into the next seat on the Ferris wheel. Nick eyed the chipping paint overpowered by the flashing lights. He'd jumped out of planes in the middle of the night but somehow this carnival ride made him more nervous than any of his stunts. He could see the headlines: Navy SEAL Killed in Freak Ferris Wheel Accident. What a way to go.

"Nick . . ."

"Sorry. I'm here. I'm with you." He slipped his arm around her shoulders and leaned back, the seat rocking a bit with his movement.

Kaylan peered over the edge as the ground slipped farther from reach. "Maybe this wasn't such a good idea," she whimpered as the basket pitched again.

He wrapped his arm a little tighter, fighting the drop in his stomach as they lurched to a halt. "Let's just play a game."

"Nothing that requires moving."

"I guess kissing is out."

She grinned, her eyes dancing in the energy twirling around them. "That might be more dangerous than this ride."

"True. We'll table that for now. How about a game of 'would you rather'?"

"You and your question games." She sighed. "All right. I'll go first. Would you rather go back in time or into the future?"

"Back in time. I don't want to know the future. Would you rather have a huge wedding and stay here for the honeymoon, or elope and have a huge honeymoon?"

"Um, are we talking hypothetical here? Because we kinda planned everything already."

He chuckled. "It's a game, babe. Relax." Their cart swung as the ride started again. Their feet hung above the ground as the ride hoisted them back into the air and stopped again.

"I would rather elope and have a huge honeymoon."

"We should have played this game before planning."

She rolled her eyes and swatted his chest.

"Kidding. Kidding." He poked her in the ribs. "Your turn."

"Would you rather wrestle a hippo or a bear?"

He threw his head back and laughed. "Where does your gorgeous brain get this stuff?"

"Hey, buddy, you wanted to play. Answer my question."

"Wrestle a hippo. You can avoid the mouth, but those bear claws could slice you up in a fight." Their cart swung to the very top and stopped. The carnival stretched below them and a black star-studded sky hovered above. "My turn." His stomach churned. "Would you rather live an uncertain, unsafe life with a man you love, or live a stable, safe life with a man you like but don't love?"

Uncertainty danced across her face. "Do you play these games just to get answers to things you wouldn't normally ask?"

He offered a nervous laugh. "I don't mean to." They started moving again, their cart quickly approaching the ground and their exit. Not enough time to answer. Not enough time to really know.

"Short answer is I would never trade you for the world, Nick Carmichael. No matter how many fights we have, how many mean mothers show up, or how many men threaten my life."

Her fingers stroked his face. He closed his eyes, his spirit weary. Strength came from Christ alone, and he would need it to lead this beautiful woman, to treasure her, and to protect her. "I'm so sorry for all this mess."

"Hey, look at me." He opened his eyes to passionate green gazing back at him. "We do this together. You and me." She slipped her arms around his neck. "I would rather you be a man who follows the Lord into battle for others than a man content to watch from the sidelines and do nothing. Following where Jesus leads is never safe, but it's always the best place to be."

He rested his forehead on hers, sharing her strength. He chuckled. "As long as we keep having these weak moments at opposite times, I think we will be okay."

Her smile lit up his world. "Come on. Let's go play some real games."

They spent hours trying every carnival game in the parking lot. Kaylan walked away with a pink stuffed elephant, a yo-yo Nick swore he would learn to use, and a small basketball. With an aching stomach due to way too much cotton candy and a night spent laughing at everything and nothing, Kaylan slipped her hand in Nick's, ready to go home.

"Step right up, step right up," a young guy in suspenders and a straw hat called from a high striker, a game Kaylan hadn't seen in ages. A twelve-foot-tall pole with a puck at the bottom towered over the man. He balanced his weight against a wooden stick with a heavy mallet at the end as he yelled at the crowd to step up and take a shot at making the puck fly up and strike the bell fixed to the top of the pole.

"You there," he pointed at Nick. "C'mon, show your little lady how strong you are. Step up and take a shot." He held out the end of the mallet to Nick.

Nick waved him off. "No, thanks. I think we're done for the night."

"Oh, c'mon. Are you chicken, a big strapping dude like you?"

Kaylan knew he'd made a mistake as soon as he'd called her competitive fiancé "chicken." While Nick didn't need to prove anything, it didn't stop him from making a point every now and then. Just for fun. She rolled her eyes as he accepted the mallet and stepped up to the base of the high striker.

"You going to cheer me on, babe?" A gleam from a night of fun filled his blue eyes.

"I don't think I need to feed your ego any."

"C'mon, don't leave your man hanging," straw hat goaded.

"He knows he can do it."

Nick took a bow. A laugh slipped before she could stop it. If he managed to hit the bell, she wouldn't hear the end of it for weeks.

A crowd gathered as the carnival man raised his voice, creating a spectacle that might keep him busy the rest of the night.

"Military?" a woman said to Kaylan's right.

Kaylan smiled. "Yes. How'd you know?"

"They have a look about them. You hang around long enough and you can spot 'em. Every branch carries themselves differently."

"Do you have family in the military?"

"My ex was a marine."

Kaylan nodded. The stout lady had a look about her, too, like she could eat Kaylan for lunch. Nick got the crowd clapping as he gripped the mallet in his hands like a bat and prepared to swing.

"It'll never last."

Kaylan turned to look at her, really look at her for the first time, but the woman's attention was firmly fixed on Nick. "Excuse me?"

"Take it from me, honey. You'll never be able to hold onto a man like that for long. Another woman will get him. Or the job will. But in the end, it's all the same."

Nick swung and the bell rang out loud and clear. The crowd cheered as he took a bow. Kaylan clapped and smiled as Nick came and placed a quick kiss on her cheek. But deep inside, she wrestled with the woman's words. She never worried about Nick with another woman. Women looked at Nick all the time, even with Kaylan present, but he never noticed them, never responded with anything other than friendly courtesy. But his job?

Kaylan glanced down at the palm of her hand, the very hand that she'd fought to open after the pastor's sermon. All she wanted to do was let go, surrender Nick and their relationship to the Lord. Surrender her fear, but at every turn something warred with that decision.

But she'd lived with the conflict long enough to realize that as long as the war raged on, it meant her fear hadn't won. She leaned closer to Nick as he walked her to their car, talking and laughing about their night. The man next to her meant the world to her, and she would keep fighting.

Even when the tiny voice within her told her the woman might be right. She might lose him.

CHAPTER TWENTY-SIX

Snow fell outside Anya's Virginia "home." Despite a step up in comfort, she found that a house too could be a prison. She'd known that for years. Her comfort came at a price. She sold her soul to stay alive, and now it just belonged to a different master. Was it really living if she was never truly free? Anya wondered.

A tree obscured her view of the street, snow coating each branch. She pressed her fingertips against the glass, her mind falling back to the warmth of her childhood home. Her mother kneaded fresh dough in the kitchen, her brother Andrei read in the corner of the room, and her papa smoked his pipe near a roaring fire that heated the whole room while snow softly fell outside. A scientist and innovator in an age in Russia where innovation had become welcome once more, he thrived. When his young daughter had been recruited by the Stasi for her brains and her demeanor, he'd been thrilled.

Anya had become part of the *Hauptverwaltung Auf Klarung*, or Stasi, at a very young age, responsible for espionage and covert operations abroad, often posing as a student. She was responsible for infiltrating Western intelligence agency operations and preparing acts of sabotage. In contrast, her younger brother, Andrei, grew up struggling against Russian propaganda and the ideals encouraged behind the Iron Curtain. In his late teens, he began to smuggle those mistreated or wrongfully hunted over the wall.

Until he'd been caught the week before Anya turned twenty-three.

She broke into a coughing fit. The room now seemed much colder, but the memories refused to freeze. Andrei had been hauled into their small home, the home she was visiting for only two days. Her superior held a gun to his head. His eyes never wavered from Anya's. He fired.

In that moment, Janus was born, a woman with no country, loyal to no man, and concerned with only one person. Herself. After that she began to spend more time near the Berlin Wall, where she met an enlisted American airman. Under the guise of gaining information, she began to flirt, but all too soon she fell for the naive boy from Kansas. Handsome and carefree with a laugh that made her melt, he stole her heart. Then one day, he was gone, and she found herself pregnant.

Her fingers traced patterns over her wrist where the faintest string of black numbers interrupted her pale skin. The squadron number of the only man she'd ever loved. She later learned of his death. Killed off duty while in the city, and she had a feeling she knew exactly who ordered the hit. The same man who now held his life in her hands.

Coughing seized her again and she doubled over. It was getting worse.

A loud rap interrupted her reverie. She jumped and fought to regulate her breathing. Jake. Too smart and too observant American. She'd outsmart him yet. She had to. But for now she'd play his game.

"They told me, you know."

"Told you what?"

"About the coughing. The wheezing. The meds they had to give you."

She refused to answer as his eyes probed her. She knew what he would find. Nothing. She'd been trained by the best, the most deadly men. If she didn't cower in front of them, she wouldn't cower in front of him.

"Cancer. Lung cancer, isn't it? You don't have long anyway. Why don't you just help us? Redeem yourself."

She could almost hear the distant shouts of men banging down her door. It became the night she vowed no man would control her. It became the night that demanded revenge.

"We will do it my way."

"Wrong." He took a step into the room, his legs spread and arms crossed over his slender chest. "We will do it our way. You don't really have a choice."

But she did. She had to get away. Death chased her one way or another. She would meet it on her own terms.

CHAPTER TWENTY-SEVEN

The buzzer reverberated through the gym as the crowd cheered. Cheerleaders shouted and waved blue and white pom poms in front of the risers as Kaylan shifted on the tan plastic bleachers. Tanner Carpenter received the ball and began dribbling it down the court as their small group cheered.

"Shoot, son! Shoot!"

With a jumpshot that promised a future in many games, Tanner sent the ball sailing through the hoop. Two more points for the Bluedevils, the local elementary rec team.

"That's my brother," Molly shouted from her place between Kaylan and Nick. She'd perched on one or the other's lap all night, eating up the attention that Nick lavished on her. Titus sat with his arm draped around Liza. Micah, Colt, and Jay stood at the edge of the bleachers next to Logan, their eyes glued on the court, yelling encouragement to Tanner. They'd been home over a week now, and quickly fell back into their routine. Their crew not only worked together but also spent free time together, and this Thursday night was no different.

On the court, a red-headed, freckle-faced kid shoved Tanner, knocking him to the shiny gym floor.

"Don't you take that from him," Jay shouted as Tanner surged back to his feet and into the game.

"Jay, rein in those protective instincts and don't encourage my son to be a poor sport," Kim warned.

Stunned, Jay looked back and forth between Kim and Logan. Logan grinned and fixed his eyes on his son. "She's the boss."

The buzzer announced halftime and Kaylan motioned to Molly. "Want to go get some popcorn from the concession stand?"

Her blue eyes lit up, full of wonder. "With extra butter?"

"You got it." Kaylan reached for her hand as they stood, winking at Nick. The fire in his eyes lit a slow burn in her stomach. If this is what nights looked like in their future—kids, friends, games—then the future looked bright indeed.

The roar and cadence of the gym dimmed as Kaylan and Molly passed through the metal doors and into the atrium of the middle school. A small concession stand off to the side served the families.

"Can we get candy, Aunt Kaylan?"

"I don't know that your mom and dad would want you eating candy this l—" she stopped cold as the man in line in front of them turned around. The same man who had visited her home less than two weeks ago.

Dressed more casually in a polo shirt and loafers, he held a box of Milk Duds. "Evening, Miss Richards. I trust you are doing well." His gaze raked her from head to toe as he popped a piece of chocolate in his mouth. He bent down in front of Molly. "And who is this beauty?"

Kaylan's fear fled and her protective instincts kicked into high gear as Molly curled against her side. "What are you doing here?"

He looked up from where he knelt and slowly rose. He smelled of peppermint and liquor and the faintest flicker of tobacco. "I wanted to take in American culture while I am here. Neighborhood sports seemed like a good way to achieve that." He smiled, but it fell flat, rippling on his face like crackling paper.

"I think you need to go."

Inside the gym, the announcer's voice boomed through the mic, announcing the beginning of the second half. The man popped another Milk Dud in his mouth. "I wouldn't want to leave when it is getting good. Little Tanner is doing an excellent job tonight, wouldn't you say?"

Anger and fear fought for prominence as Kaylan realized his question to Molly was a formality. He knew where she lived. He knew their routine. He knew their names. And he didn't want anything except to terrorize, to keep them aware of his presence.

"Kayles, what's taking so long?"

Molly dropped Kaylan's hand and darted to Nick, flying into his arms. The princess dress she'd insisted on wearing billowed around her.

For the first time since their run-in, the man took a slight step back, but his poise remained firmly in place.

Kaylan watched Nick's guard slip into place as he approached, regarding the scene in front of him. He took one look at Kaylan and turned to face the man. She held her breath, wondering how he would handle this. He held out his free hand. "I don't believe we've met. I'm Nick."

"Vlad. Pleasure, Nikolai."

Nick froze before allowing a small smile to slip through. "I'm sorry. You must be mistaken. It's just Nick. How do you know my fiancée?"

Kaylan noticed his deliberate use of their relationship as he slipped his arm around her shoulder. Molly curled into his chest, her eyes wide.

"Miss Richards and I were just having a conversation. I am a basketball fan. Chicago Bulls, actually."

Nick's smile cooled. "I guess you are at the wrong game then. This is just a bunch of kids."

"I think it's important to interact with American families when I come to the States." He shrugged his shoulders. "It makes my experience more authentic." He popped another piece of chocolate in his mouth and chewed slowly while regarding Nick.

Kaylan could feel Nick tensing more next to her. She spoke up. "Like I said, you need to leave."

"Again, Miss Richards, you are proving me wrong about Southern hospitality. But clearly what you lack in manners, you make up for in beauty." He took a step back. "I expect next time I pay you a visit, there might be a warmer welcome. Perhaps sweet tea? It will make our conversation much more cozy."

Kaylan knew the man had crossed a line, and she knew Nick had put the pieces together. He let Molly slip from his hip. "Hey ladybug, why don't you go see your parents. We'll be right there."

"But the popcorn ..."

"I'll bring it, munchkin," Kaylan reassured her.

With a nod, the little girl turned and ran back into the gym.

Nick came closer, his tall frame towering over the mousy man. "Since you've visited my fiancée at her home and threatened her, that leads me to believe you know exactly who I am and what I do."

Vlad only stared. The amusement in his eyes made Kaylan nervous. Was he here alone?

"So then you must know that within a few seconds, a few more SEALs will probably come through that door."

"I am not afraid of your threats. I am a Russian diplomat here on business. You can do nothing to me."

The squeak of shoes hurrying over tile reached Kaylan's ears and she turned. Jay, Colt, and Micah appeared and quietly stood behind Nick and Kaylan. Micah turned to Kaylan, a question in his brown eyes. For the first time in minutes, Kaylan relaxed.

Nick took another step forward, his body moving a bit in front of hers. "That's the thing, Vlad. I didn't say we were going do what we normally would to any terrorist we come in contact with." His voice remained calm but deadly as he took another step. Kaylan noticed a wariness creep over Vlad's features as he fought to stand his ground, but Nick kept advancing. Micah, Jay, and Colt followed in his wake, slipping to block her. "I did mean that we don't take kindly to strange men attending neighborhood basketball games. It can look bad, if you catch my drift." Nick stopped inches away from the man. "So kindly remove yourself, or we will do it for you."

Kaylan felt more than saw the guys around her tense ever so slightly, now clearly aware that something wasn't right. The crowd cheered from inside the gym and Kaylan heard the announcer say Tanner's name over the mic, but in the atrium, nothing sounded except the quiet chatter of the teens at the concession stand and the sound of popcorn popping in the machine.

After what felt like an hour, Vlad finally smiled. But Kaylan thought he looked more like the Cheshire cat. Her breathing stalled.

"I guess I will be going. Such a shame to miss the rest of the game." He chomped down on another Milk Dud, the box rattling as he righted it.

"I'll be seeing you again, Miss Richards." He looked at the guys. "Do tell little Tanner hello and commend his athletic performance."

"Are you serious?" Micah spat. In one quick motion, his fist drew back and connected with Vlad's face. Kaylan squealed as the man landed with a splat on the floor. Blood dripped from his nose as he stood slowly. His glare filled Kaylan with terror, but none of the men moved.

"Don't you ever come close to this family or this team again," Micah whispered, his voice deadly calm.

Kaylan glanced at the teen watching with wide eyes from the concession booth. "Micah . . ."

"He can't do anything and he knows it, Kayles. Otherwise he would have to 'fess up on why he happened to be stalking Logan's family at a neighborhood basketball game."

Kaylan slipped to her brother's side. But Nick gripped her hand and held her back. "Let him be, babe."

Micah said, "My sister and my friend have asked you to leave."

Vlad slowly stood to his feet. His hand tucked under his nose to stem the flow. His gaze landed on Kaylan. Her stomach clenched. This man wouldn't stop. With a final glare and a dip of his greasy, thin haired-head, he exited into the night.

Kaylan realized she'd been holding her breath. She released it in a whoosh as Nick rubbed his hands up and down her arms. "You okay?"

She only nodded, not sure what to think or feel or do.

"Why didn't you send Molly to come get me?"

"I was hoping he would leave without a confrontation."

"Anyone want to fill me in on who I just punched? Who was that guy and how did he know you, sis? And why was he here?"

Kaylan turned to face the guys behind her who looked more like combat-ready men than the guys that joked and laughed with her all the time. She secretly applauded Vlad for standing his ground as long as he did, until Micah let him have it. At this moment, they looked so intimidating she wanted to run back into the gym.

But another thought smacked her as quickly as her realization. He hadn't been eager to run. In the presence of these strong men, he'd been calculating, amused, interested even, but not afraid. Not until Nick began to threaten and Micah hit him. Even then, she'd only seen a glimmer of fear, before it faded into his cold veneer. That told her more about Vlad than anything, and that alone made her spill everything to the men in front of her.

Jay swore under his breath. Micah gripped her shoulder. "We are going to lock you and Megan in a padded room until all of this is over. Seriously, why does this keep happening?"

Nick's hands on her waist kept her grounded. "It's time to end it, Bulldog. We end it, all of it so that this stops. No more bringing it home with us. Life goes back to normal."

Colt shook his head. "This is not normal, and I'm getting tired of it. Next time we go out, I don't want to come back until this is finished."

Inside the circle of SEALs, Kaylan realized for the first time, that though they all operated individually and brought different personalities, strengths, and skills to the table, they acted as one.

She was still learning the SEAL community, but the more time she spent with Nick's team, the more confident she became that Nick and her brother were in good hands. That and under the protection of a good God. She slipped her hand into Nick's as the men walked back into the gym. Cheering erupted as Tanner fired another shot. Nothing but net. As they settled back into the bleachers, she heard her brother mutter to Nick, "Game on." She steeled herself for another departure, but this time, she would greet the goodbye with hands wide open.

CHAPTER TWENTY-EIGHT

Nick had imagined this moment for months in the deepest parts of his heart, never dreaming it would become a reality. Truth be told, he didn't quite know how to handle it. He'd faced down men with guns and terrorists with evil intent. He'd survived distant blasts of IEDs, the death of loved ones, Kaylan's disappearance. And just two days ago he'd stood up to the latest threat to those he loved, Sasha's right hand man, Vlad. But for some reason, meeting the sister he'd never known had him twisted in knots. A whole different kind of nervous than he'd ever experienced. And Nick didn't like nervous.

He'd driven over an hour to meet her at a diner somewhere in between Coronado and Edwards Air Force Base. Truth be told, he couldn't even list the name of the town. He'd plugged in the address, followed the direction of the automated voice drifting from his phone, and had somehow arrived. Over an hour of silence, praying, wondering, and he still wasn't prepared.

A sky blue Volkswagen bug slid into the spot next to him. The woman inside flipped down the mirror, her motions frantic as she ran her fingers through choppy, layered blonde hair that stopped just above her shoulders. She snatched her bag from the passenger seat and flew from the car as Nick opened the door to his Jeep and stepped onto the pavement.

He recognized her, and it somehow felt good that she was as nervous as he was. She stuffed her keys in her purse and took a stumbling step to the diner door.

"Natalie?" Nick's voice sounded scratchy to his own ears. His palms began to sweat and his heart pounded as she slid to a halt and turned slowly to meet him. Nick offered a wave that felt as awkward as it probably looked. He shoved his hands in his jean pockets.

"I'm Nick."

"Oh, hi." She straightened and fumbled with her hair before sliding her hands to her hips. "Well, this isn't exactly how I imagined this moment."

"Were you expecting moving music and an instant connection?"

She chuckled, but he suspected nerves leaked through her now confident veneer. "Yeah, a full choral arrangement. But I gotta say"—she motioned to the diner—"burgers, fries, and milkshakes are much more my speed."

He nodded to the door. "Must be genetic." She offered a small smile as she fell into step with him. He held open the red door as they slipped into the joint. The overpowering scent of meat and grease greeted him. His stomach growled as they slipped onto bar stools and accepted laminated menus.

Nick didn't quite know how to fill the silence that stretched between them as the latest teen pop song filtered through the speakers overhead. A few rough-looking guys sipped coffee in a booth a little ways down and a mother coerced two young children to finish their food at a round table in the other direction. Nick couldn't focus on the menu.

She slapped her menu on the bar counter. "Okay, confession. I'm not hungry. At all."

He chuckled. "Why don't we both just try a burger and go from there?"

"Probably a good idea," she acquiesced as the waitress approached and Nick ordered for them. "With cheese. And ketchup. And the fixings on the side," she called as the woman walked off, waving behind her as she went.

"Not hungry at all, huh?"

"Apparently I eat when I'm nervous. So . . . what are we supposed to talk about?"

Nick didn't know how to start the conversation or how to carry it to completion. "So you're an Air Force brat." He took a sip of the water the waitress placed in front of him.

"We can start there." She grinned and rotated to face him.

"And now you are actually in the Air Force?"

"Technically I'm a civilian. I work in public relations. I make the boys looks good. And you're a, uh, a . . ."

"Not so good at the trash talk, huh?"

She laughed. "Nope."

"Works out for me. I'm a SEAL."

She shook her head. "We didn't grow up together yet somehow we both ended up working jobs that serve our country."

"I think it's in our blood."

She turned curious blue eyes to his, eyes a shade lighter than his and clearer—the color of the sky on a beautiful day. It somehow seemed appropriate that they had met off the beaten path on land away from his ocean and her sky, finding new footing on solid ground. "How much did Kaylan give you in that file?"

She shrugged. "Not much. Enough to tell me about you and me and how we were split."

He tensed, hoping it hadn't included the note about his mother. Their mother. "Well, looks like I need to fill you in then."

The waitress placed burgers in front of them as he launched into a story about their dad, all he had learned about his time on the Air Force Base in Germany, how he died. Nick had done some digging and identified the family they came from in Kansas and had even tracked down an old military buddy of their dad's for a phone call.

"From what I heard he loved the adventure of living overseas, despite the conditions. He had an engaging personality, the base jokester, always pulling pranks and making people laugh."

Natalie flagged the waitress down and ordered cheesy fries and milkshakes for both of them. Nick smothered a grin. "And our mom? Do you know anything about her?"

Nick shifted on the stool. He'd debated the whole drive down on how much to reveal and decided to play it by ear. "She's still a bit of a mystery." He didn't meet her eyes as he polished off his burger. The meat tasted like sawdust in his mouth.

"Our dad's buddy said he met a beautiful girl, a local. Blonde hair and blue eyes." He smiled as Natalie absent-mindedly reached for a strand of her hair. She had a gentle spirit and the beauty that he suspected Janus would have had in another life, if circumstances hadn't hardened every inch of her being.

"Apparently he was smitten. He spent all his free time with her. Then one day, she disappeared, and our dad was shot, and our dad's buddy never saw her again."

"But somehow we wound up in America?"

"We were kids of an American military man. I guess when we were dropped off on base, they cut through enough of the red tape to send us home. I don't know all the details. I don't even know if that was legal at the time, but someone made sure we didn't grow up under the shadow of the Berlin Wall."

"Thank God for that." She rubbed her hands together as the milkshakes and a plate of fries arrived.

He chuckled, noting her smaller frame. "You must be like Kaylan. She can eat and never seems to gain much weight."

"She would probably disagree with you on that. I bet she pays more attention to what she eats than you think she does. Speaking of Kaylan, how'd you two meet?"

"I went to college with her brother. Then we ended up in the SEAL Teams together. I met her and her family during that time. When I visited her family for the first time in Alabama, I fell hard." He smiled, remembering how she radiated energy and joy. Her laughter still echoed in the recesses of his mind.

"And it was love at first sight." She smirked. "Typical."

"Nah. I don't believe in that kind of stuff. She doesn't either. But she was pretty amazing. I did know then that I would never get tired of that smile or her laugh or the way she loves stronger than anyone I've ever known."

Natalie nodded. "I guess struggles do that to a person. You know that chapter in Psalms where the Lord talks about refining us like silver and leading us through hard things until he brings us to a place of abundance? Sounds like he has done that for you two." She smiled. "Kaylan told me that you are a Christian."

"Good to know you are, too." He took a swig of milkshake, the strawberry flavor coating his mouth and reminding him of summer. "Natalie, I'm sorry if finding out about this disrupted your life. I'll understand if you don't want any part of it."

She played with her milkshake straw, not quite meeting his eyes. Nick sensed her internal battle. He hadn't known what to expect meeting his sister, his blood. Scientists had a lot to say about nature verses nurture, and the two of them had grown up in very different homes with different life experiences, yet he couldn't help but note their similarities. She radiated strength and surety about herself in a way that drew him. She didn't need him, but she'd chosen to meet him. That had to say something.

"I only wondered about my birth family once. When I was seven, we took family pictures with my grandparents and all my cousins. Everyone is dark headed, dark eyes, olive-toned skin. I burn like a tomato in the summer. My hair is really blonde. And blue eyes were just the icing on the cake. I think it was the first time that I noticed I didn't look like the rest of my family, and it was the first time I wondered if there was another family out there that I did resemble." She finally looked up and met Nick's gaze, her eyes studying every feature. Nick knew what she searched for. Resemblance, connection, some clue she could identify with. "I guess I finally found it."

"But you were happy growing up?"

"My family is amazing. With my dad in the Air Force we moved around a lot until we finally settled in California. My sister is two years older but a beauty and a brain. She got married three years ago and has a beautiful one-year-old that I spoil to death."

Nick chuckled thinking of how he felt about the Carpenter kids.

"I never wanted or wished for anything else, Nick."

A small piece of him sank at her admission. He had a family with the Richards, the most beautiful girl with Kaylan, but a small piece of him had always wondered about his biological family. "Hey, Natalie, I understand." He pushed his empty milkshake glass away from him. "I'm glad you grew up happy and whole. I wouldn't want anything different for you." He reached for his wallet as the waitress brought the bill and then scurried away again.

Natalie's fierce grip stilled his hand. "I said I never wanted or wished for it, but I can't ignore it now. My family wanted me to meet you, too." Her eyes searched his. "Could we maybe just take it slow? I want to know you. I can't pretend that I don't have a ... a brother out there now. Wow, that's weird to say."

He smiled and covered her hand with his. "Take your time. I've had a few months to process this, and clearly my fiancée had to act on it before I did."

"She's a keeper." Natalie slipped her hand from his as he dropped cash on their ticket. "By the way . . ." For the first time, Nick saw a determination filter across her face. "I know there is something you aren't telling me about our birth mom. Call me crazy, but I can tell."

He laced his fingers and took a deep breath. "Kaylan said you had an insatiable need to know the truth."

"Open communication was a big deal in my house. When it wasn't present, I noticed its absence even more clearly. I recognize when someone is telling pieces of the story but not the whole truth. I want to know, Nick. I don't understand the secrecy. You don't have to protect me."

Nick glanced around the diner, noticing new patrons had gathered since they sat down an hour before. "Let's take a drive."

Nick's mind raced as they crawled into his Jeep. Clouds now streaked the previously clear blue sky. They hit the highway, passing sandy, brush-covered hills. "Natalie, there's things about my job, things I can't say, can't even tell Kaylan. I go. I do what I need to do. I come home. I get ready to go again."

"I know how military life works, Nick. I was raised in it. But what does your job have to do with our mother?"

Nick glanced at Natalie as they drove, the desert landscape a far cry from the ocean he was so used to. "I get that you want the whole story. I get that you are interested in the truth, but knowing the truth could hurt you, could hurt a lot of people."

"Does this have to do with that Russian guy that showed up at Kaylan's when I was there?"

Nick exited the highway and made a loop, pointing his car back to the diner. The drive had been a dumb idea. He couldn't escape her questions. He couldn't give her the answers she wanted. She didn't even know what she was asking.

"It has a little to do with that."

"Well, then he already involved me. So spill, brother." She emphasized the last word. Nick smirked.

"That stuff doesn't work on me, sister dearest."

She shrugged, a smile he was coming to admire lighting her face. "It was worth a shot."

"Give it enough time, and we are going to be pretty good at this sibling thing."

Her eyes met his for a brief moment. "I've never had a brother to pick on before. This should be fun. Are you going to be one of those protective, overbearing, know-it-all kind of brothers?"

He thought of Janus, of Vlad, of the job ahead of him to take down Sasha and grimaced. "You better believe it."

"At least I know what to expect."

He pulled into the parking lot and threw the gearshift into park. He turned to face her. "Our parents met during a rough time in Europe." He chewed on his words, trying to figure out how much he could tell her without violating national security or her safety. "Suffice it to say, our birth mother had a hard life and it affected her decisions.

She gave us up for good reasons, Natalie. We were better off being raised by the parents we had." Nick knew that was a gross understatement the minute it came from his mouth. If she only knew, she would turn tail and run back to her family and never speak to him again. "She wasn't in the file for you to read about for a reason, Natalie. And right now you don't need to know any more about her. It isn't worth it."

But Nick needed to know more. He needed to know what Janus knew. He needed to understand her motivations. He needed to protect his growing family. He needed to protect his team, his country. And for that, he might have to give her a piece of him, surrender his sanity for the sake of the greater good. As he took in the woman before him, he knew he would do it to keep Natalie safe.

Natalie nodded slowly. "Okay. I'll trust you. For now. I don't need to look for her anyway. But about this Russian fella. Do I need to know anything?"

"If you see him, call me or Kaylan, or call the number on this card." He handed her a copy of the card he'd given Kaylan. "Avoid that man at all costs. I'm not sure what his agenda is, but it isn't anything good."

"Okay, on that note..." She unbuckled her seat belt, her hand hovering over the door handle. "Thanks for meeting me. You aren't so bad. In fact, you turned out all right."

Nick chuckled. "Gee, thanks. You aren't so bad yourself, for an Air Force brat, anyway."

"Watch it, bud. Don't those guys fly in and save your butt when you are in a tough spot?"

"It's the least they can do when we went in to save their butts in the first place."

"It's so good to see your humility bleed through. I almost thought you weren't a SEAL there for a second."

He crossed his arms and leaned against the seat. "So this is what it's like to have a sister." It felt good to laugh together.

Natalie smiled and opened the door. "I better go. I guess I'll see you soon?"

"Absolutely. Hey, Natalie?" He reached for her arm before she climbed from the car. "Kaylan and I, well, we would really like you to come to our wedding. Only if you want to, though."

She nodded slowly, a shy smile creeping over her face as she set foot on the pavement. "I would really like that. Send me the invitation. Kaylan has my address now."

The piece of Nick that had always wondered what blood family looked like soldered to his heart in that moment as he waved goodbye to the sister he'd never known but always wanted. She was better than he'd imagined. And he had a kind-hearted, stubborn, auburn-haired beauty who wouldn't take no for an answer to thank for their meeting.

CHAPTER TWENTY-NINE

Kaylan opened the door to a grinning Nick gripping calla lilies and a rectangular jewelry box. She smiled and slouched against the doorframe. "The meeting with Natalie went that well, huh?"

"Only you can pull off cute and cocky."

She took the flowers from him and held them up to her face. "In that case, I'll have to make a habit out of it."

"Don't you dare." He kissed her cheek and slipped past her into the house.

"What's in the box?"

"A puppy. One of those would fit, right?" He smirked as he held up the jewelry box. He set it on the counter as she arranged the lilies in a vase. "Just open it. It's not much. Just a little something."

She leaned across the counter from him and slipped the box open. She tugged a silver chain from it. An anchor dangled in midair.

"It's beautiful. But what's it for?"

He leaned across the cabinet, slipping the chain from her fingers and fastening it around her neck. "I figure all good things have happened to us in the water. It seems to be an anchor for us. But I wanted you to have something to remember me while I'm away."

She played with the anchor now hanging from her neck. "Babe, you don't have to give me things to remember you by. I think about you all the time." She slipped her fingers through his.

"I was reading in Hebrews this morning before I went to meet Natalie, and I ran across Hebrews 6:19. I don't think it has ever hit home for me quite like it did this time."

"Is that the verse that says hope is the anchor of our soul?"

He nodded. His fingers traced patterns on her hand, doing crazy things to her nerves. She loved that butterflies still took flight every time he touched her.

"I don't think I had ever paid attention to the second part of the verse before. The veil used to separate the Holy of Holies in the Jewish temple. Before Jesus, only the priest could enter and atone for the sins of the people. But when Jesus died, the veil was torn, and nothing separates us anymore. I guess when I wonder if I will come home to you or in those times when you struggle to let me go, I want us to cling to Jesus, our anchor, and not one another."

Kaylan knew she loved Nick, but in the moments when he let her in on the deepest conversations of his heart with the Lord, she loved him even more. Hope in Jesus. An anchor she could cling to, no matter how much the waves buffeted her. It somehow seemed appropriate for her relationship with her SEAL, for her relationship with the Lord. She leaned forward and bestowed a feather-light kiss on his lips. "I love you, you know."

His slow, lazy grin set her heart racing. "I know." He groaned. "I would love to curl up on the couch with you and not share you with anyone tonight. Do we have to go to Logan and Kim's?"

Kaylan pulled a foil-covered dish out of the oven. "I don't think you will regret going tonight."

"And why is that, gorgeous?" He brushed a loose strand of hair behind her ear.

She waltzed to the door. "Let's just say that for once I know something you don't know. Will you grab my jacket?"

He slipped her jacket from the back of the kitchen chair and opened the door for her. "Hey, no fair keeping secrets."

She stopped on her way to the car and looked back at him.

"Never mind. I'm going to be quiet now." She opened the back door and carefully situated the hot glass dish on the floor before climbing into the passenger seat. Molly had asked her to make Gran's lasagna, and she just couldn't tell her no.

"Let's go, Mr. Frogman. I'd hate to keep everyone waiting." She enjoyed watching him bite his lip as he closed the door behind her.

"This is torturing you, isn't it?" she teased as he climbed into the Jeep beside her.

"So, so bad."

"Good." She grinned and settled back in her seat.

After he started up the car and began to drive, his hand drifted over to rest on her leg. "I could make you tell me." His low voice held a warning that Kaylan didn't like.

"I will not negotiate with handsome men trying to use their charm."

"Who said anything about charm?" He squeezed the place right above her knee that always made her shriek and laugh.

"Nick, stop." She laughed. "You're going to have a wreck."

"Just tell me then." He squeezed her leg again, laughing with her this time. "Come on, babe. Just spill."

"This is cruel and unusual punishment."

He wagged his finger. "No, cruel and unusual punishment is when you lean in to kiss me and then won't let me actually kiss you until I do something for you. That is just pure torture. This"—he squeezed again and she shrieked—"is just payback."

"Nick Carmichael, let go." She pried his fingers from her leg and held them in her lap, forcing him to concentrate on the road.

They pulled into the Carpenters' neighborhood and stopped at a stop sign. He turned to face her, the glow of the street lights casting an evil glint to his mischievous blue eyes. "Just wait till we get there and I can use both of my hands."

She leaned in close to him, unable to stop a smile of pure joy as she hovered inches from his face. His gaze drifted to her lips and his grin matched hers. "You, my handsome fiancé, are going to wait. Just like everyone else." A car behind them honked before speeding around them. She leaned back in her seat as he blinked away the fog.

"I think you stopped long enough."

Nick groaned and accelerated. "Now see, that right there, that was just mean, Kaylan Lee Richards."

She massaged the spot above her knee where he'd dug his fingers. "It's only fair." They parked and got out of the car. Kaylan balanced the hot casserole dish in between pot holders and they headed up the wheelchair ramp to the house.

As they waited at the door, Nick whispered, "I can't wait to marry you." His lips brushed her ear as Kim opened the door.

"Great. You guys made it." She looked back and forth between them. "We really need to get you two married fast."

Kaylan felt heat spread through her cheeks as Nick grinned and squeezed her waist. She stepped through the door. "Only a few weeks away."

Within seconds, kids swarmed Nick and Kaylan. "Ah, girl, let me have that hot plate," Liza said as she swooped in and rescued Kaylan from Molly's reaching hands.

"Aunt Kaylan, come play with me."

Kaylan looked to Kim, who had Nadia balanced in her arms. "We're waiting on Jay and Colt, so you have a few minutes."

"They're late again? Shocker." Nick kissed Kim's cheek and Nadia's forehead as he moved into the kitchen. Kaylan grinned at the loud greeting she heard from Logan, Titus, and Micah, while Liza hollered for them to keep it down.

Somewhere in the past few months, this group had become inseparable, friendships forged by sacrifice and fire. Kaylan was discovering that those friends made the best ones. There wasn't a reason to hide anything.

Kaylan settled on the floor in Molly's room in the middle of a circle of stuffed animals. A crib now sat in one corner. Molly had her wish—a real-life little sister that sometimes doubled as a doll. Molly might not like it as much when Nadia learned to crawl away from her.

"What are we playing, ladybug?"

"In order to save the princess, the prince has to give himself over to the wicked troll." She pointed at one of her teddy bears.

"And that's the troll?" Kaylan pointed at the fluffy teddy bear just to be sure.

Molly nodded as she picked up her doll. Kaylan couldn't help but think Molly looked like a little doll herself—with her beautiful blonde curls, big blue eyes, and porcelain skin, Kaylan just wanted to squeeze her. "You're the prince, Aunt Kaylan." Molly pointed at a Ken doll lying discarded a foot away.

"And who can I be?" Liza entered and settled in the circle with them. "I can't handle those rowdy guys right now."

Molly rolled her eyes, her flair for the dramatic in full force. "I know what you mean, Aunt Liza." She sighed and shook her head. Kaylan and Liza smothered grins.

"You can be the troll, Aunt Liza."

"The troll, huh?" She looked around the cute stuffed animals, no doubt searching for something ugly. "And which one is that?"

Molly giggled and pointed to a fluffy brown teddy bear. "That one."

"Oh, of course. This one." Liza picked up the bear as Molly began to tell the story. The princess was locked in a tower and the prince had to give himself to the evil troll in exchange for her freedom. But the prince had a trick up his sleeve. He wouldn't surrender until he knew the princess was safe. So they went to the tower to release the princess, and the prince tricked the troll into entering the dungeon. He immediately slammed the doors, locking the troll away.

"And they kiss and live happily ever after," Molly finished. "The end."

The doorbell rang. "Molly, come wash your hands for dinner," Kim called as Colt and Jay's voices filtered into Molly's room.

"Coming, Mommy." Molly dropped her dolls and skipped off, the story already forgotten.

"That girl has quite the imagination." Liza straightened the teddy bears in the circle.

"And romantic streak." Kaylan stood and pulled Liza to her feet. "You and Titus thinking about kids yet? Y'all have been married a few years."

Liza looked away, a pained expression on her face. "I want to. We just haven't been able to get pregnant."

Seeing the pain on her friend's face, Kaylan pulled Liza into her arms. Liza and Titus had started coming to church more with Nick and Kaylan since the events of the past fall. Kaylan couldn't help but think that her disaster had turned into a wakeup call for several around her. When she looked at it in that light, she could let go of the lingering anger and fear. She wouldn't repeat the kidnapping for the world, but she didn't wish to change it now either.

"I'll be praying for y'all," she said, giving a final squeeze before she stepped back.

"Thanks."

They walked toward the kitchen, where Kaylan heard the strains of male laughter.

Soon everyone formed an assembly line and began to dig into the food. Nights like this reminded Kaylan of evenings in Alabama. Her mom and Gran believed in celebrating and enjoying life with a full spread. In these moments, Kaylan knew that wherever she and Nick moved in the future, she would have a home, a family, and nights like this. Laughter and conversation rang like a symphony before her as she studied faces she'd come to love.

The Carpenters gathered around the table, Logan helping Molly cut through pieces of her lasagna to make smaller bites and the boys pinching one another with mouths full. Liza cooed over Nadia, and Titus, Jay, and Colt stood with plates in hand, joking. Nick and Micah stood next to her, her little slices of Alabama in California. Kaylan overheard pieces of Nick's day with Natalie as Micah listened and asked questions.

Kaylan played with the anchor now hanging from her neck. Hope. Jesus was her anchor, her hope. But he provided these people to be the chain that kept her ship from drifting away in the tough moments. She hadn't realized it until now. She had everything she needed. She lacked nothing. And hope rested like an anchor in the hard moments that would come for this group, a group that had committed to something bigger than just themselves. Kaylan leaned into Nick, for the first time fully appreciating the story God had called her to, the honor of loving and learning to understand a warrior's heart. The more she learned to love her own story, the more she gleaned of Nick's bravery.

Nick was full. Full of food. Full from his day with Natalie. And overflowing with gratitude for the people in his life. Kaylan and Liza washed dishes at the sink as Kim and Logan whispered in the corner.

Conner and Tanner ran up to Micah and Nick, baseballs and gloves in hand. "Hey, want to go throw the baseball outside?"

"Sure thing. Maybe grab your coats." Micah tousled Conner's hair as they scurried off.

"Boys, hold up," their mom yelled and sent them to a screeching halt. "You can go play in a few minutes. Can y'all please come over by your dad and me?"

"Is it time?" Conner grinned and rushed over to his dad.

"You bet, champ."

"Being quiet is so hard," Molly said, smiling at her dad from her place in his lap.

"Molly knew the big secret all night and she never said a word?" Micah asked in shock.

"Way to go, ladybug. Our new secret keeper."

She grinned. "I'm pretty good, aren't I?"

Logan squeezed her. "The best. Do you want to tell everyone?"

She squealed, her big blue eyes energizing the room. "Daddy gets a new leg!"

Shocked silence greeted the room for a fraction of a second before everyone exploded.

"Ow, ow," Jay hollered. "Best news I've heard in weeks."

"Congrats, brah. It's about time." Colt fist-bumped Logan as the congratulations continued. Nick watched months of worry and anxiety for the Carpenters bleed from the team in a rush of celebration. Logan had never complained after losing his leg. Not once in months. He'd gone to physical therapy. He'd helped Kim with the kids when she went back to work. He'd remained involved and available in the SEAL community.

"That's not even the best part," Tanner shouted over the din.

"My turn?" Conner looked to his dad.

"Tell 'em, champ."

"After dad gets his leg, he's going to be an instructor at BUD/S."

"Those tadpoles couldn't ask for a better instructor." Nick shook Logan's hand and caught Kaylan's eye. She'd known. She'd known this would be the best news he could receive. A friend and brother had found life in the middle of catastrophe. He breathed deep for the first time in months as the kids helped Kim pass out saucers of cake and ice cream.

Nick slipped next to Kaylan and wrapped his arms around her. "How long did you know?"

"Since before you got home. He wanted to tell y'all himself."

"Maybe you need an award for being the best secret keeper." He kissed her cheek. She leaned back against him, her eyes focused on the Carpenters.

"I wouldn't want to take Molly's new title. But it was pretty fun." He didn't have to see her smile to feel it reach all the way through him. She'd been there, loving this family even when he was gone. She'd integrated with his world, despite her struggle with this new life. Her actions told him more than her words ever could. She would weather this just fine, and she had a whole family to help her.

"I love you, you know."

"Keep on telling me, handsome."

"Always." He squeezed her tighter.

The evening passed with more stories and laughter than Nick could remember swapping in a long time. A cloud had dissipated, leaving Logan an intact and active member of their community. A mentor of warriors.

"Think you will catch him this time? The Kahuna?"

Nick kept his voice low, the kids now in bed and the adults gathered in the Carpenter's small living room. "I hope so."

"It's time to end this," Jay affirmed.

"How you doing with all this, Hawk?" Logan asked. All eyes turned to him.

Kaylan slipped her hand into his as he met the eyes of the men in the room. He read only confidence and personal concern. They knew he would do what was necessary. "I'm ready to never see her again. To get this Russian guy off our backs. I'm ready to slow the slaughter of women and children and Americans over in the Middle East. And all of it stems from one place."

Titus stood to answer his phone as quiet banter broke out in the room, punctuated by loud laughter from Micah and Kim's shushing.

Nick came alert as Titus re-entered the room.

"Time to go?" Logan asked, straightening in his chair.

Nick squirmed, knowing that despite news of his leg, Logan would never join them in the field again, a reality that Nick knew Logan would wrestle with and accept. But he couldn't erase the ache that accompanied the longing in Logan's eyes. He almost expected his friend to stand and walk out of the house with them.

"That was X. Grab your bags. We are out of here."

Men stood all over the room saying hurried goodbyes. Micah pulled Kaylan in for a quick squeeze and kiss on her cheek before following the guys out the door.

"Wait up, Bulldog. I'll catch a ride with you."

Nick pulled Kaylan onto the front porch with him and into his arms. "There's no time for goodbyes." A part of him braced for her frantic pleas for him to stay.

She wrapped her arms around his neck and kissed him. He felt her fear and then her gentle release. "I'll see you when you get back," she whispered near his face before stepping back from him.

"I love you."

She smiled, but this time he saw peace fighting for prominence. "I love you, too. Now go. End this."

Nick met Logan's eyes at the door behind them. "We'll watch out for her. Go get him, Hawk."

With a final nod, Nick handed Kaylan his keys and ran to the idling car. He slammed the door behind him as Micah shot toward their home. It was time to cut off the head of the snake.

CHAPTER THIRTY

They landed on the USS *Dwight D. Eisenhower* off the coast of Spain a little after seventeen hundred on Sunday, February 6. Sun shone and glistened off the deep blue of the Mediterranean. This was Nick's kind of deployment. Despite the versatility of the SEALs, under the cover of night and water remained Nick's favorite time to strike.

X met them on deck, his red hair whipping in the wind stirred up from planes zipping to and fro on the flight deck. The ship teemed with life, men and women going about their daily tasks, ready to answer a distress call or respond to orders at any given second. It felt good to be back.

"Let's go, ladies. We've got to get you operation-ready in just a few hours. This meet goes down at zero two hundred." They followed him below deck to a room complete with a screen and chairs. "Take a seat, ladies."

Nick found a seat, smothering a yawn as fifteen other guys from Support Activity 1 gathered around. Anticipation had built throughout the long flight as the comforts of home receded. The only thing Nick could focus on was the picture of Sasha. Sasha and locking Janus up for good.

"All right, at twenty-one hundred two days ago we received confirmation that Sasha, aka Kahuna, arrived in Marseille. We believe him to be traveling with his wife and one of his associates under the guise of a family holiday. Pleasure, not business, is the official line."

He hit a button on the remote, and the screen changed to a photo of a young man with Mediterranean good looks who couldn't be more than twenty-two or twenty-three. "Meet Milo Kozma. Milo is a small fish in a big pond, but last year he became the courier between an al Qaeda group and their dealers. Drugs, sex trade, weapons, you name it, he arranges it. Poor kid converted to Islam after rooming with a radical in college. Claims God told him to rid the world of infidels. We think if we can capture him, we can flip him, hence why our good buddy is here again with us."

Nick turned slowly, meeting Jake's gaze before colliding with Janus's. Now after meeting Natalie, he noticed the resemblance. Both blonde, small-boned, blue-eyed, and tough. But one had a sweet demeanor, the other an icy veneer and killer instincts. Physical qualities signified the end of their similarities.

X nodded to where Janus stood. "Janus will go under cover, pretending that she escaped from prison and is working for Sasha again. She will convince Milo to set up a place to meet the Kahuna to make the final sale. Now after our little victory in Afghanistan, the Kahuna is running scared, his trust in his associates frayed. He won't risk sending anyone else to make the deal. We will be there to capture and kill if necessary. We have confirmed that enough evidence exists to take him down, and naturally the French want nothing to do with this little escapade, so they are turning a blind eye. We get our guy. We get out clean and make as little noise as possible. Got it? Things with the French are strained enough as it is, and we're lucky to get this much."

Jake and Janus slipped from the room as X continued his briefing. "Jake will get Janus in place now to set up for the meet tonight. Sasha will most likely have his wife with him to continue the romantic getaway bit. His associate is most likely his most trusted bodyguard." The screen changed to a new photo.

"Meet Boris, trained by the KGB and now working for Sasha. He is one tough cookie. Highly skilled. Highly dangerous." X scanned the room. "Don't underestimate him."

He crossed his arms over his chest and leaned back against the wall behind him. "I know this isn't the way we like to move. Too much can go wrong with Janus in the game." Nick caught the briefest glance in his direction as X continued. "But we need to end this and end it now. This will protect countless of our boys in the Sandbox and send terrorist cells all over Latin America and the Middle East in a frenzy to regroup and find a new weapons supplier. Our sources tell us this might be instrumental in stopping a pending attack on the U.S. Everything hinges on our enemy obtaining these weapons."

Nick tensed, his worry easing over Kaylan and his concern growing for the larger implications of not catching this guy.

"Get ready. Get some shut-eye. And be ready to roll out at nineteen hundred hours."

Men stood slowly, massaging muscles as they grabbed gear and headed to bunks reserved for their short visit. Titus, Colt, and Jay turned around in their seats in front of Micah and Nick.

"Well, what do you think?" Jay addressed the group, rubbing the two-day-old stubble growing on his jawline.

"I think nothing good can come from working with Janus," Micah answered.

Nick nodded. "I've seen what she is capable of. There is nothing selfless in her. She will sell us out if it means saving herself. But she'll be smart about it. We won't know until the last minute."

"It seems to me that Jake has her under a tight enough leash." Always the voice of reason, Titus calmed Nick's nerves. "If we worry too much about her, we won't do our part. X told me this is taking place on one of those fancy yachts anchored in the bay."

Nick snickered. Of course it was another yacht. But this time, he would make sure their prey didn't escape.

Or he would die trying.

The *thowp* of the blades roared in her ears as Jake gave her last-minute instructions over the mic. Back to Marseille. She couldn't believe she was back. She knew exactly where to find Milo. He'd be at the bakery he loved to haunt on his way home from working at the docks. She also knew much more was at stake.

"Anya, do you understand what I'm telling you? We need to make sure everyone gets on and stays on that yacht. And we need to make sure Milo does not tell Sasha that you are alive and free until we board. Do you understand?"

Anya hated being talked to as a child. She had gathered and infiltrated many Western agencies over the years to collect info. She was anything but stupid.

"I understand the severity of the situation much more than you do. It is my neck on the line if anything goes wrong. And do not call me Anya anymore. Call me Janus. It is what all my work associates know me as."

"We are not associates, Anya," Jake responded as the bird landed and deposited her on the outskirts of Marseille. "We'll be watching," he shouted as the helicopter rose back into the sky.

Janus tugged her coat tighter around her and took a step forward, basking in the freedom, if only temporary. She knew someone had eyes on her. Knew she would have to lose them at some point, but she quickly slipped out of captive mode. She was a highly trained operative, associated with one of the most dangerous arms dealers in the world. She'd survived the Iron Curtain and years under the authority of the man who killed her brother. All to bide her time. All to plot her revenge. Stupid Americans. This helped her and them. If all went well, Sasha would be dead by the end of the day and Janus would be on a plane to a beach somewhere under an alias she had never used with an account she'd stored money in for years, and whatever life she had left would be lived under the warmth of a coastal sun.

She forced a confidence to her step that she hadn't truly felt in months. Her mind switched into predator mode. Milo would be easy to convince. Sasha not so easy. She would need to play her part well. And she would need to be ready to pay.

Anya Petrov would experience true freedom for the first time tonight. With the scent of bread and sweet rolls wafting on the breeze, she could almost taste it.

CHAPTER THIRTY-ONE

Silvery white light filtered through the darkness, casting an eerie glow beneath the water as Nick and his team sliced through Vieux Port in Marseille. Notre-Dame de la Garde stood on the top of the hill as a silent sentry, lit up like a lighthouse in the dead of the night. The gold Madonna and Child watched over the sleeping harbor as if taunting Nick and his team. Nick didn't like the number of boats surrounding the yacht or the closeness of the shops. Keeping this quiet and under the radar became a greater challenge by the second.

Nick's head crested the waterline, and he bobbed in the gentle waves. Titus motioned ahead to the yacht where a single light glowed within the main cabin. Nick, Micah, Titus, Jay, and Colt prepared to board. Another small team waited on land, ready to step in if necessary, while the rest of the team waited with Zodiacs ready to extract any and all who came willingly.

At Titus's signal, Nick grabbed the railing and tugged his body over the side of the ship. His muscles burned as he slipped to the deck without a sound. A puddle grew beneath him as he reached for his weapon. Intel had confirmed five people on board—Sasha, his wife, Milo, a server hired for the night, and Boris. Titus motioned to Colt and Jay to follow him toward the main cabin while Micah and Nick stayed to clear the deck. Nick crept around the bow of the boat while Micah slipped to the stern. Nick remained alert for Boris, too aware that they were out in the open in what usually doubled as a busy harbor. They were looking for a killer and a way to silence him that didn't draw attention. Impossible.

Nick thrived on impossible. Their one saving grace remained the mutual desire of all parties involved to keep their covers intact and undiscovered. Any attention drawn to this boat could mean questions Sasha did not want to answer and could not answer without great cost.

The squeak of a rubber sole scraping against the deck caused Nick to spin. Boris stood in front of him. Nick noticed the faintest twitch in his arms and tension in his shoulders. His black suit blended in with the night around him, highlighted only by the glow cast from the other boats moored nearby. The glint of silver flashed in his hand and Nick ducked as a knife whizzed past his face. A faint plop sounded as the metal struck the water's surface. An ugly grin cracked his weathered skin. He was making it a game. What was with these men and their games? Nick knew he hadn't thrown his only advantage. He had another knife, if not more than one, on him somewhere. He tensed, prepared for every twitch.

"Stern is clear. Coming to you, Hawk."

"Preparing to breach the cabin. Stand by," Titus replied.

Nick didn't dare respond. His breathing hitched as Boris produced two more knives and held them in both hands. Knives weren't really Nick's thing.

"Let us dance, you and me," he said in Russian. "The one left standing is worthy to live. The other . . ." He shrugged.

Nick leveled his gun at the man, a silencer already in place. "And if I shoot?" he responded in perfect Russian.

"Then we both attract attention we do not want."

Nick rose from his crouch. "You could just put down your knives. Come with me. You will get a better deal than if I kill you now."

"You Americans and your rules," he chuckled. "If you were going to kill me, you would have done it by now."

"I think you sorely underestimate what I will do." As he talked, a black shadow crept behind Boris. " Just a few more feet and . . .

Shouting erupted from the cabin, and Nick heard the muffled sound of a silencer and a scream. Boris pivoted as Micah pounced. The Russian swung his hand through the air. A rip appeared in the fabric of Micah's suit and an ugly red gash spread across his chest and began to bleed as Micah backed up, his military-issue knife now firmly fixed in his right hand.

Nick fired at Boris's right arm. The man turned and tossed the dagger in his left. Nick hit the deck as it sailed past him and embedded in the wood of the deck. The man swung at Micah again. Micah lashed out, stabbing the man in the belly before flipping him, his arms firmly wrapped around the man's windpipe. The man turned purple, his hands flailing as he tried to find a contact point with his remaining knife. Nick advanced, catching his hand. With a snap and muffled cry from Boris, the knife fell. Nick knew he'd just broken the assassin's wrist. His cry turned to a gurgle as he slumped. Micah brought his body down to rest on the deck without a sound. His eyes rolled up in his head. They quickly bound and gagged him in case he woke up, and tied him slumped against the deck rail. They needed information from him.

Nick assessed Micah's chest. "Leave it. It's a cut. Let's go."

The two crept towards the cabin and slipped into the richly furnished room. The waiter lay crumpled in the corner, a single bullet wound in his chest. Mrs. Baryshev sat sobbing on the bed, closely flanked by Colt, his gun still held at the ready. Milo glowered in a chair, a red stain blotting the once ivory fabric from a wound in his arm. Every eye fixed on the center of the room where Sasha knelt, his hands linked behind his head.

"Hawk, translate this crazy Russian," Titus commanded, hate rippling in his eyes.

"It isn't good to harass my friends when you are the one on your knees," Nick said in Russian, lowering his gun as he stood in front of the man who commanded Janus, who had set a tail on Kaylan and Natalie, who provided weapons to kill thousands and somehow still slept at night. How did God view men like this and not look at them with hatred? Nick's blood boiled.

"Nikolai Carmichael, we meet at last. Tell me, is it everything you had hoped for?"

Nick didn't want to chat with the man. He wanted him dead. But in American hands was better than nothing.

"What do you want, Sasha?"

"What every man wants. Money, power, freedom."

"Not every man wants that. I'm tired of your games. You're coming with us." Nick nodded to Titus. "Cuff him and let's get out of here."

Micah slipped from the room to secure Boris before he regained consciousness while Jay searched the downed waiter. "He started shooting when we came in. I don't think he was just hired for the night."

Titus wrestled Sasha's hands behind his back as Colt and Jay pulled Milo and Mrs. Baryshev to their feet. "Stay silent," Nick said in Russian to the trembling Russian woman. Tears streaked her face as her frantic gaze darted to her husband. She nodded as Colt led her from the room.

Over the radio, Micah announced Boris had been secured on a Zodiac.

"Three more coming to you," Jay said. He yanked Milo's arm. "Keep your mouth shut, or I'll make sure you are absent a few teeth. Understand?"

"Yes." Hatred flashed from the young man's eyes, as Nick studied him. Milo hadn't been willing to go down in flames. He'd surrendered. There might be hope to flip him and use him as an asset after all. Jake would have his work cut out for him.

Titus wrestled Sasha to his feet. The man sneered. "You know what will happen to Kaylan and Natalia should I disappear, Nikolai?" Nick's blood chilled at the man's smug grin. "Vlad has orders to terminate." He spat every word. His eerie confidence even in custody raised a red flag in Nick's head.

As Titus went to tighten his hold, Sasha yanked his arm free, grabbed a small gun, and pointed it at Jay's retreating back. Nick didn't hesitate. He pulled the trigger. The bullet hit Sasha's head, and he fell back.

Jay whipped around, his gun at the ready, his breathing even as Nick and Titus both approached the Russian, ready for another fight. But the body did not move, and the eyes were vacant. "He must have had a gun stashed in a holster on his leg," Titus said. They lowered their weapons as Titus shook his head. Nick stared into the eyes of the most-wanted arms dealer in the world. Blank. Nothing.

The snake was dead.

But had Nick just signed a death warrant for Kaylan and Natalie?

They arrived back at the USS *Dwight D. Eisenhower* as the sun began to peek its head over the Mediterranean. The adrenaline had faded, leaving Nick with a dull pounding between his eyes and a growing worry for Kaylan and Natalie. His feet hit the deck, and he ducked on instinct as the blades twisted above him. Micah winced next to him.

"We need to get you to the doc." Nick slapped him on the back. "You're going to have a pretty nasty scar."

"Chicks dig scars." He winced again, his hand resting on his stomach. "But seriously, it's a good thing I just got my tetanus shot. Next time, I'll let you deal with knife-wielding crazies all by yourself, and I'll handle the fancy shooting."

"How nice of you."

Nick helped his teammates pass off a now catatonic Mrs. Baryshev and a sullen Milo. Nick had broken the news to Mrs. Baryshev once they'd cleared Vieux Port. She'd tried to jump overboard three times before they finally managed to sedate her.

After paperwork and a hurried explanation in Russian to Mrs. Baryshev, Nick followed his team below deck to debrief. As they entered the room, Nick knew something was wrong. He scanned the activity. Maps, charts, computers, and hushed tones, and Jake in the middle of it.

A sick feeling formed in Nick's stomach as he scanned the room once and then again. He fought down panic. "Jake."

One look said it all.

"How?"

"She slipped her tail, ditched the tracking device we hid on her, and disappeared."

Fear ripped through Nick and after a long night, control slid to the background. He grabbed Jake's collar and slammed him up against the wall. The room came alive with shouts. "I told you not to trust her! I told you not to use her! But you didn't listen. And now look."

"That's enough, Hawk. Get off of him." Jay and Colt ripped Nick back, his arms firmly pinned. Titus stepped in front of him, his hand on Nick's heaving chest. "Pull it together, Hawk." He looked to Jake. "How can we help?"

Jake straightened his now wrinkled shirt and slipped a button back in place. His gaze found Nick's. "We'll find her. But I need your help."

Nick fought for clarity. Colt and Jay maintained a firm grip on his arms and the pressure smacked him back to his senses. He took a steadying breath and straightened. He felt Colt and Jay's eyes on him and knew the moment they trusted he was back in control. He needed coffee. He needed to call Kaylan. He needed this nightmare to end. Now.

"I need someone to check in on Kaylan, keep an eye on her. And my . . . sister." A few heads swung in his direction. He saw Titus temper his surprise. "I just found out a few months ago, but she's Anya's daughter, too. And Anya wanted to see her. I'm not sure if that was a ruse or the truth. But I need to know they are both safe. Anya has gone after Kaylan before, and Sasha intimated Vlad would put a hit on both Kaylan and Natalie if he didn't check in after tonight's meeting."

Jake fired orders to a couple of people in the room. "Someone get on the phone with Caden and make sure he has a protection detail watching the girls. Check the airport and all her known aliases."

"She's smart, Jake." Nick took a step towards his friend. That term was relative at the moment. Colt and Jay stepped with him, and Nick smirked. "I promise I'm not going to bite him."

"I'm not entirely confident in your assessment of your emotions right now, brah. But I'm tempted to let you." Colt glared at Jake.

"Remind me never to tick you guys off again."

Jay crossed his arms, danger written in his stance. "Someone should have warned you of that in the first place."

"It took years to find her," Titus chimed in. "That woman knows how to blend in to her surroundings. She won't use an alias you are aware of or any accounts you know of. And I highly doubt she will set foot anywhere near California now that she's free and we got what we wanted." He turned to Nick. "But either way, we need to get home."

Jake nodded, shame and pride fighting for prominence in his expression. "We'll find her again, Hawk. We'll put her away for good this time, if she doesn't die on us first."

"What do you mean die on you?"

Jake turned and studied a map laid out on a table. "She has cancer." His gaze collided with Nick's. "She doesn't have long either way."

At Jake's words Nick braced himself to feel something—disappointment, pity, regret—but a hollowness seeped in. She deserved it for all she'd done. And yet . . . no. Nick shook his head. She deserved it. The world would be better off if his mother were dead.

CHAPTER THIRTY-TWO

Anya Petrov tugged the navy silk scarf around her head, tying it fashionably to avoid detection. Donned in an outfit better fitting her previous wardrobe, Anya stepped onto the private runway of her long-ago friend Sebastian. They'd met when she had masqueraded as a student at university ages past. Back when she was pregnant but not showing. Back when her heart ached so much from losing Thomas and Andrei that she wondered if she would survive.

"Thalia, my beauty, so good to see you again." She hadn't heard that alias in years, but she'd learned to don each new name like a thicker layer of skin. It was no wonder after all these years, little affected her. At least little that she acknowledged.

As Sebastian grasped her hands in his, she mustered a smile. "My old friend. The years have been kind." She searched his face for the boy she'd once known. The boy who could talk French politics, European business, and dreamed of owning his own company one day. A dream he had turned into a reality judging from the mansion that adorned the distant horizon. "Thank you for offering your plane. I lost my son recently, and"—she held a hand to her heart, feigning emotion—"I just need some time."

"Of course, of course, *ma chérie.* Anything for an old friend." He gestured to the plane. "It will take you as far as Iceland, where my pilot will stop and take care of some business for me. From there you will be on your own. I trust it will at least get you started on your journey."

"You are so kind." She gripped his hand as he ushered her up the steps and into a small but nice private cabin.

"It's lovely." My, how she had missed the finer things of life. She mustered energy to finish her ruse. She'd forgotten how exhausting this alias had once been.

He kissed her on both cheeks. "Ah, the memories you arouse in me. We were young once."

"Such a long time ago."

"Ages gone by. *C'est la vie.*" He sighed. "*Au revoir* and *bon voyage.*" He waved at his pilot as he exited the plane.

Anya sank into the couch as a young woman approached. "Can I get you anything?"

"Bourbon," Anya croaked as she lay down and closed her eyes. Seeing Sebastian made her remember the early days. Because of her size, she'd hid her belly beneath loose clothes until two months before her due date. She disappeared but continued to send reports to her officers from the field. A middle-aged woman, a neighbor in the hovel Anya had hidden in, helped her deliver not one but two squawling babies. It had taken three days for Anya to devise a plan. Three days to determine the best chance for herself. The best chance for her babies. She secretly delivered them to the U.S. Mission Berlin, which operated as a sort of embassy in West Berlin during the Cold War, with a message that their father was a soldier at the wall with the last name Murphy.

A few months later, she returned, meeting with a secret contact within the embassy. She'd learned of two babies who had been dropped off. She'd learned of their return to America, of the Murphys wanting nothing to do with them, and of their placements in homes. Separate homes in California.

Satisfied, she buried the memory of two red-faced infants as she continued her work for the Stasi, posing in a variety of roles to garner information, sometimes at the expense of lives. She asked few questions, only doing what she was told, operating on auto pilot until the day Sasha made her an offer she couldn't refuse. She left the Stasi and began working as his right hand, selling weapons to many of the contacts she'd established over the years. With a growing pocket, she grew accustomed to luxuries, an even greater degree of anonymity, and the power her gender brought her when necessary.

"Madam?"

Anya opened her eyes and accepted the crystal glass as the pilot asked them to take their seats and buckle up. The plane taxied down the private runway and lifted into the air. Anya breathed a sigh of relief, memories of the past left in ribbons in the French countryside. She didn't have time for regret or nostalgia. She only had time for escape, for she would need every bit of luck and skill to avoid the traps Nick and Jake might lay to catch her again.

CHAPTER THIRTY-THREE

"It's too early to be up," Megan groaned as Kaylan held open the door to the coffee shop on Tuesday morning.

"If you hadn't stayed up watching Netflix until all hours of the night, you wouldn't be this tired."

"Wrong." Megan pointed at her roommate. "If we hadn't run out of coffee, I wouldn't be this tired."

They slipped behind a woman in spandex still rocking back and forth from her morning run. "I hate morning people."

Kaylan laughed at her roommate's grumbling. "Cheer up. We'll get some coffee in you, grab a bagel. We'll both get to work on time. And I'll even swing by and grab some coffee tonight before I come home. Deal?"

"Can you grab creamer? And some cookies? And maybe a pizza?"

"Why don't you just make a list?"

"I'll text it to you once I set up a caffeine drip."

They stepped up to the counter and Kaylan scanned the menu options. "I'll take a vanilla latte and one of your poppy seed bagels, please." Kaylan pulled money from her wallet as Megan slumped against the counter top.

The shaggy-haired guy behind the register winced. "That rough a night, huh?" The spacer in his ear made his lobe dangle at an odd angle. Kaylan watched it swing as he addressed Megan. "What's your poison?"

Megan selected something strong and sweet with a pastry, and the two stepped out of the way.

"So what's new at the aquarium?"

"It's cleaning day. We inherited a seal from the San Diego zoo. I guess he wasn't getting along, but I think he just wanted some attention."

The barista called their names and Kaylan and Megan grabbed their orders and slipped into a table in the corner. Kaylan took a sip of coffee. "I'm rubbing off on you."

"In what way?"

"A myriad of lovely things, but you are adopting strays now, too."

"I won't be bringing a seal home, Kaylan. At least not of the flipper variety."

Kaylan offered a knowing smile. "Uh huh."

Megan glared. "What do you mean 'uh huh'?"

"I've seen the way you and Jay flirt."

"Please. That is fighting not flirting."

Kaylan just shook her head. "For you, it can be the same thing. Be careful with Jay, Meg. Y'all are in two different places now."

"I know. He doesn't love Jesus." She took a gulp and gasped. "Too hot."

"Hopefully someday."

"Hopefully."

They ate in silence. Megan became more alert with every sip. Kaylan relaxed into her chair, enjoying the time to people watch. It'd become a hobby since she moved to California. People fascinated her, but an unusual breed seemed to flock to the West Coast, and that fascinated her more. Whether they came for the sun, the surf, or the freedom of expression, they came in droves, quickly making the sunny state their home. She'd added to their number, but she missed the Southern ways of Alabama.

The bell chimed above the wooden door, and a man in a suit stepped into the sunny, casual interior of the coffee shop. Kaylan bolted upright in her chair, causing Megan to swallow hard. "What's wrong?" Her gaze swung to the man.

"Is that . . ."

"You have got to be kidding me."

"Please tell me this is a coincidence."

But Kaylan only shook her head. Nick didn't believe in coincidences, and consequently, neither did Kaylan, especially not where nosy Russians in designer suits were concerned. "Call Caden, Meg. We need to go." They stood to leave, grabbing their coffee.

Vlad's gaze swung to them as they hurried to the door, and Kaylan's suspicions were confirmed. Either he was a pro at hiding his emotions, which she suspected was true, or he wasn't surprised to see them at all, which Kaylan suspected was also true. He stood up and blocked their path to the door.

"*Zdrastvutye,* Kaylan and Megan. What a beautiful morning it appears to be." He stopped in front of them and clasped his hands behind his back.

Megan hung up and nodded at Kaylan. Kaylan watched her swallow the fear swirling just beneath the surface before turning to face Vlad. She rolled her eyes. "Another morning person. I knew I didn't like you."

Kaylan smothered a smile, despite the situation. She tried to move past him, but he blocked her again. "What are you doing here, Vlad?"

He glanced at his Rolex. "I'm awaiting an important phone call."

"And you had to do it at this coffee shop? By our house?" She tried to pass him again, but he stepped closer.

He smiled slowly, and Kaylan was once again reminded of the Cheshire cat. "Why, yes. Still diving into American culture and all. It's best to experience it in a normal American neighborhood and visit the places the locals inhabit."

"I think you need to inhabit someplace else," Megan suggested, but her tone spat ice. "And you need to move. We called in the cavalry, they'll be here any minute."

"A pity I won't meet them. Besides, I should be gone soon." He held up his phone, the screen as black as his intentions. "The next phone call will let me plan my departure as well as what needs to take place in the meantime." His friendly mask disappeared. "I suspect we will be seeing one another very soon, Miss Richards." With a final glance at his watch he turned on his heel and joined the line.

"That is not good," Megan muttered under her breath as they hurried out the door.

Kaylan nodded, anxiety weighing heavy. She was careful not to give Vlad a parting glance as they exited the coffee shop and walked to their cars. "I'll call Caden and tell him we got out of there and are leaving. But the men he dispatched will probably show up to question this guy."

"What's with this guy, Kayles? Why does he keep showing up?"

"I think it has to do with wherever Nick and Micah are right now. And unfortunately he made it personal."

"I don't want to do this again."

Kaylan pulled her in for a quick hug. "It's going to be okay. I promise. Caden will probably give us a protection detail now. The guys will be home soon. Then hopefully it will all be over. We just have to hang in there." Kaylan reassured herself with the words.

Wherever they were, the guys had left in a hurry to finish something big, something that somehow included Vlad. That he remained behind filled Kaylan with dread. She fired a text at Natalie to remind her to be on the lookout. Something wasn't right, and Kaylan wouldn't rest easy until the guys returned and Vlad left. Sooner rather than later, she hoped.

Anya deplaned in Iceland on a small runway. A couple of smaller commercial planes and a handful of private planes sat on the tarmac. Despite the wintry February weather, only a light snowfall mixed with rain fell to the ground. She thanked the powers-that-be for the warm coat she had thought to purchase before leaving France. She shifted her bag on her shoulder and hurried to the small building that took care of baggage and booking. Her contact would meet her there with the necessary means to get to Canada and then to the Caribbean. She would breathe easier when she shed this coat and walked into balmy weather. Literally. The cold air clawed at her lungs. She coughed into her glove. Struggling to level her breathing, she stepped through the glass doors into warmth.

"Elsa, it has been years." Gregor's bottle-dyed hair hid one aspect of his aging but could not hide the toll it had taken on his face and hands. Wrinkles abounded. Anya ran her fingers over her face, scared for a moment that the aging was contagious. Years of treatments and surgery kept her features somewhat smooth, but the past few months in jail had aged her.

"Good to see you. Do you have what I need?" She slipped into another old alias, recalling her cover and the memories with Gregor in the early years of her work with Sasha. His grasp of finance and quick climb into the ranks as one of the most trusted financial advisors in Iceland made him a prime candidate to gather information. And a prime source for funneling shipments.

He extended an envelope. "The envelope you mailed me a year ago. Passport, bank records, all never used and waiting for such a time as this. Just like you asked." His mouth turned to a thin line. "I trust no one will know I aided you?"

"You will not be suspected." He'd been out of the game a long while, and Anya had been careful over the years to erase any tracks that might lead to him.

"Your plane to Quebec leaves in two hours. I trust you have plans from there."

"*Da.* All is arranged. *Spasiba*, Gregor."

His pale gray eyes grew watchful as he studied her. "We will not meet again in this lifetime, I suspect."

She forced her muscles to smile. "*Dasvidanya,* Gregor. I'll see you in hell."

He chuckled. "The only place for people like us."

She couldn't resist the hand she rested on his cheek for only a moment. His eyes held a hint of surprise that Anya felt deep within. He might be the last familiar face she would see, maybe ever. She turned on her heel and hurried away. She was growing sentimental in her old age. But sentimentality had no room in escape.

CHAPTER THIRTY-FOUR

"How many more boxes do you have?" Megan huffed as they entered Kaylan and Nick's apartment on Wednesday night.

"Hey, I'm just bringing things over little by little. I don't have that much."

"Millionaires have less than you." Megan rested her hands on her hips and took a deep breath as Liza entered with another box.

"Girl, what's wrong with you?" she asked, laughing as Megan took another deep breath.

"Megan needs to go running with me more often. That's the problem."

Liza dropped the box on the couch and straightened. "Then how do you stay ramrod skinny without working out?"

"Who says I don't work out? I don't exactly have a desk job, you know."

"Uh huh."

Kaylan laughed. "All right, all right. Let me pop the pizza in the oven while we unpack these, and then we can hang out or call it a night."

"Titus isn't home, so I don't have any plans." Liza shook her head, her kinky black hair swaying with the movement. "You just wait 'til you and Hawk get married. Your universe will start centering around him, and unless you are hanging out with us, you won't know what to do with yourself."

Kaylan closed the oven. "That doesn't sound so bad."

Megan sighed. "One half of an old married couple already, ladies and gentlemen."

"Just wait until it's your turn, smarty." Kaylan shoved her friend. "Let's clean out these boxes so we can eat when the timer goes off."

Kaylan lifted the flap and pulled out a few blankets and picture frames. Liza held up a photo album. "What's this from?"

"Haiti." Kaylan smiled, the memories always a little bittersweet. Not even the earthquake could shake the joy of the people she'd fallen in love with or the place that felt a little like home, but an ache still filled her as she remembered the images her lens hadn't captured, the images that sometimes still haunted her dreams.

"Mind if I . . ."

"Be my guest." Kaylan joined Liza on the couch as she began to flip through photo sleeves.

"Oh, look at that little darling with stickers all over her face. Isn't she cute?" Liza pointed to the photo. "Is that your friend, Sarah Beth?"

"Yeah. And little Sophia. She loved to let us braid her hair. Sarah Beth was her favorite." Megan plopped down next to them on the couch and leaned over Liza's shoulder. "She's actually the one who got help when Sarah Beth and I were trapped."

"How old is she here? Three?"

"I think she was four or five."

Shock flashed across Liza's face. "Shoot, she is small."

"A lot of the kids we worked with there are smaller than their age. That's pretty common in Haiti. Because of a lack of proper nutrition, some kids can look two or three years younger than they actually are."

Liza flipped through more pages. "How do you fix that?"

"Slowly. One person at a time."

As Liza turned pages, she remembered moments with Abraham and some students from the local seminary and little Reuben and his soccer games.

"Who is that handsome baby?"

Kaylan leaned in to see the photo Rhonda had snapped of Kaylan, Tasha, and baby Kenny after their first meeting with the moms. Tasha's eyes glowed. It was the night Eliezer had come, the night Tasha told Kaylan she believed in Jesus. "That's baby Kenny and his mom, Tasha. She died in the earthquake." Talking made it easier to purge the sorrow and remember the good. Honesty could do that to a person.

The timer dinged as Liza turned the last page. "So much for getting everything unpacked," Megan said as she stood and stretched.

Kaylan popped open the oven, the scent of pepperoni and cheese wafting through the apartment. "Good thing we have fuel to help us unpack the three boxes we brought in." Kaylan rolled her eyes at her roommate. "You whine a lot."

"Just keeping you on your toes, Kayles." Megan grabbed a few paper plates and napkins and set three place settings on the small table right outside the kitchen nook. Liza joined them at the table.

A ring tone cut through their chatter. Kaylan glanced at the caller ID. "Hey, Natalie. What's up?"

"That creepy Russian guy showed up while I was at the grocery store today. I mean, what is that about? I live like three hours away from you!"

"Did you call Caden?"

"Yeah. There are a couple guys following me around everywhere now, thank goodness."

"Good." Kaylan looked out the apartment window and noticed the car parked near their building. She knew Caden had guys close for her, too. He wasn't taking chances after this morning. "He dropped in on Megan and me yesterday morning at our local coffee shop." Kaylan hit speaker and set the phone on the table.

"He's creepy and threatening, but all he did was make small talk and say he was experiencing culture and something about waiting on a phone call. Complete and total nonsense. I told him he could find far better ways to integrate into American culture than stalking me at my grocery store. That didn't seem to faze him much."

Kaylan smothered a smile. "That was brave."

"Are you kidding me? I was shaking in my really comfy Converse. I'm ready for this to end, Kayles. Is Nick there?"

"No." She glanced up at Megan and Liza. "Hopefully he is in the process of ending all this as we speak. I'm so sorry I got you involved in this, Natalie."

"Yeah, well. The guys following me are pretty cute. Who knew brothers could be so much trouble."

"I could have told you that."

"When he gets back, tell him I'm cashing in on his first act of brotherly protection. He has an annoying, creepy Russian that I would like out of my state."

"I'm sure he will be more than happy to take care of that for you." If he could. Kaylan worried what Vlad's threats actually meant. His words to Kaylan and Megan kept replaying through her mind. Something was off. He wouldn't leave until he accomplished why he came.

"Keep me posted, Natalie. Why don't you come spend the weekend with me and Megan?"

"Oh, you know. I have such a crazy social life, I'll have to clear everything." Her sarcasm made Megan laugh.

"I'll be there. See you sometime late Friday night."

"Deal." The call ended, but the worried look on Liza's face only increased.

"Girl, you tend to tick off the wrong people. You've got some sort of danger magnet attached to you."

Kaylan stood and grabbed their empty plates. "I think it is actually attached to Nick and I attract the trouble by default."

"We need to hire you a permanent bodyguard."

"I'd settle for Nick being home, but the guys Caden got will do for the time being."

"That, too." Liza rose to unpack the rest of the boxes. "I heard they might be home pretty soon. No promises though. I don't want them to come home until they finish their business. All of them are too distracted otherwise."

Kaylan agreed. Her wedding was only weeks away, but with the danger surrounding them, she was more concerned with living that long than she was about the final details. She silently prayed for protection for her, for Nick, for their loved ones, and for justice to be served and the threats to end.

CHAPTER THIRTY-FIVE

Anya's plane touched down at Jean Lesage International Airport in Quebec City. She deplaned, clutching her shoulder bag like a lifeline. One more stop. She scrolled through the list of flights displayed on the screen and grunted in disgust. Two. Two more stops. A flight to Cancun departed at 3:30 p.m. She checked the time glowing on the digital screens. She had an hour. From Cancun she would head to St. Lucia, where a beautiful beach condo awaited her.

"Elsa Eriksson, you have a message at Information," a voice over the intercom relayed in three different languages. The bustle of the airport continued around her, but Anya couldn't move. Someone knew she was here. Was it a trap?

No.

The only one who knew that alias after all this time was Gregor. Maybe he forgot to tell her something. She didn't have a phone, after all, wouldn't even dream of it with the CIA on her tail. She forced one foot in front of the other, noting exit routes as she went. If she needed to find a place to lie low until she could get to the Caribbean, then so be it.

She brushed her hair out of her face, wishing for a tube of hair dye to cover the gray, and tugged the scarf back over her head. She stepped up to the Information counter, recalling her French. "You have a message for Elsa Eriksson."

"*Oui.* Can I see identification?"

Anya breathed a sigh of relief that she hadn't yet switched passports. The woman checked her photo and name and then handed her a sealed envelope. "Someone dropped it off for you."

"Probably my friend who flew out before me. *Merci.*"

She checked her steps as she slipped inside the nearest restroom and cocooned herself in a stall. The roar of the hand dryer vied with the rush of people trying to make their flights in the concourse just outside. Anya ripped into the envelope.

My dear Elsa,

Information reached me after your departure that may be of some interest to you. Sasha's men have identified your son and daughter. Orders to kill them have been issued since no one has heard from Sasha in twenty-four hours. I know you have not had contact with them since their birth, but I felt you should know the information.

Yours, Gregor

Anya crumpled the note and stuffed it in her bag. Of course it didn't matter. She'd been no kind of mother. They'd chosen to go after Sasha; they must now deal with the consequences.

She swung open the metal stall door, stalked from the restroom, and made her way to the ticket counter. It didn't matter. She would board a plane for Mexico and put this life behind her. She'd done what she set out to do all those years ago. She'd been patient, earning the trust of the man who killed her brother, all while benefiting from the contacts and money she made under his business. She'd earned their loyalty, earned his. And now, she had orchestrated enough to see him dead. Or at least she assumed.

Nickolai and Natalia would have to learn what she had—the weak do not survive. Only those who look out for themselves. She stopped behind two people in line at the ticket counter. The flight list shifted every few seconds on the board above the luggage belt.

A flight to British Columbia departed in forty-five minutes. She could do it. Be a mother. She could fly west to British Columbia and then south to San Diego. Redeem a life of greed and running and plotting revenge. Or she could live out the rest of her days in peace and freedom. It was what she deserved after all this time.

"Next."

Nothing stood between her and her condo. She stepped up to the ticket counter. "Yes?"

She couldn't find her voice. She glanced at the flight list again. Cancun or British Columbia? She could use the alias, either way. If she flew to California, she would never be able to use her alias again, and her carefully laid plans for escape would be for naught. And they would be waiting for her, ready to take her back into custody. She wouldn't be able to save her children. She wouldn't be able to save herself.

With a last look at the digital screen, she pulled her new passport from her bag and slapped it on the counter. "One ticket, please," she said in her best French.

Anya would do what she'd always done. She would choose her freedom.

She just hoped she wouldn't regret it.

CHAPTER THIRTY-SIX

Okay, okay, my turn." Natalie jumped from the couch and stuck her hand in the bowl. She opened a folded piece of paper. "Shoot. I'm going to have to think about this one for a second."

"You have thirty seconds." Megan turned over a plastic minute glass on the coffee table.

"I'll check on the cookies." Kaylan tossed a pillow at Megan as she stood from the couch.

"Make sure they are good and gooey!" Megan called after her.

It was ten on a Friday night, and they were two games into charades, one bag of popcorn down, and on their second batch of chocolate chip cookies. Kaylan deemed the night a success. She fired up her phone and scanned through her emails. Nothing from the guys. She wondered when they would be home, wondered more if she needed to postpone the wedding if Nick didn't make it back by the week before.

"Time is up," Megan shouted.

"How can you tell? That thing is supposed to give you a minute," Natalie argued.

"I eyeballed it. It looked about half full on the bottom and half full on the top. So now you have to go or forfeit your turn."

"Fine."

Megan waited until the last grain slipped through the narrow passageway. Kaylan sank into the couch and grabbed a handful of popcorn. "Okay, on your mark, get set—"

"Knock, knock. Got room for two more?" The door hinges groaned as Nick and Micah stepped through the door.

Kaylan jumped off the couch and into Nick's arms. Sandy danced around their legs, barking. "You're home! Why didn't you tell me?"

"We wanted to fly under the radar. Everything quiet? Anything I need to know about?" He glanced around the room and his gaze collided with Natalie. "Hi."

"Hi." Natalie's quiet response had Kaylan scrambling to fill the silence. "It's quiet. Our friend is around and watching the house. You can relax. Unless there's something I need to know?"

Nick only raised a brow and squeezed her hand, his shoulders still tense.

Micah bumped Nick aside. "If I don't get a hug in the next five seconds, I am boycotting this wedding. I'm your older brother. I still rank."

"Yes, you do." Kaylan wrapped her arms around Micah's chest.

"Ow." He pulled back a bit. "Just maybe be more gentle about it."

Kaylan felt the crackle of a bandage beneath his shirt as her hand fell from his back. "What happened?"

"Oh, you know. Got in a fight with a ninja. He got in a good slice, but I crushed him. Ladies dig scars, right?"

Kaylan fought back frustration, knowing she would probably never get the straight story. "At least a ninja is slightly more believable than the shark story you told me last year."

"Dang, I'll have to get more creative again next time."

"Seriously, Micah."

"Seriously, Kayles." He lowered his voice. "I was just doing my job. But if you really want to take care of me, you can help me take my boots off and bring me a few cookies." He sniffed the air. "Those smell delicious." His grin appeared, his humor firmly in place.

"No to your boots. Yes to your cookies. Have you met Natalie?" She pointed to the blonde still standing in the middle of the room taking everything in. "Natalie, this is my brother, Micah."

"Nice to meet you." She extended her hand. "I'm his sister, I guess?" she pointed at Nick.

"Oh, now all the pieces are falling into place. Welcome to our merry band of misfits. The Air Force thing might be a problem, but we won't tell anybody," Micah whispered.

"I see my reputation precedes me."

Nick shook free from his shock. He approached and put his arm around her shoulders, patting her awkwardly for a second. "Good to see you."

She wrinkled her nose and grinned. "We'll have to work on that hugging thing."

His baritone chuckle warmed Kaylan to her toes. He was home. He was safe.

"So did you take care of business?" She plopped down on the couch across from Nick, her eyes taking in every inch of him, making sure he was intact.

He nodded slowly. "We did. We're done." His eyes drifted to Micah for the slightest moment.

"So no more Russians stalking us at coffee shops or grocery stores?" Megan chimed in.

Nick narrowed his gaze at Kaylan. "That counts as something I need to know. He's still doing that? When did you see him?"

Kaylan glared at her roommate, not wanting to focus on that right now. "Caden took care of it. There are still guys around here somewhere. Vlad may be gone by now. None of us have seen him in a few days."

"We are done with him now, right?" Megan prompted again. This time Nick and Micah didn't answer.

Micah cleared his throat. "So what are we playing?"

"Charades. Now we can do guys versus girls," Natalie answered.

"Um, I think we may need to divide into different teams," Nick said, casting a wary eye on the bowl filled with torn pieces of paper.

"C'mon, Hawk. We can totally take them. We've got this."

"I mean if you are too chicken to play against us, I understand. We can divide the groups," Kaylan teased.

"Or how about we add two more?" The screen door slammed as Vlad and a bearded man stepped into the room. True to character, Vlad appeared ready to attend a high-level business meeting in his designer suit and tie. The man next to him stood in head-to-toe black, a gun with a silencer at the ready in his hand.

Micah and Nick bounced to their feet, and Sandy charged, hackles raised and vicious barking echoing through the house. In one quick move, the man next to Vlad aimed and fired, the silencer muffling the sound.

Kaylan screamed as Sandy fell and whimpered. Nick and Micah started forward, but Vlad held out a hand. "Slow movements, gentlemen. My colleague is highly trained but not in the mood to be killed tonight. You will be on the floor next to the dog if you take another step."

Nick held up his hands, moving in front of Kaylan and the girls. "Let's go outside. Leave the girls alone."

Vlad shook his head. "I am sorry, but I cannot do that. I warned you if you continued to pursue my employer, I would be forced to act." He held out his hands. "Alas, I am acting, which means I assume Sasha is dead."

Micah and Nick only stared. Kaylan saw controlled rage in their expression. She fought to stay still, her focus trained on the scene in front of her. If she could just get to her bedroom and the gun, but she wouldn't make it two steps without being stopped by Vlad's colleague holding a much bigger gun. Or maybe Caden's men would come? She looked to the door, her heart sinking. If they were able, they would be here already. Vlad must have taken care of them before coming inside.

"Why are you here?" Micah spat, his body now blocking the view of the living room, where Natalie crouched on the floor and Megan and Kaylan huddled on the couch. Kaylan could barely breathe. She fought for calm and clarity, her instincts tuned to any movement the guys made.

"We know that Janus helped you kill Sasha. It recently came to our attention that she had two children that she gave up as infants. It seems she kept tabs on both of you"—Vlad's eyes roamed to Natalie—"your whole lives. Since we can't find her, we can make sure she gets the message that her treachery will not go unpunished."

Kaylan bristled at the way Vlad looked at Natalie. "Nick and Natalie have nothing to do with her. She is related in blood only. Natalie has never even met her."

Vlad's attention fixed on Kaylan, which she preferred. Anything to get Natalie and Megan out of this mess. Neither of them had asked for any of it. Kaylan had accepted it when she said yes to a SEAL with a complicated past.

Vlad smiled. "That may be true, Miss Richards, but her attentiveness to them over the years, though calculated and distant, suggests that cold-hearted traitor cared on some level. I am sorry, but you are just another means to an end. Since we cannot just take two of you, we must take all of you. If you please ..." He indicated the door.

"Leave the girls. Take us." Micah stepped forward. The man with the gun tensed but remained stationary.

Vlad looked Micah up and down. "Like I said, Natalie and even Kaylan are now non-negotiable. You on the other hand . . ."

"Why, you . . ." Micah jerked to a stop as the man in black leveled the barrel of his gun at Kaylan's forehead.

"Careful, Mr. Richards."

With one swift move, Vlad nailed Micah on the head with the butt of his gun. The crack echoed in the room, and Kaylan screamed in outrage as Micah slumped to the ground.

"Don't move, Miss Richards, or I'll make it a bullet to the head instead of just a bump," Vlad reiterated as tears began to trek down her face. Micah wasn't moving, and she couldn't tell if he was breathing. Everything in her screamed to run to her brother. She caught the slight shake of Nick's head out of the corner of her eye and forced herself to stay put.

Chills swept over Kaylan's body as she stared at the cold metal aimed at her face. She felt Nick's fingers thread through hers and squeeze from where he stood by the couch's armrest.

"Let's start over, shall we?" Vlad grimaced. The gun lowered and Kaylan sucked in a breath, immediately aware of her galloping pulse. "You will drop your cell phones on the table and come with us. You will not scream or yell or make a noise to arouse any suspicion from your neighbors, including"—he narrowed his already squinty eyes at

Kaylan again—"that nosy woman next door. Does everyone understand? And you"—he motioned to Nick— "will disarm and tie your friend in case he wakes up. We can't have him alerting anyone that you are missing for quite a while. By the time he can, we will be long gone."

Nick stiffened even more. Kaylan waited, and finally Nick slowly removed his phone and tossed it on the end table next to the couch. "Now if you please, my associate will ensure that we do not get ourselves into a complicated situation with any hidden weapons before we enter the vehicle."

The man with the gun holstered the weapon and began patting Nick down as Vlad drew his own weapon and pointed it at Micah's forehead as he lay still on the floor. Then he moved to Micah, removing a knife and cell phone from his pocket before throwing them to the corner of the room.

Vlad tossed zip ties to Nick. "Bind your friend's hands and feet. Tightly." With a slow step Nick knelt in front of Micah and did as he was asked. "That's right," Vlad continued. "Now stand slowly, and no one will get hurt." His tone held a warning that couldn't be ignored.

Kaylan fought panic, praying Nick wouldn't do something rash. Nick's expression was chiseled in stone. Kaylan knew his mind was on overdrive, thinking through scenarios and solutions. She also knew he would sacrifice himself before he let anything happen to one of the girls. A sinking feeling flowed through Kaylan. He might die tonight.

"Ladies, if you please." Vlad motioned that they should stand and discard their phones. Without a word, they followed his instruction.

Vlad aimed his weapon at Megan and Kaylan. "Now it's your turn." He nodded the girls over to the man in black.

Megan immediately bristled. "I don't think so. There's no way I'm letting him run his hands all over me."

Vlad turned cold eyes to Megan, and Kaylan found herself wishing Megan didn't have such a big mouth. "And how do I know you aren't carrying a knife in your pocket?"

Megan crossed her arms, but Kaylan saw a slight tremble in her fists. "I guess you will have to take my word for it, but he is not touching me." Kaylan remembered the men in the boatshed and the bruises she and Megan had both sustained. A sick feeling pulsed through her. Her roommate didn't think they would make it out of this either, and she planned to go down with a fight and her dignity intact.

Vlad stood toe-to-toe with Megan. Natalie flinched in Kaylan's periphery, but she didn't dare move. Her legs trembled, and she prepared to pounce if necessary. Vlad's hand shot out and pinched Megan's cheeks, her lips puckering under his grip. "Your word, my dear"—his voice was deadly calm—"means nothing at all." He nodded at the man in black, his grip never lessening on Megan's face as the man checked for concealed objects.

"Let her go. She didn't do anything," Natalie said.

"Ah, Natalia. I wondered if you had the same fire as your mother and brother." Vlad tossed Megan's head back as he released her. Red fingerprints marked his presence. Megan licked her now trembling lips.

"My name is Natalie. And I don't know about any mother, but if I have the same fire as my brother, I think I'm in good company. Leave Megan out of this. She's got nothing to do with it."

Kaylan had to smother a smile, despite the severity of the situation. A flicker of hope hovered in the air. She was surrounded by fighters. They might make it out of this yet.

Vlad turned his focus back to Megan. He cocked his head to the side like he was examining livestock instead of Kaylan's friend. "Natalia has a good point. On second thought, my dear, we don't need you to come." Before any of them could move, he raised his hand, the butt of a pistol flashing, and brought it down on Megan's head. She slumped to the floor next to Sandy, her face pasty and her body too still.

"Megan!" Natalie and Kaylan shouted. They both moved toward their friend, but Vlad leveled them with a look.

"Natalia, you would do well to remember that while the others are collateral damage, you are the true prize. Your friend is lucky. She isn't dead. I can't say the same for your condition by the end of the night." He pulled a gun and two zip ties out of his pocket. He tossed them to his buddy and nodded to Nick. "Tie his hands in front. I want them where I can see them. Then tie up the girl. And these two"—he eyed Natalie and Kaylan—"you might as well bind them too. We don't want them having any heroic ideas on our drive."

Nick didn't so much as flinch as the man slipped the plastic over his wrists and pulled until Kaylan could distinguish a white band of skin. She didn't have to ask him to know he was furious. His eyes raged as stormy as a hurricane despite his deadly calm expression.

Kaylan silenced a squeal as Vlad jerked her head back. Pulling her body back against his, he placed the barrel of the gun against her forehead. His stature put his mouth right at her ear. His spit slapped against her jaw as he spoke. "It seems Miss Richards provides motivation for you to behave. You can follow my colleague out to the car. Give him no problems, and I will walk out of this house with Kaylan." His breath burned her face as he placed a harsh kiss on her cheek. "But if you do not behave, she will never walk out of this house again."

Numb, Kaylan didn't feel anything as her gaze ran over her fiancé—rage evident in the twitching muscle in his jaw, hidden beneath scruff. His gaze collided with hers. Longing swept through her for a normal life by Nick's side. But even in this, they stood together. Protecting those they loved. Possibly dying with those they loved. She could honor him in that. She read his struggle, his instinct to protect battling with his instinct to kill those who threatened the lives of others.

She nodded her head a fraction of an inch and watched his fists clench in response. They would get out of this.

Or they would die together while trying.

Anya slipped through the window in the laundry room and into the hallway in time to see Vlad yank Kaylan against him and put a gun to her head. She shoved her body as close to the wall as she could and struggled to find a better angle. Nikolai stood with restrained hands, and Kaylan's brother and pesky roommate were on the floor. And . . .

Igor Aminev. They really had called in the kill squad. He was one of the most popular men in Eastern Europe to hire when a job needed to be completed. Vlad was merely a puppet, a kept man. Igor was brawn and brains in a deadly package.

Anya silently swore. She needed a weapon, and she needed one now. In her last-minute decision, she hadn't had time to stop for one let alone allow herself to second-guess what she was doing. Moving as quietly as a cat, she slipped into Kaylan's room. The shuffling from the front told her she had little time to keep them in her sights. They were leaving, and she would have to give chase. She knelt at Kaylan's bed and lifted the comforter. If she knew her son, he had left his fiancée a weapon somewhere. She just had to find it. She dropped the material, her eyes sweeping to the closet. Maybe.

The conversation died in the front room. She had to hurry. Shoving clothes aside, she spotted a box. She threw open the lid. Perfect. She grabbed the pistol, loaded it, and crept to the hallway in time to hear the front door click closed. Stupid girl should have kept the gun with her at all times.

Anya sped to the now dark front room and watched through the window as Igor shoved Natalia and Nikolai into the back seat before climbing in next to them. Meanwhile Vlad ushered Kaylan to the front seat. Keeping one eye on the window, she snagged the knife from the floor and quickly cut through Micah and Megan's restraints. Maybe they would be helpful once they woke up. Or they might all die tonight.

She heard the engine start up and bolted to the back door. Watching as the Suburban stopped at the end of the street, she sprinted for her car. Her breath came in harsh gasps. The rental hummed to life and she pressed the gas as hard as she dared. Up ahead, the Suburban took a right at the stop sign and headed down the road.

Stupid. She should have boarded the plane to Mexico. This shouldn't be her problem. But all of the reasons in the world hadn't been enough to stop the words that had slipped from her mouth as she paid for a ticket in cash. She had boarded a plane bound for California, and she hadn't looked back.

They traveled several miles, Anya carefully hiding in traffic. Then they left the suburbs behind and the Suburban hit open road, driving parallel to the ocean. Silvery light cast eerie shadows from the palm trees that lined the road. Anya hung back, careful not to appear to be following. She wasn't sure what she would do, only that she had come this far. She had to do something. Those were her ... well, those were her *something*. Or they had been at one point a long time ago.

Careful to keep the car steady, she reached into the pocket of her jeans and tugged out a stitched piece of fabric. The silvery white light illuminated the ribbed cloth, a faint smudge, and signs of age. She'd kept it in the envelope she'd given Gregor with her final alias and bank information. It was the one piece of her past she'd considered worth safeguarding. The one that made her human.

She clenched the fabric in her fist and gripped the wheel. For once, she would do something she would not regret. She had a suitcase full of regrets. She couldn't, wouldn't die with one more.

They wound through Imperial Beach, the city lights glowing orange inside her car. Finally, they pulled onto Gunpoint Drive. The road wound near the San Diego Bay Wildlife Refuge. Nothing but sand and shrubs. No other cars. Nothing. Her palms began to sweat. She glanced at the pink and blue cloth that peeked from beneath her clenched grip. Now or never.

She accelerated and slammed the Suburban in front of her, sending both cars careening off the highway and into desert sand and undergrowth.

CHAPTER THIRTY-SEVEN

Nick's knees hit the seat back and he used the car's momentum to body slam the man in back in the seat next to him. He fought to wrap his hands around the gun. Branches scratched the undercarriage as the car slid to a halt. Natalie threw her arms around the dazed driver, her bound hands locked firmly around Vlad's neck.

"Kayles, get out of the car," Nick grunted. The man flailed, yelling in Russian as Nick fought for traction. The ding of a car door opening chimed. Kaylan scrambled out the back. The passenger door flew open, and Nick tumbled out of the car, landing on the man. He rolled and jumped to his feet, his eyes frantically searching for the gun.

"Nick!" Kaylan screamed. His legs flew out from under him. He lay on top of scraggly bush. Pressure overwhelmed his chest as the man straddled him, his thumbs locked around Nick's neck. Black and gray swirled patterns danced over the man's face as Nick struggled for consciousness. With a burst of energy, he jerked his bound hands into the man's rib cage. His grip loosened enough for Nick to land another blow.

"Enough!" Kaylan shouted. The man scrambled up, his face going slack as he eyed the gun in Kaylan's shaky hand. Nick pulled himself to his feet, gulping in the night air. He stumbled out of the way, remembering Kaylan's aim in paintball.

"You won't shoot," the man spat, blood and spit striking the dusty ground.

Her eyes were colder than Nick had ever seen them. "You are threatening to kill my family. You are threatening to kill me. I think you underestimate what I will do," Kaylan hissed through clenched teeth.

The man smirked and took a step.

With shaking hands, she fired. The man jumped and the tire deflated with a pop as Kaylan prepared to shoot again.

"That will be all, Miss Richards." Vlad appeared from the driver's seat with a bloody Natalie. Her hands were now cut free, but her nose dripped red, and her hair appeared as if she had put up a good fight. The glazed look in her eyes had Nick worried. She stumbled as Vlad prodded her with the barrel of the gun.

"Igor, take the gun from Miss Richards, please."

He ripped the gun from her hands and pointed it at her chest. Kaylan sucked in a deep breath but refused to close her eyes. Nick had never been more proud. He took a step toward her, but Natalie called out, drawing the attention of both men.

"You wanted me." She jerked from Vlad's grip and slid in front of the gun, in front of Kaylan. "Take me. Leave them here."

Her blonde hair glowed like a halo in the moonlight. Nick glanced at the car that had hit them. He had hoped the passenger would call 9-1-1. Where had they gone?

Nick took another step, eyeing the gun held on his sister and fiancée. "This started with me. It can end with me. Janus never contacted Natalie. She wanted to taunt me. I'll be enough of a prize." He stopped next to his sister. "I'll be your revenge card."

From behind Igor he sensed movement from the still open back seat of the Suburban. Before he could react, Janus flew from the backseat, more wiry and stronger than he'd given her credit for. Firing a shot that went wide, she landed in front of Igor. More shots echoed in the desert air, but Nick had no idea whose weapon discharged. He rushed forward to help. Another gunshot sounded, and Janus fell. But she'd taken Igor by surprise. Nick pressed him to the sand, his arm wrapped around his neck and back of his head. An ugly red stain spread near his stomach. He didn't have long, but Nick wasn't chancing it. Igor thrashed, but Nick clung tighter. Within seconds his body went limp. Nick released and flew off of him, taking in the scene around him, ready for the next fight.

Natalie now had a gun pointed at Vlad, who was on his knees, clearly crippled when his muscle man had been disarmed. Kaylan knelt next to a woman crumpled in the sand.

Janus.

Nick's legs felt like lead as he stumbled to Natalie and quickly used ties that fell out of the car in the scuffle to secure Vlad. Then he moved to Janus. She'd fought for them. She'd sacrificed for them. He fell to his knees, Natalie slumping down next to him. Tears stained his sister's face as she looked at him, Janus's hand gripped in hers. "Is she our mother?"

Nick only nodded. Kaylan propped Janus's head up on her legs, her fingers stroking back her hair.

"You. I can't believe you . . ."

"Pocket," she rasped.

Natalie dug her fingers in one pocket then the other. She tugged loose a dirty, wrinkled piece of cloth, and gave it to Janus. As Janus folded it in her hands, Nick noticed the piece of cloth was actually two pieces stitched together—one side blue and the other pink.

Pain ripped through him as he met her eyes. She nodded slowly, breath wheezing through her lips. She'd kept pieces of their baby blankets all these years. He swallowed the growing lump in his throat and surveyed the damage. Blood poured from a wound in her side. He wasn't sure what had been hit, only that she wouldn't make it.

Anya lifted both hands, resting them on Nick and Natalie's faces. The cloth rubbed against Nick's cheek. Tears welled up unbidden. This woman who had killed so many had spent her last moments to save children she'd given up years earlier. Yet, she'd kept a piece of them. In her final moments, she'd tried to make it right.

Anger and guilt ripped through him, stronger than any pain. How did he look at a woman he had hunted to kill and see his mother, his blood? Red trickled from her mouth, but her lips twisted in a smile. Her eyes were clear. Clear blue. Unmasked. As she gazed up at him and Natalie, he saw adoration.

"My babies," she croaked in Russian. A tear trickled down her cheek. "Look at what you have become." Before he could stop himself, Nick covered her hand with his own. He could feel the life draining from her. She looked small, fragile, vulnerable.

"What did she say?" Natalie asked, choking back a sob.

"She called us her babies."

Nick focused on Anya, her glassy blue eyes, the way she couldn't stop looking at Nick and Natalie, that she hadn't taken her eyes from them since they appeared at her side.

She was dying. For him. For Natalie. She'd come when she could have run. The last pieces of anger fell from his heart, and emotions crashed over him like a wave. This woman lying bleeding before him didn't deserve his forgiveness. But he could give it. She'd sacrificed, her dying act one of selflessness. He could be brave. Forgiving her would take every ounce of courage he had. It battled common sense, but it was right.

Every muscle in his body fought as he leaned over the woman before him. He smoothed her hair and brushed his lips against her cooling forehead. "My mother," he murmured in Russian. A tear trickled down his cheek and landed in her hair.

He felt the breath leave her body as she sighed. "Andrei," he heard before the light faded from her eyes, eyes no longer cold, but at peace. She was gone.

CHAPTER THIRTY-EIGHT

White lights cast a hazy glow in the setting California sun. Mason jars danced in the trees, each with a tiny lit candle inside, daring the wind to snuff the dim glow. Kaylan's breath caught as she stepped onto Nick's back porch and surveyed the scene for their rehearsal dinner.

"Do you like it?" Nick's voice drifted on the breeze as he stepped from the shadow of the tree in the corner of the yard. With one quick breath, he extinguished the flame dancing on the end of a lighter.

Kaylan stepped into the grass, the leaves tracing a silky trail on her sandaled feet as she approached Nick. "It's gorgeous. Y'all didn't have to do all this." She shook her head, taking in the picnic tables waiting for her family and the wedding party. They'd rehearsed earlier in the afternoon and then took a break. Now Kaylan knew why.

She came to a stop in front of him. His hands settled on the small of her waist, pulling her closer to him, and she rested her hands on his chest, feeling the cotton t-shirt soft beneath her palms. "You outdid yourself." She finally met his eyes and her breath caught. The smoky blue danced in the firelight, his defenses completely down.

"You deserve it. After the last few months of putting up with all this." He rested his head on hers, his fingers tracing lazy patterns on her lower back. Chills raced up and down her spine despite the warm night. She tried to focus, pushing away from him a bit.

"It's part of the deal, right?" She snaked her arms up around his neck, burying her fingers in his sandy blonde hair. "I marry the man, his God, and his country. It's a total package." She smiled up at him, the stress of the past months bleeding away in the safety of his arms. It had been four weeks since the events of that fateful night. Four weeks of resting and processing the news of Nick's family and reclaiming peace now that the personal vendetta had finally come to an end.

"You're thinking about it again, aren't you?"

She smiled and ran her fingers over the worry lines now crinkling his forehead. She couldn't hide anything from him anymore. "I am, but not in the way you might think. It seems like a dream." Her gaze drifted to the twinkling trees again as she tried to explain.

Nick's calloused fingers brushed her cheek and gently tilted her chin. "Does it scare you? That it could happen again. Does it make you second-guess us?"

Kaylan slipped her arms around his waist and met his anxious gaze. "Nick Carmichael, I love you with all my heart. I think we have seen the end of this. I know other things will come, but we'll handle them." She traced lazy patterns on his back and felt him shudder and pull her closer. "Does it scare you?"

He wrapped an arm around her waist, threaded their fingers together, and began to sway with her, their steps drifting under the tree. Kaylan leaned into him, letting him think, loving the quiet moment. Country music drifted from the porch, and Kaylan grinned as David stepped away from the iPod speaker and slipped back into the house.

"I like your family."

She could feel the rumble of emotion in his chest and laid her head on his shoulder as she followed his lead. "They like you, too. I think I'll share starting tomorrow." She felt his smile without seeing it as his grip tightened on her waist—protective, possessive, almost desperate.

"You aren't going to lose me, you know. You haven't scared me off yet."

He chuckled. She felt the brush of a kiss on her forehead, and shivered. How could she not feel safe and treasured with this man? "You didn't answer my question, Nick. Talk to me."

She could practically hear his racing thoughts. He stopped and led her over to a bench framing one of the wooden picnic tables they had rented for the night. He settled them and reached for her hands, his thumb brushing over the back. Finally, his eyes found hers. She could see the storm swirling within the blue-gray—confidence and uncertainty fighting for prominence.

"You've said you're scared to lose me, but truth is, I'm terrified you'll lose me, too. I'm terrified that I will miss big moments with you or our kids. I'm terrified that I won't be here when you need me. I'm terrified . . . that you'll change your mind before tomorrow." His voice dropped to a gruff whisper.

Kaylan's heart ripped as Nick acknowledged his fear. She framed his face with her hands, her fingers gripping his cheeks. "You listen to me, Nick Carmichael. I can't let my fear dictate my actions. I have in the past, and the only thing it jeopardized was our relationship. I don't want to live in fear. I want to live for a bigger purpose. I want to live with you."

He leaned into her touch. "That's why I exist, Kayles, to answer a bigger call—one few want to answer—whether it's for my God or my country. Are you ready to answer with me? This is your last chance to back out, babe." He chuckled but she heard the nerves.

"And here I thought you would be the one with cold feet." She watched the fog dissipate as his laughter filled the backyard.

"No cold feet. I'm ready." He stood and held out his hand. "Are you ready to do this with me?"

Emotion swelled in Kaylan, ripping through her. How could she not respond to this, a call to serve a God who had already overcome her fear, a call to love a man who trusted God enough to let his faith drown out his fear? She placed her hand in his, stood, and slipped into his waiting arms. "Together. I'm ready."

He pushed a strand of hair behind her ear and tipped her chin up. "My warrior princess." His lips met hers, and any remaining shreds of uncertainty fell with his touch. Her future was sealed. "I'll see you at the altar tomorrow," he whispered.

"I'll be the one in white," she teased, her lips hovering over his. She felt his smile before he dipped her, deepening their kiss.

"Ow, ow, now that's a kiss," Seth howled as he stepped onto the porch holding a basket of rolls. "Just save it for the honeymoon, Carmichael," he warned.

Nick and Kaylan chuckled as Nick brought them upright but kept his arms wrapped around her waist. "You're just jealous, squirt."

Kaylan watched Seth's brows shoot up into his rusty hairline. "I don't even know where to start with that statement," he said as the rest of his family and the wedding party appeared on the porch behind. "But I think we can all agree that I can kick your butt any day, bro."

Micah whistled. "Hawk, you might want to be nice until after the wedding. Don't rile the linebacker."

Kaylan chuckled and pulled away from Nick. "All right, you two. Let's eat."

Two families—the Richards and the SEALs—converged on the picnic tables, but Kaylan couldn't help but notice how well they blended. Logan and his family, Titus and Liza, Colt, and Jay mixed with the Richards crew under the white lights. Kaylan basked in their laughter as they passed dishes and settled into banter and conversations. Pap and Gran sat at the head of the table talking to Logan and Kim. And Natalie, the newest member of the family, sat across from Nick. Even Sandy made an appearance, though he didn't make it farther than the porch before lying down.

Safety, familiarity, strength, and adventure—that's what these two families represented. Truthfully, she could no longer tell where one ended and the other began, but at some point the people surrounding her had become her entire world.

Nick tucked her against him. "I love you," he whispered, his lips hovering over her ear. She could feel his pleasure, his peace. He had a home, a family; they had one another. If she'd known what to dream, she would never have imagined it coming true quite like this.

The tinkling of silverware on glass brought conversations to stillness as Pap rose at the head of the table. "I'd like to say a few words to my beautiful granddaughter and her groom." He reached for Gran's hand and squeezed. Tears pricked Kaylan's eyes at the love radiating from Pap. If she and Nick still loved that fiercely in fifty-five years, she would count their marriage a success.

"I've watched you two during your relationship. I've watched the fear and uncertainty, the love and playfulness. I've watched the growth, and I've watched you two fall in love, a love that has been tested and tried and come out shining like gold." The tea in his glass sloshed as he motioned to them. "I know you both realize that this won't be easy. In fact, we may need to add a line to your vows that includes 'in war and in peace.'" His audience chuckled and Kaylan smiled, leaning into Nick.

"Marriage is accepting every part of the other person. Their dreams become yours. Their fears become yours. Love requires sacrifice, something you two have learned. But more than that, love *is* sacrifice. It is more than a feeling. It is more than a one-time action. It is a recurring decision to put the other person before yourself, and I have watched you both practice this as you have determined whether or not to move forward in this journey." His gaze landed on Kaylan. "Sugar, I've never been more proud of the woman you've become, and I can't thank God enough for bringing this man into your life." A tear slipped through Kaylan's guard and danced down her cheek. Tears filled Pap's eyes as he raised his glass to her fiancé. "Nick, welcome to our family."

Whistles and clapping filled the air as David and Seth slapped Nick on the back and Micah pulled Kaylan into a hug and placed a kiss on her cheek.

Logan used the table and stood carefully, still adjusting to his new leg. "My turn to speak on behalf of Hawk's family." He nodded at Natalie, who smiled in response, accepting his relationship and longevity in Nick's life. Kaylan felt emotion welling in Nick that he stuffed down.

"Hawk, you and Kaylan have been there for me and mine in more ways than I can count. You have loved us, but more than that, you have loved the team. Kaylan, I know you have struggled with our world and the demands of the job, but honestly, I've watched you spread your wings in our family, for that's what it is. You can't do what we do and not understand that family is more than blood; it's a bond that stretches deep, and, Kayles, you are a vital part of this family."

Tears threatened Kaylan again as the SEALs around her bobbed their heads in agreement. "You are good for Hawk, Kaylan. Keep giving him a hard time. Make him work for it." The guys laughed. "May you be a safe place for him to come home to, a constant encouragement, a rock, and his best friend. You are one of us now. Welcome to our adventure."

He slipped back into his seat as the guys shouted their agreement. Kaylan mouthed a silent "thank you" to Logan and Kim and received a nod in response.

The crew fell silent again as Nick addressed them. "Thank y'all for coming. For loving and supporting us, for calling us family." Kaylan squeezed his hand. "You don't know what that means to me. I agree with Pap. I think the biggest thing I have learned in falling for Kaylan is that love is sacrifice. I didn't want to love Kaylan Richards," he joked. She poked his side, and he jerked away laughing.

"Seriously, I was terrified that I wasn't good enough for her, but surrendering my insecurity to the Lord made me stronger." His blue eyes collided with her. "You make me a better man, Kayles. Your love points me to Jesus. You call me a warrior, babe, but truth be told, I'm only the warrior I am because I look at your heart, your trust in the Lord, and your love for others, and I find a passion and a strength to fight harder, love deeper, and follow Jesus more for you and for the men I work with." He turned back to the people around them. "Thank y'all for being part of this journey. I'm ready to do this!"

He leaned over and kissed Kaylan, and their family cheered, bringing the meal to a close. As their families rose to clean off the tables, Kaylan wrapped her arms around his neck and leaned in so only he could hear. "I only have that heart because I see it in you, Nick Carmichael. You help me be brave."

He kissed her again. "Then we'll keep reminding each other."

"We've got a lot of time to practice," she said and watched his eyes light up.

He smiled the smile he reserved for her. "Forever, Kayles. We have forever."

EPILOGUE

Kaylan's hands shook as she clutched cream satin and chiffon. Their wedding day had finally come, but she couldn't force herself to look in the mirror just yet or the dream would disappear.

"Do you want these or these?" Megan posed as she held up two variations of the same earring to her ears. One set boasted a pearl stud encased in a bed of muted gold, while the other dangled with pearls and faux diamonds.

"The pearl studs."

Megan grinned slyly as she fitted them to her friend's ear. "These are from Nick. I just wanted to see if you would pick the ones he sent."

"Meg! What if I picked wrong?"

Kaylan's friend rolled her eyes, her dark eyeliner causing her almost black eyes to pop with depth. "You two are thicker than dolphins off Hawaii beaches. He knows your taste." She fixed the last one in place and reached for Kaylan's hand. "And you look beautiful."

A smile touched Kaylan's lips at Megan's unusual, gentle gesture. "Is that a tear I see?"

"What can I say?" Megan sniffed and took a step back, shrugging as she dabbed at the corner of her eye. "Ever since this Jesus thing, it's just a whole new me. If you would've told me I would cry all the time, I would have run away from you."

"Jesus melts even the toughest hearts. And you just needed someone who knew how to love yours."

"All right, you two. Stop fussing," Marian Richards said as she waltzed into the room. Her hands flew to her mouth. "Kaylan, sweetheart, you are gorgeous."

"You sure it looks all right?"

"Let's put it this way," Natalie interrupted as she came to stand in front of Kaylan. "That new brother of mine is going to pass out when he sees you."

"Maybe I need to see this for myself." Kaylan took a slow breath, closed her eyes, and turned to face the mirror in her bedroom. *Please don't let this be a dream, Lord,* she prayed. *If it is, I don't want to wake up.*

"Kayles, open your eyes," David's girlfriend, Melody, said.

Kaylan slowly blinked her eyes open and then held her breath. She didn't recognize the woman in front of her. Her auburn hair had been curled, twisted, and swept back in an elegant but natural updo at the back of her neck. An ivory rose stood in stark contrast to her hair color. Her green eyes popped beneath dark lashes and creamy skin, the freckles momentarily obscured. Her ivory strapless bodice was crusted with jewels along the bust before gracefully twisting around her torso, slimming her waist then fanning out and falling in loose chiffon lines to her feet. She raised her dress just enough to see her one non-negotiable—cowboy boots, her little taste of home. They would make the sand difficult to navigate, but it was worth it.

She ran her hands down the loose folds of her dress. "This is happening." After all the tears and laughter, growth and heartache, deployments and homecomings, her warrior, Nick Carmichael, would become her husband in just under an hour. Her heart raced, sending color into her cheeks.

Her mom slipped her arm around Kaylan's shoulders as Kaylan's bridesmaids exited the room. "Have I told you lately how proud I am? We couldn't have prayed for a better man for you."

Kaylan's eyes flooded. "It seems impossible. Not fair somehow." Her eyes traveled the room she had lived in for the past eight months and landed on an unsealed box sitting next to her empty bookshelf. She wandered to it and lifted the picture frame resting on the top of the box—Sarah Beth on the beach in Haiti on a beautiful, sunny day. The days Sarah Beth lived for.

"She's watching, sweetheart. She wouldn't want you to be sad."

"I know. I'm so thankful for Meg and Natalie. Sarah Beth just knew my heart better than anyone."

Marian lifted the picture from Kaylan's hands and placed a finger under her chin. Kaylan met hazel eyes framed by tiny smile wrinkles. "Nick knows you better. Loves you more. Wants a lifetime with you."

Kaylan let her mother's words drift over her soul. She'd wrestled with loving a man who could lose his life at any moment, would willingly lay it down if the situation called for it. She'd cried into her pillow, wondering if she would lose the love of her life the way she had lost her best friend. It seemed almost cruel that God sometimes took the best people, the most dedicated. But if she believed there was more to life than weddings and wars and work, then she had to believe that it wasn't punishment to die early but a beautiful gift to spend even more time with Jesus in eternity.

She would have eternity with Sarah Beth and an eternity with Nick Carmichael. She was marrying a man who inhaled the Bible and exhaled more of Jesus. He knew the heart of a warrior was not measured by his actions but his character.

"How do I deserve him?"

"Oh, baby, sometimes I wonder how he deserves you. But that's the beauty of marriage. Two sinners join together to fight a battle here and share Jesus with as many people as possible, while glorifying the Lord. You are marrying a fighter, and you, my girl, are a fighter."

A low whistle sounded from the door and Kaylan turned to find her dad. "Will you look at my baby girl? I can't believe I'm giving you away today."

Kaylan walked into her father's arms, so safe and strong, the same arms that had comforted her and protected her all her life. "Never giving me away, Dad. Just passing me off."

He placed a feather-light kiss on her forehead and then turned to lead her from the room. Her girls gathered in the living room.

"Ready, Kayles?" Megan grabbed hers and Kaylan's bouquets from the table.

"I think so." She studied her roommate in her one-shoulder coral dress, her short, black hair curled and pinned away from her face. "Have I told you that you look amazing in pink?" She grinned.

"For starters, it's coral. But it's close enough to pink that payback is going to be awful for you."

"Yeah, yeah. You talk so tough." She waltzed past her parents and friends and threw the door open, revealing a limo outside. "Let's do this!"

The drive to the beach was short and sweet. She and Nick had chosen to get married in Coronado on the beach at sunset, truly a testament to her love for Nick. But she wouldn't have it any other way. Friends, family, and SEALs had gathered from Alabama and other states around the country. All in all, the gathering fit Kaylan's style—small and intimate.

As the car pulled onto the beach, Kaylan smiled at the small, marked-off section of shoreline. White wooden chairs sat in rows with wedding guests on each side of the aisle. Sea shells marked the aisle with a white runner that ended in an arbor laced with ivy, wooden vines, baby's breath, and calla lilies. A small quartet sat off to the side playing music from *Pride and Prejudice.* Next to the bride's side, a white tent glowed and friends bustled to set up the cake and an hors d'oeuvres table. Everything was perfect.

They'd decided against a military wedding. While it was fully part of their lives, it didn't need to dominate every part.

Kaylan sat in the car, straining to see over the heads of her guests for eyes as blue as the ocean in a fog. Eyes that could storm one moment and lend utter calm the next. She knew her brothers would be next to his side along with Logan, all dressed in khaki pants, white button downs with the sleeves rolled up, and khaki vests. She knew her family and friends would flank the aisle, but she longed for only one person.

Nick Carmichael—Navy SEAL, surfer, love of her life. Her best friend.

Music began to play. Gentle strains of a violin mixed with the lap of the tide. Kaylan took a deep breath. This was happening. Her dad squeezed her arm as Liza walked down the aisle in her coral strapless dress. Natalie, Melody, Kim, and Meg slowly followed, each clutching a bundle of three calla lilies, grains of sand kicking up under their flats. Little Molly skipped down the aisle tossing petals, her ivory dress flouncing around her and her blonde curls billowing in her wake.

And then the music changed.

"Ready?" Her dad reached for her hand and pulled her from the car. He placed her hand in the crook of his arm and caught her eye.

She clutched his tan jacket under her fingers, holding on for dear life as she prepared to walk toward her future. "I couldn't give you away to a more deserving man. You know that, right?"

Her eyes flooded with tears. "Dad, don't make me cry right before I walk down in front of all these people."

He brushed away her tears and kissed her cheek. "It doesn't matter what they think. They're all here to witness a miracle anyway."

Kaylan paused. "What miracle?"

"The miracle of two people coming together in a covenant before God. The picture of Christ and His church."

The music swelled and Kaylan's heart jumped to her throat. "Here we go, baby doll," he said, as he led them behind her guests. As they rounded the last row of chairs and Kaylan got a clear view of the aisle, her breath stopped. She paused as her gaze locked on the one she sought. His eyes were bluer than the sea behind him and more beautiful than the sun sinking low in the sky. And they were only for her.

Her boots found the runner as she took her first step toward her future.

She floated towards him and he could only think of one word: pure. Kaylan Lee Richards stood for everything pure and good in his life. In a career torn by war and the need to be strong to accomplish what was hard yet necessary, she made it worth it. His white lily, shining in the darkness.

His.

Tears filled his eyes and he blinked them away as she drew closer and he tried to say all he wanted to with his eyes locked on hers. She glowed. Light from the setting sun caught her auburn hair and set the red highlights aflame.

He barely heard the minister as Kaylan's dad passed her hand into his. It felt small and delicate, but he knew the strength it housed, the comfort her grip possessed, and the healing touch she worked to administer. He couldn't believe she'd chosen him. He only knew he would never let her go.

A gentle breeze brushed his face and sent a lily tumbling from the arbor above his head to land at their feet. He grinned, turning to face her and gripping both of her hands as the minister began to speak. As he told a story, their story, Nick heard the gospel—a Father sending his only Son to die on Nick and Kaylan's behalf. That's how he understood love. That's how he understood sacrifice. That's where he drew his courage. From the cross and from the love of Kaylan Richards.

Her gentle smile drowned out everything else. Her eyes glowed like emeralds as she mouthed the three words he once thought he might never hear. His lips sent the words back to her: *I love you.*

As the strains of another song filled the air and a woman from their church sang a love song, Kaylan and Nick walked to a table just beyond the arbor where two jars of sand stood with an empty vase. "Nick, are you okay?"

Nick blinked, realizing he was walking in a daze. No wonder people said they couldn't remember their wedding day. Everything felt like a surreal blur. Too good to be true. Too fast to catch hold. He squeezed her hand. "Can you believe we're doing this? Finally." His voice crested above the song, drawing chuckles from the audience.

Kaylan blushed and grabbed her jar of Alabama brown dirt. But he couldn't let her go yet. He traced his finger down her cheek, feeling her pulse flicker beneath his touch. An amused smile graced her lips. "Babe, the song is going to be over soon."

"They can wait." Keeping his gaze locked on hers he lowered his face near hers and kissed her cheek. "I love you, you know."

He felt her breath catch as she moved closer to him. "I love you too."

He reluctantly let go of her hand and grabbed his jar of California sand. They took turns pouring their elements in a slim, twisting vase. As the dirt and sand intermingled, he could clearly see the dark and the tan sections shrink as they neared the top. Nick placed a rubber stopper in the top. Then he pulled Kaylan to his chest for the last few moments to pray with his bride for God to bless the marriage.

As the strains of the song ended, Nick helped Kaylan back to the place in front of the minister. The glowing red sun sat on the ocean behind them shooting rose, gold, and crimson into the sky around them. Dusk descended as Nick pulled his vows from his pocket and cleared his throat.

"Kaylan, from the moment I met you, I knew you were special. Something about you on our first day just sparkled. Vibrant and pure, Kayles. That's how I would describe you, but I wasn't a man who could lead you or love you well at that time. Thank God, he is never finished with us. And thank God, he never ceases to write beautiful stories with our lives, for he led me back to you, and I returned a stronger man because of what he led me through.

"As we stand here before God and our family and friends, I commit to love you for the rest of my days, however long God gives me to live and breathe. I promise to lead you as I seek to follow our Father. I promise to love you to the point of death, because I would give my life to keep you safe and happy. I promise to honor and cherish you because you are a daughter of the King and my sister in Christ before you are my wife. I take seriously my responsibility to lead our home. I promise to partner with you, never rule over you, to enjoy life with you because it is fleeting. I promise to go to war with you, recognizing that we are called to share the gospel with every person we meet. I promise to push you closer to our Father and realize that you must love Him before me. I promise to watch *Dancing with the Stars* even when I don't want to and paint a room pink if we have a little girl." The audience chuckled and Kaylan grinned, a blush coloring her cheeks. He squeezed her hand with his free one, letting the hand holding his vows fall to his side so that nothing hindered him from looking at his bride.

"I promise to love you, Kaylan Lee Carmichael, in sickness, in health, in war, and in peace, in high tides, and low tides, and everything in between."

His hands shook as he threaded his fingers through hers but noticed her gaze was averted. He tipped her chin to meet his eyes and brushed her tears away. She smiled, her green eyes shining as dusk took hold, and the candles behind their wedding party cast a warm glow. Her turn. His throat went dry as Megan passed Kaylan her vows. Nick took a deep breath as her gentle voice washed over him.

"Nick, I never believed I deserved a man like you, especially not after the last two years. But in the midst of my most broken moments, God gave me a gift. He gave me you."

Nick couldn't help it. He pulled her close to his chest as she continued to read, the world around them fading as stars began to appear.

"You fought through my fear and my anger. You reached to my heart and encouraged me until it beat again. You didn't leave. You were a man of your word, and I realized that I could trust you because you trust Jesus first. I learned courage from you, Nick. I learned that a warrior's heart is both strong and gentle. And you are both of those traits with every person you meet. So as we stand here before God and our friends and family, I promise to submit to you, Nick. To follow you as you follow Christ and be solely devoted to you. To love your SEAL family as much as you do, and to let you go because I trust our God is good, even if you don't come back. I vow to esteem no one but Christ higher than you, to trust your leadership of our home. I vow to love you, Nick Carmichael, to respect you because you are a mighty man of God, a man who cares more about his character than his bank account, resume, or physique. A man who values others. I vow to partner with you in ministry. To go to war with you because we do not fight against flesh and blood. To honor you and cherish you in sickness and health, in loss of limb or wholeness, in your absence and in your presence, all the days the Lord chooses to give, knowing I get to spend eternity with you, my soulmate, my best friend, the love of my life."

Silence descended over their friends and family. Nick looked to the minister, who smiled and looked to Megan and Micah. "Do we have the rings?"

Nick turned to his best friend, brother in arms, and soon to be brother-in-law. Micah winked as he dropped Kaylan's band into Nick's waiting palm. "Almost there, Hawk," he whispered.

Nick gripped the band and winked back. "You're almost stuck with me." He pivoted before Micah, David, or Seth could say anything else. As his eyes met Kaylan's again, she rolled her eyes and shook her head, clearly having heard the conversation.

"Nick," the pastor's voice broke through their silent teasing. "Place the ring on Kaylan's finger."

Nick reached for her left hand and slipped the band over her knuckle. "With this ring, I thee wed. Finally." Their guests snickered. Kaylan reached for his hand and slipped the tungsten silver band on his finger. "With this ring, I thee wed." She smiled shyly. "Finally."

They both looked to the pastor as he rocked back on his heels, dragging the moment out. "Well, I guess that about does it. You know what comes next, I suppose."

Nick didn't wait for permission. His arm slipped around Kaylan's waist as he tipped her face to meet his. Their lips met and he dipped his bride, lengthening the moment as the audience whistled and hollered.

"Hey, that's still my sister," Seth shouted over the noise. Kaylan broke away from Nick, causing both of them to laugh as he set her upright, his fingers slipping through hers.

"Ladies and gentlemen, I introduce Mr. and Mrs. Nick Carmichael!"

"Woo!" Nick threw his fist in the air as he led his bride, his wife, back up the aisle.

Kaylan couldn't quite take in everything around her under the white tent on the beach. Lights hung beneath the canopy, mirroring the stars studding the black sky. The roar of the waves mixed with the DJ playing pop, country, jazz, and everything in between. About one hundred guests sat around round tables with white, wooden folding chairs or milled around food tables. Her parents, Pap and Gran, her brothers, and Natalie all sat at a table, talking and laughing. They'd cut the cake, Nick successfully spreading icing all over her lips. Her small bite had tasted like heaven.

Nick had danced with her mom and Kaylan with her dad. But now, it was their turn. Kaylan sat in her chair surrounded by her family as her groom advanced, his eyes connected to hers. He'd lost his vest somewhere over the course of the evening. His white shirt made his ever-present tan skin glow. The light danced over his dirty blonde hair and the light dusting of scruff on his face spoke of a disciplined man that couldn't quite be tamed. She wouldn't have it any other way. His blue eyes appeared fathomless as he bent and offered his hand.

"May I have this dance?"

She slid her hand in his as she rose to her feet, her boots abandoned for slippers. "I thought you didn't dance."

"Only with you, gorgeous."

He pulled her into the middle of the floor and into his arms as the strains of a Michael Bublé song filled the air. Kaylan forgot the rest of the room watched. She forgot the details she needed to cover with her bridesmaids for their getaway. She forgot everything except Nick's arm around her waist and the cadence of his heart near hers. She'd never felt so loved, so safe.

Nick was her husband. Husband.

That title carried weight. For better or worse. No matter what. But she loved the certainty, the permanency. The cords that had bound her since she said those three words were now encased in gold. Unbreakable. And she loved it.

"You remember the last time we did this?" His warm, rich voice whispered near her ear, sending shivers down her spine.

Kaylan smiled. "Before Haiti in the dance studio when you wanted to kiss me." She pulled back and looked into his eyes. "And I made you wait."

He groaned. "Ugh, pure torture." He smiled back and lowered his face to hers, whispering against her lips. "But well worth the wait." As the last strains of the song rang out underneath the ivory canopy, Nick dipped her, kissing her. A kiss that spoke of promise, ownership, and respect.

They both came up breathless and smiling to a round of cheers and Seth's exaggerated groans. As the guests began to mill around under the tent and the DJ kicked the dance music up, Nick squeezed Kaylan's hand. "Slip away with me for a few minutes."

"Babe, we can't. We need to be with our guests."

Nick rolled his eyes. "They'll be fine for a few minutes." He looked around at all the guests engaged in the electric slide on the dance floor. "They won't even notice."

With a final tug, they slipped out from beneath the canopy and hurried a little ways down the beach. Kaylan finally tugged on Nick's hand, laughing. "Nick, it's hard to run in this dress. Slow down."

He stopped and pulled her into his arms, his grin electric in the moonlight. He turned her to face the tent they'd just left. "I want you to look at this for a moment." Kaylan leaned back against his chest as she watched their guests and laughed. Micah, Seth, and David hammed it up on the dance floor. Megan, Jay, and Colt played with the Carpenter kids as Logan and Kim watched and laughed, Kim sitting in Logan's lap. Titus and Liza joined in a growing dance circle as Jay and Colt busted moves that sent the whole room laughing. Micah enticed Gran onto the dance floor while Seth worked on their mom, their dad and Pap looking on and laughing. Other SEAL families and friends from Alabama sat and ate or joined in the festivities. A lump formed in Kaylan's throat as she snuggled against Nick's chest. "If that's not proof that we are loved, I don't know what is."

Nick turned Kaylan to face him again. His eyes, gray blue, were cloaked in shadows. "I want you to remember this moment when you feel alone, when I'm deployed, when you're missing Sarah Beth. I want you to remember that you have a whole family around you, bound by blood or commitment. And I want you to lean on them."

She reached up and ran a finger down his jawline, feeling the faint stubble. She didn't know how she could love this man more, but every day her love for him grew. She still struggled with loving a warrior with a sacrificial heart, but in this moment, she knew he gave her a gift. A gift to let others be part of her life, to love with abandon the way Sarah Beth had taught her, and to trust the Lord. No matter what came, she was not alone.

"You're pretty amazing, you know that?" Kaylan whispered.

"Keep telling me, Mrs. Carmichael."

"Oh, wow. That's weird."

"Good weird?" His voice held a hint of uncertainty.

She slipped her arms around his neck and stood on her tiptoes. "Amazing weird."

"Good." He swooped in for a quick kiss. Then he pulled back and began to remove his shoes and socks and roll up his pant leg.

"What are you doing?""

His smile changed in the moonlight and Kaylan spotted trouble. "Nick . . ." But it was too late. She squealed as her feet left the sand and she settled in his arms. Her dress fell heavy around them, but Nick didn't seem to mind. "Nick, don't you dare toss me in the waves like you usually do. This is not a moment for that."

His smile quirked at the corner. "Now that would be a great memory."

"Nick Carmichael . . ."

"I guess we can save that memory for another time. I had something different in mind. A tradition that dates back in time."

"And what tradition is that?"

"Carrying the bride over the threshold." His voice grew gravelly.

"Babe, I think you are confused. You do that after the honeymoon."

"True. But you see, Mrs. Carmichael, you just happen to be with a Frogman in his natural habitat. And this great expanse"—he nodded at the ocean—"is the birthplace of our life of adventure."

"Oh, I see." She hugged his neck. "And just where will this adventure take us?"

He walked to the edge of the surf until his ankles were under water. The stars studded the sky and the moon hung low, its reflection buoyed on the water. "That's a mystery, gorgeous. But here's to a beautiful future."

His lips met hers under the starry sky, and Kaylan knew in that moment that shooting stars couldn't compete with the fireworks she had with Nick Carmichael. And this moment was only the beginning.

ACKNOWLEDGMENTS

Everything is better together, and no book comes together based on the sole effort of the author. As this series ends, I want to give a huge hug and thank you to all who have been part of the adventure.

My family: Dad, Mom, Toby, Jaryn, Chasya, and now Jordan, as well as all my extended family. You have consistently encouraged, challenged, and enabled me to pursue this dream. Thank you for believing in me even when I didn't. These books wouldn't have seen the light of day without you!

My community: Thank you to those in the two church communities I've been privileged to be part of—my community groups, volunteer teams, childhood friends, and all who poured into me while growing up — you have greatly shaped my life. To my roommate who put up with my tears, panic moments, brainstorming sessions, and numerous late nights, you warrant your own mention. To my friends from Focus, my college friends, professors, and coworkers, you entered my life as this part of my story began. Thank you for helping me through the growth pains.

My writing mentor: DiAnn Mills, you have been a blessing! Thank you for pushing me and encouraging me in every step of this process. I couldn't have done this without you. You were an answer to prayer!

My publishing team: Sarah and WordServe Literary and all those at Realms and FaithHappenings—thank you, thank you, thank you for taking a chance on a rookie. You brought this story to life. And I can't thank you enough. To my editor, Lori, thank you for sharpening me, learning with me, growing with me, and teaching me. You made these stories better than I could have made them alone. To those who helped me with research and provided an extra set of eyes to make sure things were accurate, you know who you are.

To the Master Dreamer and Creator: Good stories stir my affections for the Lord, and I pray these stories bring glory to You. Thank you for making us in Your image and instilling us with the desire and ability to create and dream things that are a reflection of You! Thank You for the story You are penning with my life and for choosing to use me, even when I'm broken. May these stories be proof of You!

ABOUT THE PUBLISHER

FH Publishers is a division of FaithHappenings.com

FaithHappenings.com is the premier, first-of-its kind, online Christian resource that contains an array of valuable local and national faith-based information all in one place. Our mission is "to inform, enrich, inspire and mobilize Christians and churches while enhancing the unity of the local Christian community so they can better serve the needs of the people around them." FaithHappenings.com will be the primary i-Phone, Droid App/Site and website that people with a traditional Trinitarian theology will turn to for national and local information to impact virtually every area of life.

The vision of FaithHappenings.com is to build the vibrancy of the local church with a true "one-stop-resource" of information and events that will enrich the soul, marriage, family, and church life for people of faith. We want people to be touched by God's Kingdom, so they can touch others FOR the Kingdom.

Find out more at www.faithhappenings.com.

50851890R00200

Made in the USA
Charleston, SC
10 January 2016